The Hunter and the Wild Girl

Also by Pauline Holdstock

Fiction
Into the Heart of the Country
Beyond Measure
The Turning
Swimming From the Flames: Stories
House
The Burial Ground
The Blackbird's Song

Non-Fiction
Mortal Distractions: Collected Essays

The Hunter and the Wild Girl

PAULINE HOLDSTOCK

Edited by Bethany Gibson.
Cover and page design by Julie Scriver.
Cover illustration (swallow) and epigraph illustration (wing): thegraphicsfairy.com
Printed in Canada.
10 9 8 7 6 5 4 3 2 1

Library and Archives Canada Cataloguing in Publication

Holdstock, Pauline, author
The hunter and the wild girl / Pauline Holdstock.

Issued in print and electronic formats.
ISBN 978-0-86492-862-7 (bound). —ISBN 978-0-86492-801-6 (epub).
—ISBN 978-0-86492-842-9 (mobi)

I. Title.

PS8565.O622H86 2015   C813'.54   C2015-901808-0
                          C2015-901809-9

We acknowledge the generous support of the Government of Canada, the Canada Council for the Arts, and the Government of New Brunswick.

Nous reconnaissons l'appui généreux du gouvernement du Canada, du Conseil des arts du Canada, et du gouvernement du Nouveau-Brunswick.

Goose Lane Editions
500 Beaverbrook Court, Suite 330
Fredericton, New Brunswick
CANADA E3B 5X4
www.gooselane.com

*À Marie, Régine, Jacqueline et mes nouvelles
amies du Languedoc*

Once a boy brimming with light. He shimmered with it, shone. Eyes blue as a polished sea under a summer sky. Beaming wonder on flower and bee, on caterpillar, on worm.

One

WITH A SHRIEK of splintering boards, the girl breaks into daylight and stands blinded, panting, sucking air as if it were a great hot soup, her chest heaving. Three breaths, harsh as the scrape of wood on stone — and then she is running, naked limbs a hieroglyph in motion across the scrubby field beside the house she had not known was there, through the alarmed and protesting sheep, running, leaping, until she reaches the cloudy cover of an olive grove where she draws a breath and, breakneck, reckless, races on. Desperate, unfledged harpy. No destination, no thought, only 'away.' Away from the darkness of the hovel and its reek, away from the old man and his snarling dog. She can hear it yammering back at the house. Up is where she needs to be. As high as she can go. Climbing is what she knows. On the other side of the trees she turns toward the limestone cliffs rising abruptly from the far side of a stream bed. She is across the stream in two bounds, slipping in mid-stride, unaware of the grind of ankle bone on rock, her mind ceasing to register, her mind already climbing, looking for handholds, for places to wedge a hip, lever an elbow. She climbs past places where swallows nest. She hears the man and his dog crashing through the olives down below and then her hands are on the topmost ledge. She uses the strength of her toes first to push herself higher and then, with her elbows tucked in close, supporting her weight on her palms, she heaves herself up and tilts, throwing her upper body flat on the solid ground, inching forward and drawing her legs to follow. She lies panting. An ecstasy of blue above her. She knows it even before she rolls over and opens her eyes. Blue. Air again, sky. She gulps them both and they taste of salt.

She has no way of knowing how long she was kept there in the stinking hut. She does not count. She does not mark the days. But she can remember the bright cold day when she was shut into the dark. She had seen dogs that day outside a wretched hamlet. Dogs mauling some rag of a creature, baying dismal memories of sinew and bone. Dogs in a pack. And so she ran. The dogs did not give chase, but she kept on running, not stopping even to look for food. When she came upon the stone hut, the sun was sinking, the air cooling. She saw the hut as a refuge from the bitter wind, but the stench repelled her. Fetid it was, sour and festering with a smell she did not recognize, so she had huddled instead at the foot of the lee wall and absorbed the last stored warmth of the sun from the rocks.

She had not woken again until night was falling and then it was too late. The old man's hands were already on her. He gripped her upper arms from behind and though she clawed and bit she could not loosen his hold. So rigid, so unyielding, like a dead thing found in the woods. He pushed her into his hut and let go and it was then that she might have darted free but for his dog that suddenly showed itself, snarling in the doorway behind him. The old man growled at the dog and it cowered while he backed out and shoved the door shut. She heard him spit and growl again and then she heard the dog's breath at the cracks in the door. The old man began to laugh and then she heard him walking away. After a while the dog too was gone.

When night came it was absolute. Morning offered only knives of light slicing through the cracks in the door, ghosts of stones looming from the walls. The old man came with a mess of food and with water. He prattled and burbled and held both out to her, and she saw his jagged teeth as he laughed and she began to imagine herself being eaten. He left the dish and the wooden bucket on the floor and closed her in again. All of it reeked.

He came again in the days to follow, sometimes with food, sometimes with a bucket of sand or ashes to throw over her dirt, but always with the dog at his back. She began to eat the food he brought, though it turned her stomach. The first time he reached to touch her she clawed him, her nails strong as a dog's. The next time he tried she flew at him again and bit, and after that he kept his distance. Sometimes he moaned softly in the thick dark. She could not breathe with him near. It made her long for the vast clear emptiness of sky and the small birds calling.

She tried at last to spring for daylight when he opened the door. The dog did not hesitate. It leapt on her at once and tried to close its teeth on her arm. The old man struck it away with the rail that barred the door. She heard a crack and the dog yelped and ran off, but the old man was quick and she found herself shut in a second time. She knew by the tenderness there on her arm that an ugly bruise was blooming. When at last she fell asleep she dreamed she was on a mountainside where the sunlight fell like rain. She dreamed thunder, the crack of it, and when she woke her head was filled with a memory: the sound of breaking wood. She got up and pushed at the door. It seemed to her that it gave a little. Again and again she tried. She used her legs. She drove her uninjured side against it, hurling herself at it over and over until wood exploded into sky and she sprang into the dazzling world.

Up on the bluff now, the wind finds her as soon as she stands. She runs with it at her back. By afternoon she is far away, at one with the high garrigue, the rough sanctuary of scrub and rock that is her home. She moves with ease along the ridge where there seems no path. At length, seeing a small bush where yellow leaves have withered, she stops. She finds a sharp stone and with her back always to the wind she begins to worry and chisel at the base of the bush. She pinches humpbacked bugs from the crevices between the rotten roots. They try to squirm away as fast as they are revealed, and just as fast she eats them. Bitter and husky they are and not to her taste and she goes on. Her life is returning to her whole and unforgotten, like waking to a day as ordinary as another. She sees a runnel of greener, denser foliage cutting across the scrub lower down and meandering on toward the valley, and she hurries there in search of water. She can hear its faint rilling as she breaks through the tangle of green to plunge her face into the shock of it. A brightness cold as stars. Ice in her veins. She takes a mouthful under water and opens her eyes to see the grey and glacial stones seeming to move, to shift in the flow. She comes up gasping, only to submerge her face again and show the stones her teeth, ridding her body of the memory of the foulness of the old man's food and his filthy wooden bucket. When she has drunk enough, she sets to digging for roots at the base of the plants along the bank. But her fingers now are slow and stiff and she finds nothing to sustain her. The shade deepens and cools. She walks on in the thickening dusk until the tremors in her legs force her to stop, the cold now mountainous. Under a low overhang of rock, she tucks down, curls against the night, and sleeps.

In the next days, her path traces a wild jag away from the suffocating darkness of the hovel and down from the ridge where the foraging was so poor, the wind so keen. She runs between low broom and juniper, vanishes in thickets of white oak and boxwood, reappears in a maze of rosemary, shoulder-high. Only a hawk flying over could pick her out. For more than six days she runs, each day following the same pattern: travelling east first, then south to follow the sun; stopping only to search under likely rocks or dig for roots where wild boar have rummaged; in the failing light seeking shelter.

On the evening of the fifth day, she sees in the sage-grey distance the tawny scar that means roofs. She trots on for as long as she can, rests, then travels on again with the risen moon. At dawn on the sixth day she begins her approach. The houses are strung out in a rough line, bunching in places more thickly and then continuing, tracing the edge of another crooked scar, this one deeply shadowed. Villages mean danger. But they mean eggs too and an abundance of tender leaves, perhaps sweet roots, perhaps even milk to lick from an empty pail set down and forgotten, grain to lift with a wetted finger quicker than the fowl. The girl, six days hungry, remembers fowl. Not the name for them, those heavy grounded birds, so busy, so stupid — names are not what she knows — but the beaky voices of them, the feel of scaly legs in her fist. And the taste. Above all, the taste, and the warm, moist feel of them in her mouth. Once, when ravenous she had come upon a place where every man, woman, and child was stepping high while a man sawed at something on his shoulder, making a crying sound that fed her hunger. She had carried away a chicken by the neck and when she was well away from the village she had swung the bird high behind her and brought it down hard on a rock. She swung it down twice more before it stopped moving. There was a split in its breast where she could pull the flesh away with her teeth. It is a memory she relives often.

As she draws closer, she sees that the houses are crammed along the overhang of a deep gorge that cuts the mountain from its twin on the other side. She can see the river now bright in the scar. It runs from below the village and passes under a low stone bridge before widening to a shoaly bend in the valley not far below her. Across the bridge, on the opposite flank of the gorge, near the base of the towering cliff, a great wheel stands idle beside a small house. She has seen these wheels before, water and sunlight flashing from the paddles as they turn.

Keeping to the high ground, she surveys the village.

When she closes her eyes she can see it laid out in every detail, from the single house where it begins near the bridge, to the others that follow the incline of the hill, to the tight twist of stone buildings shouldering for room farther on. Where the road ends, another building, larger than a house, seems to emerge from the very rock that bars the way.

She can see some hens behind the first house just past the bridge, but there are dogs too so she goes on, savouring the rich and riotous smells of village. Smoke from the chimneys sharpens the air. The cold has driven every inhabitant to keep the shutters closed. Still she is careful and keeps low to the ground when she darts forward, pausing only where there is cover. Here at the top of the road up from the bridge the houses are squeezed between the gorge in front and the slope of the mountain at their backs. A narrow strip of level ground runs behind them—where there might be good things to snatch before she moves on. She sees a pile covered with sacking. A store of something tasty? Her mouth waters at the thought and she clambers down. It is good to be out of the wind.

The shutters of the house are closed. She lifts a corner of the sacking at the same time as she sees, from the corner of her eye, the dogs from the first house trotting delicately in her direction. And now she hears footsteps inside this house. A cough. The door opens just as her fingers find a large sandy potato. The man begins to yell and she runs. She finds herself in a narrow passage between a wall behind the cottages and the cliff that rises beside it. She wants to climb back to the safety of the mountain, but it is too sheer for that. The only way is forward along the line of houses. Now all is uproar. Shutters bang open, neighbour calls to neighbour. The dogs excite one another with their alarms. The face of the cliff rising beside her is undercut, arching over in an impossible vault above, and so she runs on, keeping between the muddle of walls and outbuildings and the obstructive cliff. There are doors up ahead that might open at any moment. Behind her, other dogs are out and picking up her scent. Her only haven is in the bare, airy heights of a fig tree—and capture then the only outcome. She knows it instinctively and races on, sucking air through her teeth, her face raised as if to suck in sky itself. A group of villagers see her break from behind the last houses and into the square in front of the church. They start toward her, shouting. But she can hear the dogs' own rasping intakes of breath at her heels and she turns abruptly toward the gorge and covers the open square in strides. The dogs, distracted by the men and women, lose enough momentum for her to reach the edge of the gorge. The men and women as they watch are already in the future, reaching for the words they will need later to tell one another what they are seeing. Only a boy, Felip, is caught in the long instant, feeling his heart soar within him as her feet leave the ground.

Some said later that she jumped to the side and sprang down the rock face on all fours like a hoofed creature, her limbs stiff. They said she sprang from rock to rock, never pausing even for a breath, sometimes airborne, her head turning, searching for the next landing place. Others said no, she fell straight down, she fell like water, a human waterfall skimming the rock until she came to rest on the Devil's Snout, and there they said she raised her broken bones up and flung herself, leapt straight out into empty air above the thunder of the water. And some of these said that as she fell she looked as if her legs were trying to descend invisible stairs, while others said she went down flat, spread like a handkerchief floating from a window. But perhaps they had not seen at all, for she had sprung from the cliff with the terror of all the dogs in the world concentrated in her feet, and it was terror itself that saved her, giving her the distance she did not know she needed to clear, just, the promontory beneath her, the ledge she had not known was there and still did not see as she gathered her last courage to spring, with legs rigid as bound stakes and feet pointing resolutely to where she wanted to go. Certainly no one described how she brought her hands instinctively to cover her face from the sight of the river so that she dropped like a rod into the deep water that pooled beneath the Snout. It was far more interesting to hurry on to the next turn of the story where they saw her surface—every one of them swore to it—a hundred yards farther downstream, one arm raised up like a crooked branch on a bough.

The able-bodied raced away on foot to fish her out down beyond the bridge where most things washed up at the bend in the river. They were there in no time and would have clambered down beside the bridge to make their way along to the shoal, but what was the point? They could see what was stuck there. No one could deny the similarity of a jammed tree limb to a torso with one arm raised aloft.

Yet she would have surely been swept downstream. They decided to go on farther. Fernand le Boulidou said it was a pity that they had brought no wine, and Gustave Thibéry said that his wife would have certainly packed up some sausage and bread for them all, had she known it would take a while. When they reached the great bend they made a good show of examining between the rocks and among the tight, rustling canes. Le Boulidou lumbered away up a narrow cut with Thierry Sanis to a place where truffles could be found. They came back with their pockets stuffed. It was not long before one or two began to remark on the briskness of the day, not to mention the time. All the talk of food did wonders for the appetite. And so they returned in time for lunch, convinced that they had made a thorough search.

Back in the village a meeting had been called at Blind Henri's. The mayor, Ramon Pailhès, knew it was the way to get things done. He had held office for forty years. Assemblies were messy, often disputatious, but they rarely ended without a toast to the success of the venture. It was the way affairs were conducted where people had an embarrassment of time on their hands—and Freyzus, once a thriving mill town serving the needs of its neighbours, Soulières and Gougeac, now had all the time in the world. Nothing noteworthy had occurred in the town since the year an anthropologist with calipers had arrived from Lyons to measure the heads of the inhabitants. The girl was a welcome diversion. Here in Freyzus the business of one person was always the business of all — only in this case it was the business of all from the start. The girl had sprung into the village from nowhere. No one and therefore everyone was responsible for her.

Henri kept the tavern on the ground floor of his mother's house. His mother kept the inn above. She welcomed any assembly, for though times were hard the mayor always found the means to buy another round of drinks. Ramon Pailhès listened to each and every version of the girl's sudden appearance, and her equally sudden disappearance, while he waited to see if the search party would return with the girl alive or dead. Only one course of action was obvious and could be decided ahead of time. If they returned with her dead, she would be buried outside the town. God rest her soul.

When the men came back without her it seemed as if that had been the only possible outcome all along. But the question of her whereabouts remained. Conjecture turned once more to the missing body and the question of where — if not at the great horseshoe bend — it could have surfaced. Since it had not come to rest there, it might never be found. Mayor Pailhès was just saying he would call for volunteers to undertake a more extensive search, perhaps as far as Soulières, when Blind Henri voiced the thought that no one wanted to entertain: perhaps her body was not carried away by the river at all. Perhaps her body hung even now in the still deep water beneath the Snout, ready to rise bloated and ghastly when it swelled, as a body would. They lived in this valley, didn't they? They had seen drowned carcasses, drowned children, once a woman.

Stéphane Foix, youngest and the boldest of the men assembled, said, Well, then, let us look. What are we waiting for?

Thierry rang the steeple bell on Sundays and holy days. He knew ropes. He said he would make a sling if someone would find a lad who could be lowered over the edge to see. It would need to be attached, he said, to an exceedingly long rope—and all of it would need to be properly spliced, for they did not want a second accident on their doorstep.

And so a lad was found without much difficulty. In fact, there was one loitering just outside the door. He had been there all morning when he should have been in school.

The lad's mother, Madame Maraval, wrung her hands while she considered the risks, weighing them against the possibility that the operation would succeed and that Monsieur Maraval, when he returned from the quarry that night and learned of the heroic feat, might then be moved to love his son Felip a little more and ease his beatings.

In a couple of hours the men were ready. They had drawn a wagon close to the edge of the cliff and overturned it, anchoring it with a chain running back to the iron ring at the fountain. They passed the freshly spliced rope through a block attached to the harness and then through another secured to the axle. The air was filled with the mild commotion of orders and counter-orders, the plan revised in progress, the plan contested. They would not let Felip look over at the drop but made him turn backwards, present his rear to the gorge, and then one foot (and here the commotion increased as the men hollered to him to hold fast, to not look down, to — *any*thing, as long as they themselves did not have to go over), and then the other as he backed himself off the cliff. The voices coalesced and fell into a rhythm as the men paid out the rope, letting the boy down in sudden jolts for the physics were all askew.

The joints of Felip's fingers whitened and his mouth went strangely dry, although already in his head he was holding court with the men on his return, telling them how it had been nothing, nothing at all, and then the next day at school telling it all again, his friends listening and knowing, for they would surely know, how fine a thrill it was to dangle above the drop. If he had seen how the rope sawed at the edge of the cliff as it ran over, he might never have opened his eyes again.

Each time the men paid out, the boy's heart snagged in his chest. But he did not have to descend far before he could see the still dark pool. He shouted up to them to stop. He looked directly below and his heart leapt again though the rope was still — but no. It was only his reflection hanging in the deep water, his own clumped body far under the surface. Little bits of straw that had been caught on the rope twirled downward to his drowned body. Nothing else moved. How he wanted to report the girl crouched there on a ledge below — better, her naked body streaking through the water like a fish. But what if he saw her body swollen, her dead eyes seeming to look at him!

Bring me up!

He was shouting it. He could not stop. Once over the Snout, both knees scraped raw and his fingernails bleeding, he felt better. He used his legs to help himself up the face of the cliff as the men hauled. At the top, narrowly avoiding the loss of a finger or two to the rope that was still in motion, he scrambled over. On level ground again he fought the urge to get up and run. He saw Raoul Castres standing with his feet apart, his arms folded. It was a secret fearful triumph to be observed by Raoul, the oldest boy in the school, who came and went as he pleased and persecuted lesser boys at will. Felip stayed where he was and flung himself over onto his back, panting.

She's there, he said, his eyes closed. She's on a ledge. I think she's still alive. I saw her move.

The questions now like bats round his ears. Was she conscious? Was she injured? Were her eyes open? Did she speak?

He said she moaned; he could not see her face.

He began to regret his fabrication. As the questions multiplied he saw for the first time where his foolishness would most certainly take him.

No, he said. She could not be reached. She was on a ledge. She was too far back.

Someone said, A swimmer. We need a swimmer.

They looked at each other. Raoul made sure he was looking at Felip.

I can't swim, the boy said at once. I don't know how.

And Clarius Pech began to think how the lot of them had just behaved like fools, sending a liar down to bring back a report. He had seen Felip only last July swimming down at the bridge with his brother.

Then your job is done, he said and pinched the boy's ear hard. Go on home and wash your knees.

The boy grabbed his cap and ran. The men drew together like creatures in a herd.

He's a liar.

All boys are liars.

She can't be left.

If she's down there.

We have no choice. We have to try.

I'll try.

Stéphane smiled in turn at the faces looking his way, all of them carefully serious, seriously concerned, trying to disguise their relief. But to raise up a living body on the end of a rope? The practicalities of the exercise only baffled, until the youth Raoul, overcome with a desire for glory, offered to go down as well. Success then seemed more likely. And so it was decided: one man at a time; a knotted rope the first could cling to while waiting for the second; an additional harness, and extra rope to secure the girl.

It took time to prepare a reliable second line long enough not to be left dangling out of reach, and there was a chill in the air when they started back to the cliff above the Snout. They were many minutes getting organized—and getting organized again before Stéphane, smiling at the solemn mutterings of the priest, backed cautiously over the edge.

Raoul waited, wishing he had not volunteered. He remembered a childhood prayer to his guardian angel. He had been thinking only of the figure he would cut when the job was done. But there was no going back, not unless the rope, rigid now as a pole, were to break and send Stéphane Foix to his doom. Raoul wished it would. They were to wait until the tension came off the rope, listening for Stéphane to shout that he had transferred safely, and then they were to haul it back up. Standing in the sling, Raoul would attach it to the hook knotted into the rope, then he too would go over. He was wondering how many times the line would take the strain without breaking when Stéphane's voice, still cheerful, echoed in the mouth of the overhang.

She's not here!

The words were like the sun shining out from behind a cloud. Raoul took care that his face registered only puzzlement and concern. And then he said that he should get home for his supper.

By the time the tackle was put away, the day was almost done.

Henri's tavern filled up quickly. Mayor Pailhès and his friend the doctor had foreseen it and made their way there early enough to gain the coveted settle by the hearth. The bench and chairs at the two tables were already taken when Stéphane and Thierry arrived. Glasses of fortifying wine were placed in their hands and room was made for them at the largest table, though they had to make do with an upturned bucket and a crate. Once everyone was comfortable it was no hardship for those who had already picked apart the afternoon's operation to hear it all again, to give their own opinion again, and generally to repeat every word that had already been said, adding at least a dozen more whenever they felt moved. But something was missing. It was the girl of course. There was plenty of time to repeat and elaborate and then to embroider the few details they had seen or heard in the morning. Clarius Pech, his brown eyes bright with the novelty of his invention, said he had distinctly heard her cry out when she jumped. He said it was not in their language but in a tongue at once guttural and sibilant. Gustave Thibéry agreed and said he had made out the words 'I am unclean.' They were quite clear. Even Thierry, deaf as he was, swore he had heard laughter. On one thing they agreed. She was naked. That much they had seen without doubt. Indisputable proof of her madness. A good thing then that she was drowned, for what otherwise would they have done with her? Who would have taken her the eight miles into Soulières? Le Boulidou said he would not have objected to that particular duty, not once she'd been given a good scrub.

But the question of what they would have done with her was not one they had to bother with. The priest observed dryly that they had all been well and truly duped by the boy who lied. But Gabriel the schoolteacher, long-suffering and always kind, came to the boy's defence. He pointed out how difficult it must have been peering into the gloom under the Snout while hanging on to the end of a rope. You yourself would have found it difficult, he said to uproar, everyone relishing the image of the priest with the wind up his cassock and his hat spinning into the gorge.

By the time another round of drinks was finished, they had eaten all the bacon and bread in Henri's mother's house and consumed the last of a crock of olives. It was time to go home and eat. Someone said the night would be bright once the moon was up. And then Blind Henri let loose the thought that had been lingering unvoiced: the girl of course might still be at large. She might not be dead at all. The thought went hand in hand with its yet more unsettling sister: *if not dead, then not human.*

The only answer to that was to shrug as if it was of no consequence whatever. Now that night had fallen, it was perhaps best not to talk about these things.

Le Boulidou, the largest man in the room, said he would take the road home with Stéphane, though it was hardly a kindness, his own house being first on the road past the Snout and Stéphane young and fearless anyway. The others had seen beyond le Boulidou's loud voice, his broad shoulders, long ago. They laughed at him before he was out the door—but there was likely not a man who walked home that night without at least once checking over his shoulder.

Felip was in bed with his little brother when Thomas Maraval came back from the tavern. His wife said the boy was sleeping, but Thomas was already halfway up the narrow stairs. He yanked him from the bed.

You watch this, he said to the little brother. You watch this and learn.

He took off his belt and struck Felip, punctuating each word with a blow.

And this is one for each man you lied to. All seven — though clearly he was not counting. And this is one for your mother you have shamed. And your brother. And this one — though there were two — is for me. Satisfied, he went down to his supper.

That evening, when the last door had closed and the last dog had trodden its circle for sleep, the village was more than usually quiet. The very houses, like their masters, might have been listening into the night. No creature of God could have survived the fall.

And if he was not lying? The boy's mother whispered into the thick dark above the marital bed.

Then he'll know never to try.

That's not what I mean.

Now the boy's father also understood. If he was not lying. If the girl *had* been there. And if she was *no longer* there. If she was at large.

Alone beside each other, husband and wife stared into the darkness.

No creature of God.

All through the village that night the thought broke on the surface of minds sliding toward the edge of sleep.

ACROSS THE GORGE of the Freyne, out of sight over the high ridge, Chateau d'Aveyrac commands the wide northern slope of the neighbouring valley of the Vaz. Aloof in its dignified decay, the chateau stands neglected but not quite abandoned, home to Peyre Rouff and his unnervingly lifelike creations. It is now almost thirteen years since Peyre accepted the post of steward, forsaking the cottage at the marshes, where he loved his wife and sired a son — and where he lost them both. Now, his hair salted with grey, his voice dry as if from drought, Peyre Rouff lives out his days in solitude, bearing sole responsibility for this grand though decidedly faded estate — and practising meticulous suppression of his grief, repairing the damage whenever, as now, tonight, it breaks through. It has been a practice as stringent as any monk's. Success hangs on absolute attention to his work and on scrupulous isolation from the world. So careful is he, so rigorous, that he has marked himself as strange and lost the love of his fellow man.

At first, when he moved alone into the high chateau, the townspeople of Gougeac down near the marsh had been secretly relieved, though not without pity, the blow that fate had dealt him still fresh in their minds. Certain kind souls had continued their attempts to help him even then, travelling the steep hill up from Gougeac. Some even made the effort to come across the bridge from Freyzus, where he had lived as a young lad, and take the long road round the great burr of the hill before climbing up. They carried small gifts. They brought news — though the mayor of Freyzus, it has to be said, took it as an opportunity to raise once more the old question of water for his mill. Few who came made the journey more than once. Peyre Rouff set aside the gifts they brought and did not so much as raise an eyebrow at their news. The mayor of Freyzus was roundly rebuffed.

From time to time over the years one or two others made the journey — the priest from Freyzus, the vigneron from Gougeac — always interested to see how far down the road of grief Peyre Rouff had travelled. They returned with stories of how he was populating his house now with his creatures, specimens craftily mounted and sewn to look uncannily like life. But there was never welcome there, only Peyre Rouff with the terrible vacant look in his eyes, standing ravaged and broken amid animals that looked more alive than he. Like a dead person, they said, when they returned gratefully to the imperfect comforts of their own families and of their village, where anything shot and killed was duly and rightly eaten — not stuffed and left standing on the stairs. No, the journey had no rewards. Worse, it was unsettling. All those silent creatures, the tapestries half fallen from the walls, the long curtains, heavy with dust, drawn across the shuttered windows. It would not have surprised anyone to hear one day how he had fallen into decay himself, lying dried and silent by the black drifts of flies in the corner.

Now only the postman makes the trip, providing the weather is fine, delivering the occasional orders that Peyre Rouff places for his supplies. His work is another reason to consider him strange. It is no way, people say, for a man to spend his days. Yet it is in his work that Peyre finds the release he is looking for.

Today, with the completion of the outlandish creature (the hare, he continues to call it, though now it resembles no hare on earth), Peyre Rouff knows for a short space how the rest of the world manages to breathe and walk, free of torment, through its days. Here is the hare, transformed by his art. He is at one with it, and his unruly mind is silenced. He knows this work is successful. Both strange and beautiful, it draws the eye. It introduces some new thing into this world, something unknown. A possibility where none existed.

Extraordinary, at rest but watchful, the hare is at ease on its nest, the speckled feathers of its wings folded smooth on the soft fur of its body, its long, feathered tail partly hidden by the straw and pebbles. From whatever angle he chooses to view it, its glass eye seems to watch him. He chose this leveret for the roundness still in its face and for the length and luxuriance of its ears — like exotic, fur-lined leaves. He set them laid back, almost touching the folded wings, pheasant's wings summoning all the colours of the earth. The softness of his creation invites touch, but the hand hesitates to disturb the feathers' intricate pattern of tans and greys, sand and cloud, the ordered perfection.

He knows now that it is complete that it does not belong in the orangerie as first he intended. There, in the conservatory that stands on its own patch of ground past the western wing of the house, he has created over the years a diorama, a natural glade where every living thing outside the glass is represented. But this motley creature cannot crouch there even on the margins. It would be against nature. And all his work, all of it, is to honour nature, to honour life.

After long consideration he picks it up and carries it upstairs to the library. The wall at one end of the galleried room is hung with rows of ferrotypes made by Martin de Villiers, the seigneur. Except for one, they are largely failed images, hazy dream figures made when de Villiers was teaching himself to fix a photographic plate. There is something otherworldly in their shadowy presence. Only one of the images, left by a more skilled photographer, is sharper. Peyre knows it well. It shows a group of hunters posing with a wolf. The wolf appears not to be dead. It is standing with one forepaw raised, its head lifted as if scenting on the air its coming fate.

Peyre has often thought these images would belong in an exhibition of wonders. Now he thinks perhaps the library itself can be dedicated to such wonders.

He sets down the hare and its nest in the centre of the oval table. It looks perfectly at home. All is as he intended, unified and whole, even in its waywardness. The rightness of it brings something close to joy, and for a moment, as if he has slipped his fate, Peyre knows freedom. He draws a breath and it is like flight. If he could draw another. And another. If he could soar. And then his treacherous mind produces from nowhere the image of a falcon stooping in a sudden fall to its prey, and grief comes striding back in seven-league boots, knocking everything aside, more hale than before—and all the work of many weeks is as nothing.

In the kitchen, Peyre pulls the brandy bottle from the shelf and draws the cork. He drags a cup to the bottle and pours, not minding the spills.

TO FALL THROUGH air like a dagger had not been hard. She left the ground in a single stride and aligned herself for the drop, her legs straight as if in rigid refusal to step farther into air. She pulled her torso up, away from the rushing water, clapped her palms to her face, covering the sight of it, the thought of it, and pressed her elbows close to her chest, caging her dangerous fear. The impact when she hit the surface of the water thrust her arms high above her head and she had plunged like an iron rod let fall from some celestial forge, whiteness hissing upward, ripping like sand over her taut body, her extended limbs, as if water might peel away skin, tear arms from their sockets. She resisted, with every muscle she resisted. Her arms like flightless wings returning to her sides began to break her speed and so to reverse the movement of her body. Worms of lightning burned in her skull. She clawed her way up through the blinding, the deafening fizz, broke the surface in a tumult of molten silver. Blinded, she turned to the shadowy pool and swam like a drowning dog to the smooth rock wall behind. She found a lip of slimy rock and pitched herself onto it, jamming the toes of one foot into a seam of stone to hold herself there as she lay back, heaving and shaking.

She may well have slept, she may have fallen into oblivion, for at some new moment her eyes flew open and she knew herself held as surely in a trap as a fly in a web. She lay perfectly still. In the bright opening of her cave a thick form appeared, hard to decipher against the light. A clump. A swinging clump of something, someone. It hung a moment, shouted, and drifted up past the vault of rock. She feared its return, imagined it and others like it descending together to block her way. With a low gasp against the cold she slipped into the icy water to give herself to the flood and take her chances among the rocks. She made a strange diagonal entry to the current and surrendered to its force. At times she was tumbled in the flow, and once she was swept on her side with one arm aloft, turning the villagers' earlier projections into prophesy. If she could reach the other side, climb where the trees above the mill offered cover, a safe path up and away from these clamorous men and their ropes. When she came up against rocks she used them to push herself off in the right direction and arrived aslant the flow at the other side. The limestone of the rocky bank was overhung with tussocky grass. She could feel herself climbing already. Her fingers grabbed and she dragged herself ashore, scrambling for the vegetation that spilled down the cliff and would provide her cover. She climbed up, trailing blood from a skinned ankle and knee and stopping often to look in the direction of the village and make sure she could not be seen. She climbed up where there was most cover, keeping to the side of the old water course of the mill. She longed to stop and rest, but she climbed until her way was almost sheer and her legs refused her. When she found a place where once a boulder must have dislodged, she lay down in the depression to wait for dark so she could cut instead across the face of the incline.

And so it is that, at the same hour the boy Felip is whimpering into the thickening night, the girl is carving an oblique path across the opposite face of the gorge, following the bed of a dry channel, always climbing, believing herself always near the top, but finding always another ridge beyond. Higher and higher she goes, picking her way by starlight. She passes a place where nuts are lying beneath a tree growing at the base of a cliff. She breaks the blackened shells apart with rocks, but the nuts are bitter and dry and before long her stomach is cramping. She climbs on, hoping to find something more and hoping — because even under a sea of stars it is not easy to see — that no deep gorge lies between.

At last, cresting a ridge she sees the country open out below her and she starts down. On the broad sweep of the slope, she can make out a small house, crossed sticks on its domed roof like others she has seen, a stand of trees beside it; farther down the hill a long roof, walls, where a great house looms all pallid under the rising moon, another, smaller building beside it glinting back at the sky.

She crawls beneath the silvery foliage of a shrub and

watches, waiting. The moon is bright enough for foraging. She could find a sharp stone, scrabble and jab around under rocks to find a beetle, squeeze its insides onto her tongue. But beetles are more bitter than the nuts she had found. She could work at a patch of earth, prise up stones, dig down. But the ground is dust-dry and she would not find worms. The juicy thought of them only increases her hunger and she goes on.

The way down to the domed house is not steep. The rocks make steps for her descent between low scrub. When the thought of dogs returns, she is ready to run, but the only sounds she hears at her approach are those of her own bare feet shushing on the dry turf, whispering over the rocks. Sometimes, where the grasses she treads are longer, moths flutter up like snow returning to the sky.

Beside the domed house, a low stone wall with an iron gate on the farther side encloses a plot of land, fenced from the world by dark trees. She climbs over, though she can see already that the place offers no sustenance. She has seen a place like this before: stones growing from the earth in a jumble, flattened fingers of rock pointing to the stars, stone houses, too, shut tight, some with an iron grille to show the emptiness inside. And sometimes—her skin prickles at the memory—stone children with stone birds' wings growing from their backs. She looks around. There is one of them in the centre of this garden, another in the angle of the wall and the house. She goes to each to peer in the stone child's eyes —though she already knows what she will find: a gaze down-cast and no way to meet it. She pushes at the first, dislikes the coldness of the stone against her palm. At the second she waits longer. The eyes of this child are open, meeting hers, ferocious and defiant. She sucks the spittle in her mouth to a ball and spits in its face. At the same moment, she hears the rusty clang of the gate.

She slips between the stone child and the wall and crouches there under the ivy, watches as a man comes lurching along the path. A wind whispers through the cypress trees. They bow as if acknowledging his arrival. He comes with laboured breath and blundering feet. She watches. He kicks at nothing at all and flings his arms out wildly. In one hand he clutches a bottle. He is walking straight toward her. She makes her breath shallow, silent as the air itself. He is almost upon her when he stops and looks up, rocking. His eyes sweep the stars as if he thinks to find there some lost thing, some speck. He tips the bottle and drinks greedily. His eyes closed. She might slip now out of sight, away over the wall, but she is not quick enough, for his legs seem suddenly to melt beneath him and here he is on his hands and knees, groaning, his face level with her own. He has his eyes open. He tries to push himself up but instead stiffens his arms and empties his stomach at the feet of the child. At once she turns and scrambles away. The last she sees as she straddles the wall, he is lying inches from his mess.

Once, in just such a place, she had bitten into bright red waxy berries and swallowed. A little later she had done just as the man has done, and writhed and foamed too. Some places are poison.

She runs now, not keeping to the faintly beaten track leading down to the houses but following an erratic course that takes her to whatever cover she can find, whether shrub or hollow, and on to the next. When she comes nearer to the cluster of buildings, she stops to pry up a palm-sized rock. She knows houses like this. Few people. All manner of good things. She does not know their names, only the print of their savours on her tongue — grain, olives, eggs, water in troughs, water in fountains, mounds of earth hiding potatoes. And sometimes, yes, dogs too, in distressing numbers, but in houses of their own with iron-grilled gates to keep them in. And always they smell her, and always they raise a bedlam of baying in good time for her to run at the first sound of a door opening.

She goes farther down until she can see the lie of all before her: the wall that hems the small buildings and their yards; a long low building; and then the great house itself. Beyond the house is an open expanse, somewhere out there where the moon winks, the pale outline of a road, and then the land falls away to the obscurity of valley beyond. Everything is quiet. Even when she reaches the wall, the night is undisturbed. She lets herself in at a gate. Silence. She crosses a yard. Bright feathers curl white in the moonlight. They are lying on the bare earth in front of a small outbuilding. Crouching beside a stack of sawn branches she throws a pebble at the door. Then another, then a handful. She hears small, muted plosives of alarm from inside and a noise like dry leaves gusting in the wind, but no dog comes charging.

She creeps forward, pushes at the half-open door, and slips into the thick darkness. The birds fret. Their smell makes her nose burn. She falls on the first moving thing she can make out and gets a tight hold of its legs. A wave of panicked wings beats around her, past her. She kneels on her catch and bites into its neck, then rises up quickly and runs, the chicken dangling and banging against her thighs, its feet, which will not be still, like a bunch of ghoulish flowers in her fist.

She runs on, noting even as she runs, even in moonlight, those things she can return for, the tight heads of green leaves, the delicate fronds where she will find bright orange roots, light glinting from the surface of water in a bucket near the house. She runs on out of the grounds and on until she is out of sight of the house, running away from the first rise where she had seen the man and making for the higher, more thickly covered ground to the east, and then, when her heart has stopped hammering, she finds a place to squat and begin her meal. She tears away feathers and bites through the skin. The flesh is moist, not yet quite cold, one with her own mouth. When she has eaten her fill she carries the remains up to hide among broken rocks and settles there to a dreamless sleep while the moon slides away.

Down at the house, Berzélius beats his tail on the floor when he feels the reverberations of the front door banging open. He gets up stiffly from the rug in the corner of the kitchen, shakes, and walks through to the tiled entrance hall, but the man is already halfway up the unlit stairs and leaning on the banister. The dog's hips no longer take it up there. It wanders on, past the wolf that stands sentinel in a pool of moonlight at the foot of the stairs, past the man's discarded boots, on through the open door, and down the shallow steps to relieve itself on the sandy drive. Grunting in complaint, it regains the terrace and pads back inside. The rough pine table in the centre of the room is strewn with the remains of the man's supper: two empty bottles, a loaf of black bread in pieces, a waxy wedge of cheese on its side, a pot of oily beans, the spoon still standing in it. The dog sniffs the floor around the table and, finding nothing, goes to settle again on the old rug in the corner.

Peyre Rouff is well beyond all thought of food. Peyre Rouff has grappled his way in darkness up stairs afloat beneath his feet and has gained his room. He pisses once more—surely he has been pissing all night—ineptly toward and mainly into the pot and then lurches forward onto his bed. He feels the room spin once, twice.

When he wakes with his tongue thickened and his head ballooned with brandy, he has forgotten all about the arduous ascent to his bed. He has no memory of his nocturnal walk, every rock on the tussocky hill chalked by the moon, and he has no recollection at all of the face he saw the night before. He raises his head with difficulty to look at the clock on the mantle, sees only a blur, and sinks again to the rumpled grey linen of his bed, subsiding with a groan that on his next breath becomes a snore.

All morning, while the sun makes its slow passage across his shuttered window, he lies like a marionette abandoned. There is no one to witness his disgrace. Though the cats come in turn to greel and mew their discontent, walking away, each one indignant and disgusted, to a day of hunting for themselves, and though the peacock screams its wrath from the roof peak above, Peyre Rouff does not wake again until past noon when he gets up, still in his clothes of the night before. It is not the first time he has risen to find himself dressed for the day. In the difficult work of both sustaining and suppressing memory, Peyre is able most of the time to ride his mind, bending it to the creative act or filling it with his complicated system of lists. It is exhausting work and without relent. And when it fails him, Peyre fails himself spectacularly.

Leaning over makes his head pound. With care he picks up his pot. If now he were to leave his room and descend the way he came up, taking the wide staircase down to the entrance hall, he would see at once the front door standing open, his boots lying where he kicked them, and he might remember. But he turns right when he leaves his room and walks himself and his queasy stomach and the dangerously undulating product of his night down the back stairs to the water closet, then goes on through to the kitchen, where Berzélius lifts his great head and rises creakily to his legs. Peyre sets down a plate. The dog's chain jangles against the tin rim. Its jaws snap up the scraps, its black lips loose. Peyre pours a glass of water. He can take only sips, can move only slowly. He puts on his clogs without bending and goes out to the courtyard, where his chickens chuckle and run to him. He throws a handful of grain to them. He has to close his eyes against the sun as he turns and goes back in.

When he has restored order to his kitchen, he goes to his workshop in the yard and closes the door behind him. Berzélius wanders outside and ambles away to lie in the sun in the wide doorway of the coach house, where the stones warm even in winter.

On the other side of the house, the sunlight slowly steers its wedge of light over the boots and across the black-and-white tiles of the entrance hall.

In the afternoon, the girl returns. She has gorged on her stolen bird. It tasted only richer as the day wore on. She walks down the slope at the rear of the house and lies flat on a rock to watch. No man or woman is about. No dog. It is still and quiet except for the few hens that peck in the yard. But she does not need another hen. She does not know what she wants. She makes her way down farther still and round to the front of the house. Creeping nearer she sees that the front door is standing open. No one comes or goes there. She watches for a while. The air is very still. She picks up a rock, and creeps forward again, quiet as a risen shadow, up the stone steps to the terrace. And now she is close enough to see the boots lying in the hall—and the wolf standing guard. Her feet refuse her. Yet the wolf too is rooted. It gives no sign it has seen her though its head is turned her way. Blind then. Of course blind. She aims the rock, launches it, and whirls to run. But even as she turns, the impossibility she has glimpsed in the far corner of sight stops her in her tracks. The wolf had rocked. On stiff legs it had rocked. She looks back. It remains where it first stood. And then she knows it for certain; like the winged child: not alive. To look in its dead eyes would be to feel again the thrill of power, but she dares not go closer. She flees, scuttles back to the jumble of rocks and scrub she has chosen for her lair above the house, and settles down to hide behind closed eyes from her own excitement.

IN HIS WORKSHOP off the courtyard, Peyre is atoning for his intemperance, clearing the debris strewn in his frenzy of work the day before. As a kind of penance for his debauch, he delays going to look at his creation in the library. Instead he sets about methodically gathering up feathers, laying specimens of feet and claws in their numbered boxes, sweeping up straw. Disorder can make him sick.

When the table and benches are cleared, the floor swept, and all the drawers of the cabinets closed flush again, he pauses. His stomach and his head are working toward a tentative agreement, his spirits mending. He runs his fingers lightly over the face of the drawers. He does not have a project in mind to follow the hare. When he lives without work on hand, he is in a wasteland with no place to hide from the storm that threatens always to strike him down. Finding himself wide open to thought, he rushes to close himself off. Lists help. They always have. He sits down at the pine table and opens the drawer where he keeps his notebooks. Written in a tight, cramped hand, the entries nibble their way down the pages like columns of black ants, detailing the subjects he sets himself to think about each day — butterfly wings, the shape of a falling water drop, the colour yellow, the legs of a scorpion — in order to avoid thinking about the one thing. It is a sensible plan — given the waywardness of his mind — but cumbersome, for if he does not in practice complete his thinking by the day's end he is compelled to carry over the remaining thoughts to the next day. His lists are very long, for when he *is* working, he finds himself at the end of the day having thought only of his work — that is, having *thought* of nothing at all. And the penalty for that, dictated by his complicated mental discipline, is to add six entirely new items. It is an endless process — which for Peyre is the whole comfort.

He draws a line under his last entry and dates it. He begins at once to consider the legs of the common scorpion as he goes to the kitchen to prepare his supper. The list, faultlessly memorized, goes with him.

He sets a pot of potatoes and onions on the fire, a kettle of water to wash his plate and bowl, and makes his way through to the library in the company of the colour yellow, his next item. He pictures marsh marigolds and knows himself dangerously close to the one thing. As a skilful rider steers a headstrong horse, he turns his mind to Spanish broom, mounds of it cushioning the high slopes in the sunshine.

When the girl recovers her nerve, she resumes her private orgy of excess. She tears every last shred of flesh away from the bird, wanders off in search of water, and finds none. She goes back to her lair to suck on the bones. She sleeps a little. Late in the day she wanders a long way off in the cold but finds herself circling back. In the waning light of afternoon, in its cooling air, the attraction of the great house and its silent presence grows stronger. Green-tasting water to lap from the pail in the yard? Scraps thrown out from a doorway? There is too the impossibility of its upright dead. She remembers fleetingly the complicated thrill of observing the stiff-legged creature that did not respond. But for now she needs water.

The light is beginning to fail when she squeezes past the gate hanging by a single hinge and slips into the walled courtyard at the back of the house.

Peyre in the kitchen, feeling hungry now, feeling almost normal, begins his soup. Berzélius is already settled on the old rug in the corner and will not get up again until morning. One of the cats comes to sit on the table and watch Peyre eat and he lets it, his mind occupied with the wing pattern of a swallowtail. Again. And again. And again.

When he has finished eating, he sits for a while until the particular pattern he has been contemplating is complete, then he picks up his cup and his bowl and carries them to the stone sink. He pours water from the kettle and looks out through the grime of the window, past his own reflection and into the darkness, counting the turns of the mop round the bowl in his hand.

Yellow light falls on the cobbles from one of the windows in the house. It falls on the pail beside the door. Such an expanse of yard to cross. And the yellow eye open, watching. The girl sprints across to the wall of a low building and vanishes under the dark leaves of the ivy that clambers there, draping the length of it in a thick curtain. She slithers beneath the leaves until she reaches the end of the building then, keeping low, darts across to the pail, where she drinks in huge, lumpen gulps. And then — she cannot resist — straightening a little she cranes to look in at the window. The eyes of him! And she is gone, back into the cover of the ivy.

One turn of the mop, two, three, four. And there is the girl again — if only he would look. But on four he blinks and sets the bowl aside. He picks up his cup and begins to count to ten as he turns the mop. When he looks back out a faint breeze is lifting the ivy leaves on the workshop wall. Here just once. There. As if ghosts brush by on their absorbing business. Peyre dries his hands.

The girl waits until she can make a dash for the gate and catch her breath, quiet her heart in the shelter of the wall. In another minute she is leaping away like some outlandish gargoyle in the cold light of the stars.

*

Sleep will be good. Last night has drained the blood from Peyre's veins, replaced it with some heavy, viscous fluid that feels as if it might at any moment congeal and stop altogether. He waits for Berzélius to return to the rug and then he climbs the stairs.

In bed, grateful, the sheets straightened, the lamp extinguished, he sighs. He has scarcely begun his list before he lets go and begins the smooth descent to sleep.

Outside in the night, though she lies curled, the girl is wide awake. The eyes of him unseeing. Dead like the wolf's. Yet he a living man. Like the wolf, he was both there and not there. Like the wolf he carried no threat. Other men had eyes like bee stings.

In the long fall to sleep there is a jutting ledge where the mind catches. No wider than an eyelid, it opens yet on plains of understanding where what is known resides in brilliant light, all shadows lifted, every contour sharp. The mind sees and slides on, slips over the edge to oblivion. Or wakes. Peyre wakes. He knows suddenly and for the first time that he saw a face the night before.

It had looked at him, he is sure of it. A girl's face. Or a boy's, he could not tell. He had not remembered it when he woke earlier in a stink of alcohol. A face. He gets up and pads down the back stairs, goes out and stands in the courtyard. He stares at the moonlight on the ivy and tries to remember, then he goes inside and closes the kitchen door. He turns the key in the lock, draws the bolt home. No one had business being about the place without announcing himself. Herself? And where did he see the face? He goes through to the main entrance at the front, sees his wolf guarding the still-open door. Sees his boots lying where he kicked them. In an instant he recalls his walk up the hill, the sudden wave that overwhelmed him, breaking in a wreckage of loss about him.

There was never warning. Only ever the wave that came at him. Even when the shell of his body found quiet in the small satisfactions of his creations, the wave could break on him. Last night it had come out of nowhere, as always. One moment he was turning his handiwork over, enjoying the form, its stability, its completeness, turning it in his hands, thinking about raising a glass to toast its delivery into existence, and the next he was gagging on his risen grief and reaching for the neck of the bottle.

He knows now: he walked up the hill. O, the sky. Its endless cold beauty.

He goes out to stand on the terrace above the steps. He must have seen it at the graveyard. Where a lost face might find a home. Or a soul. He listens. There is nothing. But a thought does occur and he goes to find a lamp. He takes it outside to the barn where his four chickens roost. There are only three. He cannot find the fourth bird. And he saw only three this morning. So. A little thief about the place. He closes the door and slides the wooden bar in place, runs the chain through the socket and through the hole in the end of the bar, and padlocks all. When he goes back inside he makes sure the iron rod on the front door drops into its bore in the tiles.

It had been a broad face, squat, its eyes fierce and glittering. Angry. A girl or a boy? He tries to recall it in more detail — and begins to doubt. He could have dreamed such a face. Not his son's, though. He would have given all he had for that. Would give his life to see again just once his son's face made whole. He begins to work furiously on his list as he climbs the stairs for the second time.

Three times the girl dreams she is awake and returning to the chateau, is in the yard, is in the house where the yellow light shone. And three times she wakes. In the early hours of the morning she rises and moves away in the bloodless world, crouching to the body's needs. A finch begins to sing though the sky is still dark. Cautiously she stands and looks down the hill. She does not know what she wants at the house. Her belly is feeling slack again, but it is not that. Perhaps it is to look in again at the foreign world of edges and corners marking out space, to look at dead things that stand alive or living things that stand dead. To suddenly know again the mysterious twining and wrenching — herself both separate and at one with what she saw. Or perhaps just to see again that strange dead stare, the neutral gaze that would not flay her. But she can articulate none of this. She is only drawn, as lightning to the tree, as thirst to water, to the eyes of the man, and to the wolf standing in the hall.

In the pale dawn light, she makes first for the front of the house. Everything is closed. She goes up the flight of steps and pushes at the door, listens. There is no reaction. The thing then still standing stupidly dead-not-dead inside. She pushes at the door again. It does not yield. Now she does not know what she wants. She goes round to the back and on into the courtyard. The bucket is gone. She eyes the pump. She has seen a woman operate such a thing. The screeching and braying could be heard all over the hill. She runs through to the kitchen garden. The bold green leaves she tears are bitter on her tongue. She runs round to the chickens—and finds none. She can smell them, but the door of the barn will not open. Thwarted and angry she makes for a long low building. On a whim she tries the door at the end. She grabs the latch with both hands and it makes a click. She stops and listens. A fox is crying somewhere in the distance. Nothing responds to the click. Slowly she pushes against the door, waiting again after the creak of the wood. She steps inside carefully, her bare feet making no sound at all. The sight of bushes inside unsteadies her and she stands amazed. Here is undreamed-of plenty. Birds of every kind large and small, birds of every hue, in the trees, standing on shelves, lying in trays. And all of them freshly dead. She runs to the largest, a ring-necked pheasant, and grasps it. It is stiff and strangely light and the mystery of dead and undead returns. She holds it with both hands and brings its breast to her teeth, tears at the skin there and spits. She uses her fingers. The skin does not come away as it should. She traps the neck under her knee and rips the skin up and away from the body. Inside is nothing she expects and she is overtaken by anger and disappointment. She squeezes her eyes shut and puts it to her mouth. It is rough and dry. Withered grass bunched tight. A fine powder coats her tongue. She drops the bird and snatches up the next, a quail. Her hands know by the lightness of it that it will be the same. Still she tears with her teeth, rips away the feathered skin, and she can smell it, the strangeness. Bird-not-bird. She pulls away parts with her teeth. Though she licks and sucks at the innards, her mouth fills again with the bitter dust. She throws down the quail and reaches for another, smaller bird, this one stranger yet for it is caught in the act of flying off, its feet frozen to a dead bough that leans against the wall. But flying, therefore surely less dead. She tears it free. This time she holds the neck in her teeth and yanks the body away. Something thin and sharp as a claw springs out from the neck and pierces her lip. She yelps and flings it away, then picks up the branch and hurls it after. A pair of wood doves on a tree limb topples from the shelf it strikes. She does not like this world of the self-contained dead. They are unpredictable. She spins, losing her sense of direction in this walled space. When she sees the open door again she runs.

Peyre wakes not as the fragile toper of yesterday, nor as the uneasy watcher who rose in the night to padlock his chickens and secure his front door. He is restored. His self has returned. Intact, it can steer his dangerous mind through another day, ride it with the reins taut and its vision blinkered, turning it from the boy who lies always at the edge of sight. He starts on yesterday's list even as he leaves his bed, his body assuming the dreamlike quality of the sleepwalker while his mind engages fully with its subject — the outstretched wing of an owl, its primaries extended like fingers that would comb the air, its markings as if a painter ran a brush of white in bands across the wing half closed. His mind is tracing each feather, one for every stair as he goes down to the kitchen. But halfway down, when the image of the girl's face slides into his mind, he lets it.

Berzélius, as always, beats his tail on the floor and cranks his bones to stand and stretch, his hindquarters shaking with the effort. Peyre pours water into a dish and the dog drinks noisily, its tail gamely waving. Peyre keeps his mind trained on the contours of the face while he stirs the coals in the range. When Berzélius has finished, Peyre opens the door and the dog goes dutifully outside. Peyre continues with his morning ritual, lighting the range and setting his pot of soup to warm, filling a kettle of water, placing his bowl and his cup on the table, his spoon in position, before he goes to let his chickens out.

He knows for certain he was not imagining the face. And last night he closed only three chickens in the barn. But he can check the straw-filled corners to be sure, reach behind the stack of baskets for a sick or a stone-cold bird — though he guesses he will not find one.

Well. He was once a hunter. A trap for a thief should be easy to devise. Of course he — she? — might be accompanied. That would be more difficult. And he could not count on Berzélius to help him out. Berzélius, who loves all things on two legs — even chickens — would be no help at all. He never was a guard dog. No matter. If the thief is about he will catch her. Him? Unbidden comes the thought: not 'him.' Let it not be 'him.' If the thief is about he will catch *it* soon enough. And then what? Teach it a lesson. Make sure it never returns. That too will be easy to do. Though now his willful mind is refusing to follow the thought, is instead fixating on the face — so close in age to his son's, so close — and his resolve vanishes as he imagines taking the young face by the chin, and gently turning it to look it in the eye. But a thief is a thief, and he does not want one in the house.

The girl's lips and tongue are burning. The sun itself is inside her mouth and there is no river to quench it. If she swallows, she will burst into flame. She crams her fingers in her mouth, claws at her tongue as she runs. And there is the pump. She throws herself down and licks the green stone beneath. It is not enough. Her fingers find the handle and close on it just as the woman's had done. She pulls it down. Once, twice.

Berzélius lifts his head. He loves the sound and what it signifies. Already the muscles of his face are drawing his lips to a grin.

Three times. Water splashes her feet. As she bends to drink, she sees, framed in the arch of her raised arm, her fear advancing on all fours, hindquarters low, lips drawn back from yellow teeth. It is too close for her to turn and run. She begins to back away toward the gate. At the wood stack, her fingers find the end of a sawn limb. She snatches it up and closes both hands on the stock. She can feel its uneven weight as she swings it to her shoulder, her eyes still fixed on the dog, her mouth foaming.

Peyre comes round the corner of the coach house both a moment too soon and a moment too late, for the girl, with her feet planted square under her, her knees bent and every muscle taut, has already swung the sawn branch that so handily terminates in a clump of knots, and Berzélius has already lunged forward to greet her. A hoarse high yelp is the only sound the dog makes before it falls. The man's voice rings on. It is not directed at her. It is a voice carrying within it something unnameable and dear, something she seems to know from another time. Against every instinct to run, she freezes.

Zélu! the man is saying. Zélu! And he is down on his haunches, bent over the body of the dog. She sees the way his own body bends to it, curves, arcs itself to shelter and protect. And then his back begins to straighten and he is rising. She dives behind the pile of sawn boughs and holds her breath. The man bellows into the new morning.

Devil! Filthy devil! The words ringing like hammer blows in the sunny courtyard. And then silence. She risks a look. He has returned to the dog and is rising again, this time lifting the dog with him, the mass of black and tan hanging in his arms, the hindquarters loose against his legs. The dog's jaw is slack. Its head lolls and its eyes are strangely silvered. The man's body matches the thing she heard in his voice. He holds the dog about the ribs. It hangs against him, almost the length of him, its head askew as if its attention is caught by something on the ground. Her heart lurches with a yearning known only to itself. She watches the silent rocking of man and dog in their slow dance and she is unaware of her blistering mouth. The man holds the dog closer. His own eyes are closed. At last he bends at the knee and takes the full length of the dog in his arms and with it cradled so walks to the house, kicks open the door, and goes inside. And still she does not run. There is something there that she longs to see again, that unnameable thing that her heart knew though she has no memory to match it. She wants that. She closes her eyes so that she can see it again inside her head: the curve of the man's body as he bent to his dog, his arms as he folded it to him. She wants that. But when the man comes out he is someone else entirely. He looks wildly about him and she knows he is looking not just for her but for something to harm her with.

The makeshift club lies where she dropped it. He picks it up and roars into the blue morning.

Get away! Get away from here! Then he turns away and leaves her narrow line of vision.

Like some stark animal shorn to the white bone she springs from her cover, but she is not quick enough. He hears her and spins, hurling the club after her. It strikes her heavily on shoulder, but she, undaunted, runs on.

You! You! Get away from here! Get back to hell, damn you!

A stone too strikes her on the back but still she runs, lurching, low to the ground, her knees bent, her upper body lunging forward, hands ready to grasp at wall, at scrub, tussocks—whatever might pull her faster away. Farther off, she straightens and lengthens her stride.

Out of breath as if he has himself been running, Peyre watches her pale bony body cross the wide face of the hill beside the house.

And he does not pursue her.

BERZÉLIUS IS ALREADY stiffening on the kitchen table. Peyre needs to drink half a bottle before he can even go to the dog again, before he can even look. Where the girl's club struck, the side of the dog's head has caved completely. The jaw is askew and the mouth has filled up. He steps outside and tries to breathe deeply. His dog reduced in an instant to a carcass lying on the table. Beyond the power of any medicine to mend. But he can do something. He will not lower Berzélius into the cold ground. His hands can restore at least a semblance of life, at least an illusion. He walks for a while trying to clear his head, where everything—the girl, his dog, his son—competes to dismantle his sanity. The longer he walks, the clearer his course of action becomes. He will not take the dog apart, cannot. However marvellous his art, it can never deceive him. The eyes will never see again. The only eyes he learned to meet since his son. The only eyes. He can do nothing for the animal. It will never be Berzélius again. Neither in life or death. He will be alone. He feels a swift panic rising at the thoughts that certainly lie in wait. Action is his only salvation.

He goes to open up the barn and feed his chickens, and then he takes up a pick and a shovel.

He breaks a patch of rough ground near the coach yard, then methodically lifts away the stones and the soil. He tries to keep his mind trained on his task. He concentrates on the roughness of a pebble, polishing it with thought, but the vision is overlaid with the unthinkable. He digs until the mound of earth beside the hole grows into a small hill. He climbs into the hole and carries on, rhythmically chopping, digging, shovelling. He does not want to see the silvered eyes.

When the hole is deep enough, he climbs out and lays his shovel beside the mound of earth. He does not know how he will manage. He has no plan, can only do this one thing. He goes to the house and comes out carrying Berzélius. He walks stiffly and stares straight ahead. A dark gout falls from the dog's jaw as he shifts its weight.

At the edge of the hole he lays the dog on the ground as if careful not to hurt its bones. He climbs down and hauls the dog in with him. He bends to arrange the legs, but they will not comply. He lays his hand on the brown shoulder, then pulls himself up and out of the hole and picks up his shovel. And now he is remaking the ground furiously, shovelling the earth back in, hard and fast, his jaw tight, his arms dangerous.

The earth makes a low hill over the grave. Peyre stands breathing heavily, evenly, until the rhythm of his breath breaks apart and there is only his sharp breathing out, and breathing out, and breathing out, in one ragged chain and if the girl had been witness she would have recognized it.

His shoulders heave. She would have known this, she would have remembered. She has done the same. It comes like a storm that batters the heart inside the ribs, that shakes the shoulders and convulses the chest. The body a broken rat in its jaws.

Peyre shuts his eyes against the vision of the girl pale on the hillside, though there is no controlling anything now. He has lost control and sees her still. He carries the shovel back to the shed and goes into the house. Its cold kitchen. He lays more kindling in the range and closes the door.

The same age. His son was the same age when he died. Were it not for her strings of hair streaming he could have thought her his son running for his restored life, his white bones dirtied with the earth. Watching her, with Berzélius at his feet, he had wanted to call out. *Come back! Come back forever!* But the dream cry had lodged in his throat and the girl had run on, smaller and still smaller, and then swung to the left and out of sight. Now Peyre alone with the vision does cry out, for in the chaos of girl and dog his son has broken through.

He rams his fist against his mouth, and his stomach heaves as if he is choking on his own voice. She arrived like the weather. Like a sickness, like a birth or a death, she changed everything. The very thought of her is an iron claw dragging at the coals of his heart, raking them to red life.

The impulse to pursue her had died not long after it arose. What to do with such a poor mad creature? The same age. The same age. He grasps at his day's list, but his mind is like the face of a blind man turned to the pages of a book. Though he holds it there, it will not see, will not disengage from its own vision. He makes his hands go about their remembered tasks. The crackling of the wood as it catches in the stove is suddenly, absurdly, pointless. His hand cannot reach even for the soup pot to draw it onto the hob. Stark limbs flailing down the hill. Her bony arms. The terrible strength of them. The broken face of Berzélius. How work? How think? It is not possible. Again he sees her running. Again he wants his son, naked climbing from the river, limbs no longer a child's, not yet a man's, streaming water. He does not bother to eat. He lets the stove die. Brandy helps. Peyre drinks long and hard until the walls tilt. He goes upstairs to lay himself upon his bed and wait for oblivion. He lies on his back on top of his bedcovers and his eyes close themselves of their own accord. There is no darkness. There are no dreams. No memory to squeeze his heart.

The girl does not get far. She is a tangle of affliction and need, hunger and thirst indistinguishable from pain and cramps, nausea and fear. She lies down beneath the harsh cover of a furze and closes her eyes on the clamour of her body.

THE MEN OF Freyzus continued to search for several days. They revisited the river and then they climbed up the hills behind the village, up among the goats and the sheep. They took guns of course, not for the girl but for the chance of a mountain sheep or a chamois. Looking out over the enormous length of the valley, they considered finding her a hopeless task, and since there was very little in the way of game to be had, unless they climbed much higher and made an expedition of it, they quickly lost interest.

The women are glad when their husbands come to their senses. They have already decided among themselves the girl will not—cannot—be found. If she is not indeed a visitor from another world, she certainly behaves like one—appearing out of nowhere, then disappearing without a trace.

The schoolmaster, tired of her lingering influence in his classroom, decides that the best way to rid the pupils' minds of her presence is to organize a small search of his own. He lets both boys and girls loose on the hill. As he hoped, the sunshine and the exertion in the brisk air clear their heads. In the course of the day they enact every possibility of escape and discovery and capture. The opportunity to talk all they want about the girl loosens her hold on them. They return to their houses grubby and exhausted, and with renewed respect for their teacher, who has given them such a splen-did holiday. When they go to bed, they do not give the girl another thought.

Except the boy Felip. Felip begins to believe the lie he has told. It gives him dreams. He sees her palely glowing on the dank rock, dangerous. He sees her rise up naked and beckon-ing, then he wakes yet again to a clammy belly. Sometimes he dreams her in the village, dancing, the old men clapping their thighs in time to her feet. But here is the thing. She is alive, he knows it. She is alive and she is somewhere in the garrigue. He has seen her and now she is gone, an exotic to be hunted, to be outwitted, and at last to be entrapped.

He takes to wandering by himself up in the hills above the village before darkness falls, hoping to see her, hoping to catch even a glimpse. He does not know what he will do if he finds her. Except gaze again. But the cries of the birds and the forlorn clang of the goats' bells only make him feel more alone. She is not there. He returns home in a daze, receives clouts about the ears for lateness, and scarcely notices. Once, he stops to listen to the old men who sit under the marronnier. They sit on the two benches with their hands on their knees or with their arms folded across their vast bellies. They have the brazier burning there for its brightness and its comfort on a winter afternoon, though the chestnuts from the tree are long consumed. They are speaking about a wild child, or maybe there is more than one, emerging from the woods, from some high, inaccessible cave way up the gorge. They tap their pipes and say, Yes, it has happened before. It is not unheard of. You never know what lives in these parts.

Felip kneels to play with a little white and ginger cat, careful to keep within earshot.

No one has travelled the length and breadth, they are saying, not even the geometers who came and built their towers. No one. Remember that other man of science, someone says. The whatdoyoucallist who said there was a boy near Rodez with a head as big as a bell. They all remember that. And there are boars out there that weigh as much as a small cow and can split an oak in two. No one knows what else dwells in the deepest cover. No one.

The cat rolls in the dust. The old men suck on their pipes in silence until the thought of the girl summons other feral creatures from the hill to squat at their feet there under the marronnier — though evidence of their existence is less than robust and no one remembers on what authority it rests. The boy feigns indifference and busies himself amusing the cat with a piece of string. The old men know they have an audience and the creatures grow more exotic. There is the old man who arrived in the time the monks still prayed over on the slopes above the Vaz before the chateau was built. He appeared one day, babbling and bearded with not a stitch to cover him. He banged open the door to the chapel while the monks were at vespers and ran gurgling and chittering right up to the altar, where he turned suddenly and, seeing the monks as if for the first time, dove under the altar cloth and stayed there trembling until he was coaxed out with the blessed bread. And then there is the boy over near the Tarn, grimy and black as soot; he went on all fours and was never heard to utter a word. The doctor from Lodève took him away to Paris, but the boy died before they arrived. And strangest of all are the twins. It was long ago. Oh so long ago. Old Robert's grandfather heard the account when he was a child and his grandfather heard it from *his* grandfather. The old man had only told it once, but Robert remembers the details. The twins were girls. They too went about on all fours, for their mother, the one who raised them, was of course a wolf, what else? When they were found they yapped and whined like pups, their mouths pulled into long dog-grins. They snapped their white teeth when anyone drew near, but once they were given morsels of meat they whimpered for more and after that they began to lick at any hand extended toward them. And the wolf? the boy is thinking. Of course, says old Robert as if in answer, the two girls never would approach my great-great-grandfather, for it was he who shot their mother.

Now you're being superstitious, says Pech. Giving a she-wolf some power. Their mother! he said. What about their real mother?

I shall have to think, Robert says, getting up to refill the jug.

Felip too gets up and makes his way home in the dusk. For the first time he sees the stories for what they are — idle entertainment for old men with no lives of their own to live. The girl, it seems to Felip, does not belong in the company of legend, these less-than-human creatures, rude and grovelling. Their stories are as coarse as the imaginings of his school fellows who brag they will lead her in triumph through the village. Yes. On a leash.

But he has seen her in mid-air, free like a bird in flight, a bird from the highest air, folding its wings to plummet straight as an arrow. And in dream at least he has seen her stripped clean by the chill waters, her bones gleaming like the Saviour's, as if they might break through the translucent skin. Crouched awkwardly, clinging to her ledge, she might have risen from some subterranean passage to split the smooth dark surface of the water and slide noiselessly to her rock. Above all, the boy favours his vision of frozen flight, its declaration that she does not, indeed, belong to the coarse and rock-bound world of the village where every living thing — every donkey, woman, girl, boy, man raised on the most menial and filthiest of daily tasks — sees on the road ahead only unremitting drudgery. In his mind she has broken free of human bonds. He will think about it while he shovels pig manure. He will think about it while he goes for water. He needs her to be alive, to be for him a sign, a token at large in the world, of life redeemed from toil. But she is nowhere on this side of the gorge. He would have known. He would have felt her. No, she is on the other side. She is in the next valley where the crazy man lives all alone.

After a week of gossip she is larger than life and she takes many forms. For some she is a tall, full-breasted woman — though one who still has not acquired any clothes — serving men's needs on lonely nights. For others she is half-animal, returning to prowl the village unseen after dark. But the boy rejects all her incarnations. For him she is sufficient exactly as he saw her, complete and perfect in the purity of her fearless leap.

PEYRE OPENS HIS eyes to a thin lemony light cracking the boards of the shutters and he remembers and the day is hollow before him. It has been raining. A hole in the gutter is releasing the last of it drip by drip. He lets his eyelids fall heavy and slow, as if a vision could be quietly stifled. The girl. The contours of his life pulled out of true by her arrival and all disrupted, all.

He gets up and goes downstairs. His lists have deserted him. He is walking through absence, trying not to see it, not hear it. He lights the stove against the bleak chill of his kitchen, then goes out to the barn.

Outside the day is cleaned and gleaming, the sand lustrously rich between the cobbles, the vine fresh and glistening along the wall. All is as it should be, the white clouds bowling away to the southwest, the sky bracingly blue. The cats come to greet him and he hates them. He lets the three hens out, throws them a handful of grain, and goes back in to his breakfast.

Without appetite he eats some of the last day's soup and leaves the rest. Then he takes up a broom and sweeps out the corner where Berzélius used to lie. He takes the rug outside and shakes it for a long time before he puts it back in place.

He cannot escape the destruction she has wrought. In the kitchen garden just beyond the courtyard, where he grows a few vegetables, where he keeps the low hedge of herbs trimmed as his uncle Guilhem once had, where in summer he sows a handful of beans, he sees this morning only the plants the girl has trampled in her panic to get away. The girl who murdered his dog and summoned his son. The girl. He does not know how she was able to gather such speed with her strange, uneven gait.

He laces up his boots, takes up a stick and a rope, and sets off down the hill. She will be miles away by now. Nevertheless. He walks on, his stride suddenly purposeful, his eyes watchful.

The land, seductive in the rinsed light, holds its secrets close. One of the pair of ravens that lives up at the churchyard ratchets skyward on its throaty cry. It circles once and returns to the cypress by the furze brake. He walks forward, watching the tree. The raven rises again and circles at his approach. Again it settles. Something, then, close by. He does not need to look for long before he sees her bony feet and her shins, thin as deer shins, protruding from the cover of an inhospitable furze.

Come out!

Only the raven answers, taunting him with two short cries and flapping to a farther tree. He calls out again, glancing round uneasily as the raven mimics him. He listens, wondering now about accomplices, a trap. There is only the faint hushing of the grasses and the nattering of the small birds among the scrub. A new thought comes to him and he does not want it to be. He steps forward warily and reaches to put his hand on her foot. Clammy and cold to the touch yet not rigid, not yet dead this body—as he might be, stark naked in the morning air. He takes off his jacket in readiness, then grasps her ankle and tries to rouse her. The furze obstructs him. He has no option but to take hold of both legs and drag her out to the open. She pulls herself to sitting. Her eyes waver and her jaw hangs slack. A working of foam rims her mouth. The same face he saw two nights ago at the grave, alert and fierce, peering out from the dark leaves. The same androgynous quality. The high wide cheekbones, the broad brow, and fleshy lips. And now sightless, it stares full at him again, its expression flat. She sways. When he takes up his jacket and makes to put it round her, her eyes roll back in her head and her body collapses as if suddenly emptied of its bones.

So that here now, as if from some wayward deity, is a corporeal message laid at his feet, a call to wake from his eternal grief. He would have preferred a bolt of lightning, sulphur from a rock, serpents. He lays his jacket over her and picks her up. A fold of cloth falls over her face, and in an instant he is picking up his son again. His stomach contracts and his limbs come alive with the memory, thrumming with the force of the blood that plunges through them. This is not the same as the memories he keeps in abeyance, held offstage in the theatre of his mind. This is physical. This is here, now. It is reliving. His legs are unsteady as he climbs back up toward the house. Though she is not heavy, he staggers. His hands shake. When he reaches the courtyard, he does not know where he is going with her. Not in the house. Not in the house. He cannot take another step. He pushes open the door of the workshop with the toe of his boot and stands heaving for breath.

It is a moment before he recognizes what he sees. His trembling as he surveys the wreckage before him is volcanic. He lays the girl down among the broken bodies, the meaning of the white foam about her mouth suddenly clear. The meaning of her need for water. He sees the spittle lining the edges of the girl's mouth for what it is. The broken bodies of the birds make sense. The two phenomena disastrously joined. He would like to turn his back on her, thief, killer, that she is. Instead, he goes to the pump, keeping an eye always on the door of the workshop. He returns with a pail of water, conscious that he is going to the aid of his offender. He wets a rag, thinking how his god of torment is yet not done with him but sends this creature in some elaborate jest to plague him. He turns her face to one side and cleans the corner of her mouth, wiping firmly. Her eyes beat against their private dark and open wide. She struggles to sitting and scoots backwards until she is jammed against a box of shavings. When Peyre tries to continue, she bares her teeth and from the back of her throat aims a harsh and foul-smelling exhalation at his face. He stares hard into her eyes.

I'm trying to help you, he says, and his voice sounds unnatural and unnecessary in the air between them.

Her jaw remains slack, though her sight has returned. Her eyes are speaking as clearly as any words: Stay away. He hears again the rasping exhalation, distant, like an echo in her throat.

I want to help you, he says. He could just as well himself be hawking dry air for all the response she offers. What's your name?

But her eyes show no reaction and he wonders if she can hear at all.

Like one who is deaf and mute himself, he mimes pain all round his lips. He splashes water on his mouth and makes expressions of pleasure, relief. She makes a sudden move toward the door, but he is quicker and blocks her way and she falls upon him in a fury that flares and as suddenly collapses upon itself. He pins her arms and grabs the hair at the nape of her neck, pushing her face down toward the bucket to rinse her mouth. She struggles once and then he feels her body convulse. He brings her up for air and then — committed to getting the job done whether she understands or not — thrusts her face back into the water. The knuckles of his hand whiten. One of her hands reaches up to claw at his, bringing blood to bead on the surface. Never loosening his grip on the back of her head for fear she will turn and bite, he relaxes his pressure enough to let her lift her face for breath and as she gasps he catches her arm more securely, holds it lower so she cannot claw again, then pushes her down again to sluice her mouth. Three, five, seven times, they enact this living murder. And then it seems as if she begins to understand, or perhaps she is so weakened that she can no longer resist. Her body, understanding it is not about to die, not just now, begins to cooperate. He is the one now gasping to restore his ragged breath. He softens his hold when he feels her lean spontaneously toward the water but brings her up swiftly before she can swallow. Now her body yearns for it, every muscle lengthening so she seems like a snake to stretch forth. He pulls and drags her into the yard and over to the pump, but he cannot manage to hold her and to draw fresh water at the same time. He sees how her eyes are darting now, the glances swift as dragonflies in every direction. She will bolt. He knows she will. Who would not? And then? Run naked down into the valley like any wild animal to die curled in a convulsion of pain?

He has a low stone outbuilding that houses only crates and empty tea chests, a broken chair. It has a simple wooden door with a bar across. She is as a slippery as a fish as he pulls and drags her in its direction. When she sees what he is about she begins to fight with more purpose, but it is a sorry ballet they perform, calling for her teeth and fingernails, his hips and chest and knees, and when he pushes her inside, she is exhausted and buckles forward.

Peyre too is exhausted. Walking back to the house, he understands how he has been delivered a new torment after all these years, a special affliction, exquisite in its subtlety, calling for him to nurse this girl, this girl who dispatched his only companion, back to health. And he accepts it fully, opens his heart to it and welcomes the pain, feels the aptness of its uncanny justice. He renews an old vow: to endure, to submit to whatever trials life concocts for him and to do it with a will, acknowledging always that to die can never be enough.

Thud of wood against wood. Wands of light through the cracks in the wooden door. Chinks of it from under the broken roof tiles. She listens, hearing his footsteps retreating, and rises shakily in the silence to smack against the door, hands flat. She listens again, hears only her own heart pounding. She scrabbles at the edge of the door. It makes the smallest rasping sound. And it gives, just slightly. But though she pushes and pushes, the movement comes to nothing at all. The effort leaves her trembling and deeply nauseous as the surge of energy drains away.

She lies down in the partial dark and for the space of a breath it is enough to be free of the man's shocking grip, but it does not last. Her insides are cramping viciously. She pushes herself to a squat and heaves dryly. She licks at her lips and the burning returns. She stays there, squatting, listening for the man, waiting her chance to run from this nausea, this agony. When she hears the man returning, she crawls to the door and crouches beside it, ready.

Peyre has anticipated her. He slides in through the barely opened door and shuts it again before she can dart out, blocking her path while she tries to fix him with her dull and wavering gaze. He wonders if she is about to collapse.

He has brought water for her in a pail and he has brought a cup. Slowly he sets the pail down. Says, Water. He scoops the cup full and with both hands brings it to his lips, keeping his eyes always on her. He takes a mouthful and swallows noisily, watching her over the rim.

The girl's thirst returns to flare and rage in her throat. She recalls the water flooding her face, the man's hand on the back of her head.

He takes another drink and holds the cup out to her, willing her to cooperate. She hesitates, then in a quick movement knocks it to the floor and is down on her hands and knees, lapping. When the water is gone, she looks up at him expectantly. And here, he thinks, is something close to understanding, something as perfect and precise as any language: she wants more. It is the gaze he knew in Berzélius, has known in every living beast, a line of meaning running between them, comprehension absolute. He scuffs at the floor with his foot to make a depression, pours water into it from the pail, and steps back while she sucks at the water. He does it again. And still she is looking to him to pour again. Instead, he crouches down at the pail and lowers his face toward the water, trying to show her what he wants her to do, always keeping his eyes on her, but the water is too far below the rim and he will lose sight of her. He scoops with his palm, splashes water into his open mouth, then stands up and steps back, wipes his chin with the back of his hand. Her wariness now is tremendous—but the water in the pail so inviting. It seems for an instant as if she will come forward. Instead she pushes with her heels and snakes and rocks backwards, arching her spine, until she has the wall behind her. Her body convulses once, twice. Her hands drag across her belly as if to claw it open and release all that ails her. He slips away again. He has no idea how to help her.

In the deep gloom of the shed, the girl drags herself to the pail. Like a creature waking from the underworld, lowering its face to some elixir of life, she drinks until her belly distends and her bladder burns, her body nothing more than a conduit for the water. And still she drinks. A dark stain spreads beneath her and seeps away in the dirt.

When Peyre returns an hour later she is lying curled in the corner. The pail is overturned. He steps forward and picks it up. She does not move. Nor does she open her eyes when he comes back a second time with the pail refilled. He had trusted that the water would help. He hopes he is right. He rattles the handle and lets it fall with a clang. She doesn't stir. He lets himself out. As he slides the bar in place it occurs to him for the first time that he does not know what he will do with her if she dies — or if she recovers.

When the girl opens her eyes again, hours have passed and the gloom in the hut has turned to night. Her craving is fully awake — and it is not only for food. In her head there are stars, a moon floating above the hills. She finds the door and pulls at it, pushes it. She examines each wall, her fingertips reading the dark, her feet skirting the stacked crates. Her fingers travel from stone to the wood of the closed door and then to stone again and back to wood, and then the story is complete, is closed about her tight, and there is no way out. She remembers the panic and the terror of that other hut, before wood had splintered into blinding day. And she begins to howl.

Something peels the film of sleep from Peyre's eyes and skirls on among the stars. Again it comes, harsh and unearthly, and yet again. He listens, wide awake now. Her keening floats over the sleeping countryside. It skims the low buildings of the courtyard and rises up over the great house, travelling unchecked into the limitless night. It is hard to recognize the human voice in what he hears. He has never heard such a sound. It belongs to the creature that he saw on all fours, lapping. Every muscle serving her thirst, only her hairless skin marking her from the beasts. The sound he is hearing, neither animal nor human, is as it should be. It matches the deep bend of her haunches, the angular blades of her shoulders. It matches the movement around her mouth when the muscles there exposed her gums, drawing back her upper lip toward the nostrils and so baring her teeth in — dear God — the semblance of a snarl. But as he listens, the cry teeters on some immeasurable peak of rage and plunges from it to a place where despair rocks in darkness profound, so that his own grief comes home to lap in his most hollow place, and he begins to weep. And then he knows her fully human and he could join his voice, his grief, to hers, is almost moved to go to her again — for to console a fellow creature is balm not only for the consoled. And yet the rawness of her, her voice as naked as her body, holds him back. So self-sufficient is she in her work of lamentation. He does not go. He lies listening to the rage in it decline, hearing the passion exhaust itself until the sound that comes rhythmically through the dark is no more than the sound of a rusted gate swinging in a sullen wind. When night is restored to itself, he thinks of her sleeping, curled, her nakedness something fetal, something holy.

At dawn he has made a decision. He will feed her and after that she will need to be clothed before anything else can be done for her. He wants to help her, but he is not sure where he will take her, or when. Almost every gesture she makes, every sound, every turn of her head, every grunt, even her glance at times, is animal. He does not know if he will be able to take her anywhere, so feral is she. Yet he has seen a flash of understanding and he has heard her human grieving, and though she might yet run from him and launch herself again into the wilderness, he cannot let her go naked. Lunatic and wild. Were she to find herself taken by coarser men? What then?

He has a smock his son wore to school. In his hunger Peyre has gone to it often. It hangs in an empty armoire as if in some austere reliquary. There is nothing else in the room but the few sparrows he has preserved and set on the floor by the window, as if pecking there for crumbs. He goes to the armoire now and lifts the smock from the hook. He knows every thread of the coarse grey linen. He takes it out and holds it awkwardly between his closed palms, as if it were a bunch of flowers, or a child's face. Then he carries it to the kitchen and lays it over a chair along with a piece of rope that will serve as a belt, or a leash if need be.

There is no sound at all from the hut. He goes about his morning chores attempting to apply his mind as usual to his current list, but again he cannot recall where he left off. His mind will not be mastered, not this morning. And it is not the memory of his son that intrudes, nor even the loss of his dog. It is the girl. The girl and her overwhelming need. It is as if the boat he rowed in daily on a smooth lake, undisturbed, has suddenly been carried away in a rushing stream, spinning him on into a vast ocean where the girl eternally drowns. He can think of nothing else but how he can begin to help her.

He finds an egg for her and takes it back to the house where he gathers the other things he will need.

*

The girl hears his footsteps. There is nowhere for her to hide. She goes to the corner and urinates nervously.

The door squeals when he comes in. Still crouching, she backs away, awkward, indecent, and he is glad he has brought the smock with him.

He is carrying a basket and she watches him warily as he sets it down.

He takes out a cup and puts it on the ground, takes out another vessel and pours water in the cup. He fills it until it runs over, then he lifts it and puts it to his mouth. She can hear him swallow. He looks at her as he drinks and his eyes are so full of his purpose she cannot hold his gaze. She is hungry and she can smell something other than the man, other than the water. It is in the basket. He holds out the cup and takes a step forward trying to engage her as he had the day before, but she doesn't take her eyes from the basket. When he drops to his haunches, she springs and is at the basket before him, has the egg in her hand and is already lunging for the door. With one hand she pulls and pushes at it, while with the other she crushes the egg to her mouth, and though he rises and grabs her and pins her arms it does not stop her sucking out the contents, straining them from their shell, and swallowing them down.

He spins her round and places himself between her and the door, and she faces him there, crunching and spitting eggshell. Flakes of it stick to her chin. The last of the white slithers from the corner of her mouth and she sucks it back.

Staring him now full in the eye, she belches. Peyre smiles. He cannot help himself.

And the girl sees it, sees his smile, and seeing it is to her more astonishing, more alive, than the present egg sliding down her throat. So that in that moment everything that is to follow becomes possible. He catches her astonishment. And there it is again, the line of meaning between them.

She darts suddenly back to the basket. Peyre barely has time to realize what she is about before she has snatched up the cheese he had hoped to use as a reward and is stuffing that too into her mouth, at the same time gagging on the unfamiliar taste. When he reaches to stop her, she swallows it and the next instant is on her hands and knees retching up the cheese along with the egg. She shakes her head and shudders and tries to scoop up some of the mess with her hands, then scrambles away to the far corner. He sees her cowering there as he leaves. If he had beaten her she could not look more wretched.

On his way back to the house, the smock still in the basket, unattempted, Peyre does not know how to rebuild what he has just destroyed.

It is as well he cannot see her now.

The girl is pressing her face against the door, breathing the day through the cracks in the boards, sucking it into herself. She can hear birds. She knows the day to be vast and airy. She knows it to be clothed in sky and she longs to be in it, plundering its hidden riches. Her fingers remember the

74

firm little bodies of the quick lizards, their cool meatiness on her tongue. And she remembers sweetness, the waxy smooth whiteness inside the furred green nuts she once climbed for and, sweetest of all, the heavy soft fruit lying for her on the ground, its pink flesh inside the dark skin. She did not even have to climb for it. But there is nothing here for her, nothing. No tree or leaf, no green shoot. At the foot of the wall she digs with her thumbs in the packed earth but makes little impression. Still on her haunches she hops sideways, tries farther along. It is just as hard. She knocks the pile of crates down and searches behind them. The earth is dryer still but looser. The fine sand excites her and she digs until she exposes the nest she knows is there. Tiny white grains wobble away in all directions as if on their own momentum. An exploding nest of seething ants, each no bigger than a speck of sand. Even though the eggs are so small she grabs a handful, tasting the poison on her tongue as it rolls them round, retaining the soft white grains, spitting out the useless stinging bodies. She cannot work fast enough to stop them disappearing. And then they are gone, their tunnels collapsed, the nest scattered.

She lies down and waits. It is hours later when she hears footsteps returning. She is at the door in two simian bounds.

Peyre squeezes in through the barely opened door and pulls it closed behind him. The girl watches his other hand on the basket. He keeps very still and breathes as quietly as he can. He sees her mouth working as if it has its own memory of egg. Her tongue licks at the corners of her mouth. He stands perfectly still.

The girl looks up at him and she senses at once an immeasurable shift in the order of things, for when she meets his eyes she sees they are looking directly at her hunger — her hunger that was all hers, that she carried with her, her burden, through all the world, her hunger that was her constant companion, her hunger that was her. He is looking right at it and she knows he can see it. Yet he is looking farther in. The hunger is not her. He is looking past it. He is looking at *her*.

There is no other sound but their breathing.

At last he puts down the basket and breaks off a piece of bread and she sees crumbs fall like dirt. He holds the morsel out to her, while he tears with his teeth at the piece in his other hand. His eyes are watching her as he chews. She lunges for what is left and he lets it go.

But here is nothing she knows as food. It is sour and mealy, breaking apart all over the inside of her mouth. She spits it out, using her tongue to eject every last crumb. She looks him in the eye. He is frowning and she experiences another shift: he wanted her to eat. This new skill of seeing, of understanding, warms her belly as well as any food. She looks in his eyes again to confirm it.

Peyre knows her mind is racing. He saw that line of meaning shimmer again like liquid fire in the air between them.

With patience he induces her to take more bread. At first he feeds her small pieces that he puts on the ground for her to pick up. He can see it is not to her taste, but she is ravenous and she begins to eat more quickly as she gets used to it. He breaks off pieces for himself, eats with her. He makes small noises of pleasure. Then he tears off a larger piece and holds it out.

The girl wants it and she does not. She snatches it, careful not to let their hands touch. In her mouth the stuff is neither flesh nor leaf. She cannot recognize it. Not fruit or root. Something like a nut long chewed. Her hands reach despite herself for more. She swallows, intent on watching him.

When he leaves the shed, he is content to have achieved at least some degree of familiarity. She has lost, he thinks, that panicked look. Perhaps she has even seen in him an ally. Though it is subtle, it is not inconsiderable, this change. He guesses she has had other contact with people, perhaps not all of it good but perhaps some of it kind.

That evening Peyre does not have to resort to his lists. He rehearses over and over his strategy for pacifying the girl and eventually winning her compliance. The next day, he goes several times to the shed, each time with food, but, in accordance with his plan, never quite enough to sate her. As the day is ending he takes milk to her and they share it as they shared the bread, though 'share' is not accurate for he is careful to be in control always.

He thinks that she is mad for the milk because she is bold enough to reach out and curl her fingers over the cold rim of the cup while it is still in his hands. And she does love it. She licks furiously at the white spots that splash on her arm.

Yet there is something more that she wants, something Peyre cannot possibly construe from their wordless exchange.

She saw him wipe his mouth with the back of his hand and she saw how he bared his teeth and narrowed his eyes, but not to growl, not to growl. She wants with an ache to feel what he was feeling then.

Standing there with their hands joined by the cup, Peyre thinks it will be easy. Already in a matter of hours he has begun to bridge the gap between them. He has her attention. She has made progress. But as soon as he relaxes his grip, she has the cup tipped and she is down and lapping, lapping herself to some distant memory of animal comfort, of some sweet fragrance. She looks, with her ribs visible on her back, for all the world like a starving dog and it enrages him. He will have her clothed. He is determined. It is not too much to ask. He picks up the smock and waits for his moment. When she has finished, he fights with her. It is not what he intended. He meant to be so patient, to give her all the time she needs, and now he is cramming her head into the opening of his son's smock, forcing her arms into the sleeves. It is ugly and something fragile between them is bruising and tearing. But he succeeds. He has her clothed. He will make her human.

The girl stops flailing. Her whole body heaves with each breath. She drags air in through her nose, her upper lip quivering. She rocks. With her mouth shut tight and a trickle of blood running from her bitten lip onto the smock, she rocks.

Peyre drinks far into the night trying to drown the sense of defilement that overwhelms him. He has desecrated the last relic of his son. And in his efforts to do what is right and decent, he has desecrated something in the girl.

Two

THERE IS NO town or village in this part of France that does not know the story of how Peyre Rouff left Chateau d'Aveyrac to take a wife and raise a son, only to return one day alone. Those who can remember him as a boy see a cruel inevitability in his story. Some say he was always made for isolation — but no one, they say, deserves the fate that awaited Peyre Rouff.

There was something forlorn about him from the beginning. As a child he lived with his father, a chair-maker working alone outside the town of Gougeac. His father had resisted all offers of help when Peyre's mother died, choosing instead to raise his son single-handed there near the marshes, teaching him how to build a chair to last forever — but not how to run with other boys or play. There are people in Gougeac who can remember the day eleven-year-old Peyre Rouff walked into town to make the solemn announcement that his father would not wake up. They say it was obvious the boy knew his father was dead but he had been afraid to say the word. In Freyzus, across the gorge of the Freyne, the part of the story the villagers recall is how young Peyre came straight from his father's funeral, so quiet, so dry-eyed, and entered the house of his aunt without a word.

For the next four years—every one of them dismal—Peyre lived in the house of his aunt. She never did warm to him. He was a strange one, in her opinion. Much too quiet. Even for an orphan, she said. They get over it, children. As if she had a wealth of experience in orphaned eleven-year-olds. Of one thing she was certain: boys grew only more irksome with every passing year. She said as much to her brother Guilhem, the steward at Chateau d'Aveyrac, when he came down to visit. More to the point, she said, Peyre was eating her out of house and home. Her little kitchen garden could not keep up. She had said it the year before, but this time Guilhem listened. Peyre was fifteen, strong and healthy, and Guilhem was not getting any younger. The idea of extra help was appealing. He did not care whether the boy was quiet or not—he was not looking for conversation—and the estate would supply more than enough to satisfy the lad's appetite. It only mattered that he knew how to work. And so Peyre, to his aunt's undisguised relief, was packed off to Aveyrac.

At fifteen Peyre had no idea about the management or care of a country estate. But he began to learn. He was good with his hands, he was willing, and he seemed to love the wild high country there. Guilhem was glad of Peyre's help and over the years taught him many skills, the least relevant of which was taxidermy. It was an absorbing way to pass the time. When the boy showed he had the nimble fingers and the concentration required to work for hours at a time to produce a lively specimen, Guilhem began to send away for supplies for him; there was nothing else on which to spend his stipend and the winter nights were long.

From time to time, though at increasingly long intervals, the seigneur, Martin de Villiers, came to visit. De Villiers was a sophisticated man with a mistress who kept him in the city of Montpellier. He only played at being a countryman, using his estate as a bucolic lodge for friends who liked to hunt. He thought the mounts that Guilhem and the nephew had made—here the head of a stag, there a badger—were lending the place a certain charm. He did not seem to notice the work of maintenance left unattended. When de Villiers brought his friends to stay, Guilhem would take them hunting in the chestnut woods or arrange a duck shoot for them down near Gougeac. Young Peyre was good at that. De Villiers was a generous man. He gave his steward permission to take to market whatever could be brought down in his absence—so long as there were always birds and game remaining for his friends.

For seven uneventful years Peyre lived contentedly with his uncle—until the lightning bolt of love found him out. He was a young man in his twenty-second year when he first he saw Mathilde. She was at the market down at Gougeac, and she had two live white ducks to sell. Peyre did not need ducks. He had been up since three o'clock that morning with his gun and he had sixteen fine mallards of his own—neatly dead—that he had taken at the marshes just outside the market town and had brought in to sell. He had been doing a brisk trade and he was almost ready to leave when Mathilde arrived with her two white ducks. Peyre could scarcely remember what had brought him to town that day or why he was standing there at all. The turn of her cheek. Her throat. There among the women in their faded black. Her white kerchief. Her arms. The grace of her. He purchased the living ducks at once — to the amusement of the other vendors. His friend Frédéric was discreet, pretending not to look. The older men watched it all with interest and raised their eyebrows at one another. There followed much sardonic commentary on the transaction with not a few remarks about the mating habits of fowl. Peyre did not notice.

She was not hard to woo, Mathilde. He watched her eyes with their long lashes lift on a flash of light, only to sweep back down to her fingers hooking and unhooking the latch of the cage, hooking and unhooking. He found his heart could read a language hitherto unseen, unguessed at. And his legs no longer knew how to stand steady beneath him.

He carried the ducks to his trap and lifted the lid of the seat, dropped them inside. He closed the lid, smiling. He could not help himself.

Prisoners, he said. He handed her the empty cage, not smiling now. He counted out her payment and his fingers touched her palm.

When she walked away, he saw the direction that she took. It was to Freyzus, where he had once lived. It occurred to him that before he went back up to the chateau he too might cross the bridge today.

In the village Peyre went to the house of his aunt, intending to give her the white ducks, but found at the last minute that he could not bear to part with both of them. His aunt took one of the birds, grumbled a little that it would fly off without the other and complained — unreasonably — that she had no one to help her with the place since he had been living up at Aveyrac. He said at once he could come down from time to time to his old home. He would be pleased to.

Driving back up to Aveyrac with the duck, Peyre knew he risked his uncle's scorn. In the courtyard, he lifted the seat on the trap. The duck's white wings clattered in applause as he drew her out.

His uncle watched in silence.

She will be useful gobbling up snails in the garden, Peyre said.

Guilhem felt like cuffing him around the ears, but the lad had long outgrown such treatment. And so would you, he said. So would you.

The following week both Peyre and Mathilde were again at the market at Gougeac, he fresh from the marshes, the bed of his cart quilted with feathered carcasses, she with the pocket of her skirt heavy with his coins of the week before. And then she stood at the cart and Peyre helped her choose, shifting the soft bodies, taking his time. She walked away with a dark mallard hanging at her back, its webbed feet crossed piously at the base of her throat. The duck's head bumped the small of her back just below her waist as she walked. Everyone watched. And everyone knew.

The story reached Freyzus. It was told and retold that afternoon by the men under the marronnier. To tell it was to taste the earnestness of youth, youth's foolishness. To laugh about it and to laugh again was somehow to reach and touch a little of the joy contained within its heart. You had to be glad for young Peyre Rouff. You really did. Such a solemn lonely lad, he was, when his aunt took him. You had to be glad.

Mathilde's father was ready to let her go, having taken for himself that very year a new young wife to keep his house in Freyzus. Martin de Villiers was less enthusiastic. He was disappointed at the news of the betrothal, imagining Peyre now would be held fast over in Freyzus, where Mathilde lived. De Villiers knew only too well the power of women to dictate a man's life without ever uttering a word. He had had Peyre Rouff slipping conveniently into his uncle's shoes when the old man could no longer manage, had considered him practically raised to the job. It occurred to him that Peyre's services would still be assured when the time came if he could render the young man in some way beholden. An extravagant wedding gift was the answer, one large enough to constitute an undeniable lien. The cottage down at the marshes would be perfect.

And so on a drear November morning Peyre and Mathilde left the old stone church in Freyzus, received a farewell kiss from Peyre's aunt, and were escorted by Mathilde's father with his own young bride, Lizette, Mayor Pailhès and his cohorts, the postman and the postman's wife, and every young lad and girl in the village, treading gaily with them down the hill and across the bridge to the other side of the Freyne gorge, where they bade them goodbye and good luck.

Only Peyre's boyhood friend Frédéric Maurel remained to accompany them on the road to Gougeac in the neighbouring valley. By the time they arrived at the stone cottage beside the marsh, the massing clouds were bruised with mauve and brown. Palest pink, the colour of trout flesh, leached away below.

The child, conceived the month before the wedding, in a prickly field, under an orange moon, was born at the cottage in Gougeac in midsummer, slipping small and perfect into the midwife's hands and calling lustily for life—or perhaps it was mercy—when she slapped him. Peyre, craning in the doorway to see, was bullied away, the door slammed shut behind him, while his wife limply smiling said, Please. Please, let him. But only when mother and child were sponged dry and decently covered did the midwife open the door.

Peyre was embarrassed by the sight. Two where before was only one. An actual life. Everything about the small being announcing it. Blood. Breath. Pulse. It was a boy, wrinkled and red, a shock of black hair sticking straight up on the top of his head, exotic. Fingers made of sparrow bone. Yet soft. It was too much. Peyre could no longer look. It was inexplicable. He turned from his wife, shaking his head in disbelief, and at last surrendered to the impulse that was shaking him and laughed out loud.

Then Peyre was more than content to live his life with his small family away from the affairs of the town. The house by the marsh was all he required, his family all his world. His wife to warm him at night, his son to light his days. Mathilde told herself she too was content, though she suffered continuously from a pain in her abdomen, an echo of childbirth that diminished but never went away, there always to remind her that she might never have another child.

They called the boy Giles. When he was six, and crowned with blond curls, they sent him daily along to the crossroad, where the carter from Ysolt, on his way in to Gougeac, would lean down and without stopping his old horse hook the boy like a fish, swinging him up by the arm to join him on his seat. At the next crossroad he would stop his horse and Giles would clamber down and run the rest of the way to the school. He learned his lessons well and was soon able to read and write, do simple sums and speak a little Latin. When Peyre saw how Giles was progressing, he was proud, but he was happier still when the boy left his books to join him in his workshop or on the land.

Mathilde would watch as father and son left for the marshes. She watched them at home as they bent their heads together to solve some intractable problem—a broken axle, a stubborn piece of leather—or to admire a well-oiled fowling piece or some other inscrutable object of beauty. Mathilde had once owned the boy's attention, shared her secrets. She had shown the child tricks—how to empty an egg and leave the shell unbroken, how to snap peas from their shells. She had taught him tales and rhymes, but his father always offered more. Her own supply of wonders was limited. She would never have thought of pointing out the fat yellow pouch on the leg of a bee, the curled tongue of the butterfly. She felt herself starving for the child's rewards, the flash of delight or surprise, the sweet complicity of a secret shared. Soon she began to notice the boy's guarded glance, his impatience to be free. And she saw too plainly how his father's tricks — bringing a bright mallard to fall from the sky above, undressing a rabbit, then making it seem to live again — surpassed anything she could offer.

Mathilde was no longer sure she liked the humid airs at the marshes, but Peyre was happy. They summoned his own boyhood, when he had lived close by. He could recall the days when he was just a lad and went with his father to cut canes for making chairs. He found himself absorbed again in the world of his childhood. The marsh held its secrets close. It seemed to have saved them just for his return — the sudden whistle of feathers when pintails came whippling, skidding, onto the surface of the water, the arc of silver drops that hung for less than a second when a flock was startled into air. The treasure was everywhere, only revealed to those who looked, who listened: the canes clashing their applause to the breeze; the brown-splashed eggs of the snipe nestled at the foot of a clump of sedge; clouds of midges hovering above the sloughs, the sapphire dragonflies that hunted them. The ducks he brought down for the table were only a sampling of the riches the land possessed. Of his days he did not ask for more and he imagined them — the days, the weeks, the years — processing without interruption.

When Peyre began to school a young falcon, Giles was enthralled. Peyre gave him the job of feeding the litter of mice he intended to breed for lures during the bird's training. Giles gave the mice more attention than his books — or his mother, Mathilde noted. She was faintly disgusted that so much care and attention was lavished on creatures fated to be torn apart in an instant. In any event she could dream up nothing that would fascinate the boy more than the accoutrements of the sport: the great glove Peyre had sewn from sheepskin, the supple leather tresses that trailed like snakes from the bird' s legs, and most of all the tiny hood, plumed with the feathers of a lark. No. Shelling peas could not compete with this arcane ritual.

On occasion, Peyre returned to the chateau at Aveyrac to lend a hand. Mathilde cherished her time then, alone with the little boy. But when Giles was older, Peyre sometimes took him too, ignoring Mathilde's protests that the boy should be in school.

She wished there were women to talk to, a daughter to love, to love her back. Her days were long. There was a limit to how often the hearth might be swept, how many stockings could be darned. She could almost welcome the small aggravations, the mishaps that enlivened the hours — a sheet that blew from her washing line to drape a corner of the roof, a jar of oil that slipped from her hands to crash on the stone floor. When she scoured pots and pulled beets, it was with brutish energy. Peyre seemed to have deliberately abandoned her to her dispiriting chores. There were days when Frédéric Maurel and Isop Nogès came from Gougeac to hunt with Peyre, boys he had known in his school days, now men with lives of their own. The women of the town had no reason to come out, though they were pleasant enough at the market, or at the church where Mathilde took Giles in order to have him to herself. In the evening, Peyre sat close to the lamp, with their son curled at his feet like a dog. Peyre studied yet another book of natural history while Mathilde sewed or darned. He brought volumes of Buffon one by one down from the chateau to read at home. Thirty-six, he answered when she asked how many there might be. Peyre was not unkind, that could not be said of her husband. He was a gentle man and he smiled often in her direction, but she knew he was simply directing his eyes, while his thoughts lingered at the passage he had been reading. Sometimes it was hard to see him as the same young man who bought her white ducks, and whose coins that day burned in her palm. In the night, he came to her only when he woke from deepest sleep. And he returned to sleep at once. She wondered sometimes if he had ever really woken. And then one morning, when they were still in bed, a thought arrived from nowhere, a reason for the cold hard anger that stirred within her each morning and grew only colder and harder as the day went on: she was jealous. It was the answer to the question she had never formulated, to why she wanted always to upset their peaceful world and to throw their home into disorder. Why she burnt the bread and served the turnips cold. Why she wanted to make Peyre hate her. She almost laughed aloud. It was true. It was absurd. She was jealous. She was jealous of her husband who seemed to own now Giles's undivided love—that elixir that once was hers. She was jealous of Peyre, but she was jealous too of her own son. It was as if her husband had taken a lover. The thought was incestuous and vile. She rolled to her husband and claimed him absolutely for her own, consuming all trace of envy in the vortex of her desire.

When Giles was old enough, Peyre took him duck hunting and Mathilde knew that both now were lost to her for years to come. Peyre hunted for many reasons—for the pot, for the market, for the pleasure of his friends from the town. And now he hunted to teach his son. His son. She heard herself think it.

It was as well she did not see them together, the boy's face illumined by wonder, Peyre's face bathed in the reflected light. For Peyre, watching the boy run free on the way to the reeds sharpened the exhilaration of the bright morning. He saw the boy's growing strength, his easy agility as he pulled himself up into his favourite tree, and his own limbs remembered. As soon as Giles could carry his own gun for the duration of the trip, Peyre allowed him to hunt. He watched with pride the boy's stillness, his silent attention as they waited for a flock to approach. He marvelled at his son's speed of reaction, that collision of present and future, that exquisite fusion, the descending duck, the boy's finger on the trigger, the wingbeat, the heartbeat, the retort, the echo. Giles had no idea that anything remarkable or extraordinary had occurred. Peyre would try to recapture the moment later for Mathilde, but she made a point of treating it lightly—as if it were nothing to keep talking about.

She liked it better when de Villiers brought a duck hunting party to the marsh. Then he would engage Peyre's services for several days, and life for Mathilde was suddenly more interesting. Lodged in the hotel in Gougeac, the men would drive each day before dawn in the hotel's only conveyance—an ancient vehicle optimistically transformed into a landau when the driver threw in a few woollen travelling rugs. Crammed shoulder to shoulder, one sitting with the driver, sometimes one perched precariously at the back like a postillion, the men drove, thick-headed and bleary-eyed into the night mists of the riverside. Alighting at the cottage, they bristled at once with the firearms they drew from under the seats. And Peyre would be waiting with lanterns, his dog trembling at his side, Giles hiding his own excitement as he watched with Mathilde from the open door. The men would get themselves organized and be away on foot just before the first birds began to sing.

On their return, their game bags heavy with the morning's work, the guests would seat themselves at a long trestle outside the cottage and Mathilde and Giles would serve them a lunch she had prepared with the seigneur's provisions. The compliments and the teasing were like fresh rain on parched ground. She could never have enough. The guests ate and drank too much and wiped their lips and made foolish toasts, while the dogs, exhausted, lay on their sides and sometimes smacked their tails and sometimes groaned at the laughter that disturbed their rest.

Sometimes one of the hunters, ruddy and eager, pleased with his day's performance, would leave the finest specimen for Peyre to preserve. Then Mathilde in turn would groan, though only to herself, for when Peyre had loaded the last of the morning's haul into the landau and watched it drive away, he would retreat to his workroom. While Mathilde scoured the pots and platters, Peyre would take meticulous measurements of the bird to be mounted and then sit down to trace its outline onto paper. Giles would help him set out the materials, while his mother made her dissatisfaction known by the volume and harshness of her sighs as she went about her work.

Giles watched every step of the operation, holding the glass-bead eyes in his palm, observing how the bird, suspended by its feet, was finally reduced to something for the cooking pot—its body naked and exposed to air, the length of its own skin, still attached by the beak, hanging inside out below, all its finery concealed. His father would sever the carcass at the nape of the neck and set it aside for reference before he cleaned the skull and dusted the skin. When he started work on the form, Giles would pass him the wire or the twine, hand him the scissors or the knife. But the part Giles loved best came last when the form was ready to be clothed. Then he would watch as his father attached the form to the skull and drew skin back again over it, down the false neck, over the false back, the feathers springing into sight, and time reversing until the bird came miraculously to stand before them.

And his father would sigh, but not at all in the same way as his mother.

After a day of carcasses tumbling from the sky, it was a restoration of sorts.

Martin de Villiers, though not much of a hunting man himself, did like to please his friends and every two years he arranged for a boar hunt up at Aveyrac, where, he liked to tell them, they would learn the best kept secrets of the hunter. But Peyre had no arcane wisdom to impart. What he had learned from Guilhem was simple: Know the habits of your prey; know the limits of your skill. The hunt when he was engaged was always successful.

For the boar hunts, he would take both Mathilde and Giles with him to the chateau to help Guilhem make ready. Two days before the hunt, a dozen guests would arrive. There were guns to clean and to check, knives to sharpen, boots to rub with oil and to relace. There were cartridges to fill and ammunition to assign. And there was always food to prepare, and wine to bring up from the cellar, fuel for the work. At five in the morning on the appointed day, the hunters would rise and set out on foot for the chestnut woods, more than an hour away. Mathilde and Giles would stay behind at the chateau.

But the day came. She knew it would. It was at the hunt that took place in Giles's twelfth year. He was old enough,

Peyre said. Mathilde said she needed Giles to help her prepare the next day's breakfast. The hunters were so many this year. But Peyre was adamant. The boy should not be deprived of this experience. The seigneur did not arrange these boar hunts often. The knowledge would be invaluable.

The sun had been up for several hours when they returned. She heard their voices long before they appeared.

The hunters were in good spirits. They had killed two fine sangliers. Though it would have been easier to dress them in the forest and carry the carcasses divided among them, they brought back the two boars in wheelbarrows that creaked under their weight and they laid them on the terrace to toast the occasion of their slaughter. The men were ravenous and fell readily to the lunch Mathilde had prepared. In the afternoon, while Guilhem and Peyre attended to the sangliers, the hunters snored in their rooms.

It was an easy matter to butcher and dress the first animal, which was to be shared among the guests. The second demanded more care. They measured it first and Peyre made careful annotated sketches. The skin was destined for a commissioned mount, the flayed carcass to be roasted whole on the spit that night. Guilhem and Peyre worked almost in silence while the boar was born again naked into the world. On the spit it glistened and almost smiled. Guilhem and Peyre raised a glass to the success of their endeavour, and the guests began to wake at the aroma of roasting meat. At supper each detail of the hunt was rehearsed, relived. Even Giles had something to add to the endless retelling of the kill.

That night Mathilde received many compliments from the men as she served them. They were deep in their cups, their desire only lightly disguised in joviality. The only woman in the hall, she could not help but glow.

At the end of the evening Giles, long exhausted and with far too much wine inside him, found a warm spot on a rug in the corner of the kitchen and could not be woken. Curled against the warmth of his belly lay the seigneur's gift of a water dog, a pup barely weaned. Peyre and Mathilde went up to their room on the third floor without him, and Mathilde was glad. She had read the men's desire easily and it had stirred her own.

In the small room under the rafters, she said to Peyre, I am yours. Only yours. He smiled and held her.

They should see what we can do, she said. Prompting, hopeful. What you can do to me.

Peyre smiled again, his eyelids heavy. I claim you, he said, still smiling. I claim you, and his eyes slowly closed.

His arm was heavy across her belly. She could feel the weight of his exhaustion.

Mathilde lay awake in the dark while he slept. After a while she removed her nightgown and began to bite softly at the back of his neck until he roused.

The next morning the men went out again. Mathilde, sleeping soundly, did not stir.

For three days the party hunted. Mathilde had never felt more alive. She worked harder than she had ever worked at the cottage and yet her energy was boundless, as if it fed continuously on the hunters' excitement, the vitality they exuded in their pursuit of death. And each night she made sure her husband turned to her in the room under the rafters. On the last night she insisted that the lamp remain lit, casting their shadows on the yellow walls.

On the fourth day, with the last of the kill duly shared among them, the guests departed, already anticipating the welcome of their wives. Peyre took Mathilde and Giles home to the cottage so that the boy could return to school, then he went up again to the chateau to work with his uncle on the skin of the boar.

Mathilde wondered that Peyre had not marked the attention of the men. He did not treat her like a woman to be protected. Alone at the cottage, she missed the excitement of the hunters. She had not minded that they stank, some of them. Nor had she minded when one of them passed her in the doorway and rubbed his thigh across her hip. She locked the memory away. Believing that her life continued to diminish, shrinking from the thing she had hoped it to be, she needed every sustaining crumb.

When Giles came home from school and sat at the table reading, she did not see how life was transforming to some quiet beauty of its own, Giles at the table there concentrating, the pup at his feet, sleeping, content. She saw only how neither of them needed her, and she imagined Peyre up at the chateau in easy conversation with his uncle, not thinking of her at all.

While they waited for the cleaned skin to cure, Peyre and Guilhem worked on the armature for the sanglier, binding tow and wood shavings onto the frame of willow and wire until they had a facsimile of the body. They stopped often to measure and recheck—the length of shin here, the width of shoulders there. Peyre's sketches were detailed, indicating the contours of muscle, the distension of the belly, every fold of skin. He and his uncle worked as precisely as they could. In the next days the old skills came alive, the old habits returned easily. It was detailed work and they spoke little, knowing how to assist each other, exchanging glances of satisfaction or relief when some new stage was successfully accomplished. After two weeks they had their frame. They prepared a bucket of soft slip dug from the clay of the old reservoir. While Guilhem soaked the skin with arsenic water and soaped the inside, Peyre applied the clay to the armature, smearing it over the frame to building and shaping every muscle of the sanglier. He worked quickly and by the end of the afternoon it was ready. Guilhem helped him pull the skin over the damp form.

There were days of labour still but the animal already had taken life. It stood with its head lifted. To look at it was to hear the twig crack like gunshot underfoot.

FOR TWO SHORT weeks Mathilde had the boy to herself but she did not have his attention. That belonged to the pup. It consumed him. She chafed to hear him repeat Peyre's instructions: Un maître seul. One master only. Et c'est moi! Giles said, beaming as the pup licked his face.

Mathilde, who never prayed, took to praying. She began that winter, in the chill days when only hunters deemed the days worthwhile. She talked to Our Lady as if she were a neighbour. She acknowledged that she was blessed with a husband to provide for her and with a son to bring her joy. She acknowledged the two short weeks of the boy's exclusive company and she excused herself for complaining. She said, Holy Mary, Mother of God, I'm not ungrateful for the gifts your Son has bestowed, but I am lonely. I do not belong out here on the edge of the marsh. It is no place for a woman to serve God. She did not have a clear vision of the form her service would take. She was only sure that she would be happier if she had some human intercourse and were not surrounded all day by bundles of voiceless reeds and dumb animals only partly created. She said, *Holy Mary Mother of God, whose Son will refuse you nothing, intercede for me, I pray.* And then she crossed herself and waited.

There were days when life seemed sweet again. Once she went reluctantly on a cold morning to help Peyre cut rushes for his chairs. Giles's pup ran ahead of them. Mathilde went with a muffler wound tight across her face against the cutting wind. She walked with her head down, watching for patches of ice underfoot. She worked hard in order to warm herself. When she looked up at a sound, she had forgotten where she was. The dun rushes were everywhere furred with frost. The sky blazed above, transforming to a geometry of white and black as a flight of storks beat over. Peyre was standing too. The two of them alone, together, receiving a gift from the world. The exultation of the moment carried her through the morning until the sun warmed their backs. They went back to the cottage with a laden cart. Soup had never tasted so good.

But such days were rare, not in themselves, for they existed always, in every season, but in her knowing of them, her living of them. When Giles was not occupied with his school work, he was helping Peyre, or he was with the pup, throwing his cap for it to retrieve, again and again and again, the two of them, boy and dog grinning with pleasure. It was hard to accept, this feeling of life going on without her. She could not shake the feeling that she had lost her son to her husband, her husband to her son. And then some savage god decided to teach her how it might feel in truth.

It was a still October morning. There were not many hunters. Peyre and Giles had gone with the dogs and with Frédéric to meet de Villiers and one or two of his guests at the marshes. So still it was. She had heard the retorts, and she had heard the silence. And then their boots upon the road, and their laboured breathing, like a monstrous many-legged creature from hell approaching. It was Frédéric Maurel, who had walked ahead, who pushed open the door and made her start.

Madame Rouff, he said. His hat was in his hand. And the catastrophe of knowledge came upon her like a rockfall. Her own name was echoing, rebounding without meaning from the walls of her skull as she looked past him and saw her husband, white as any corpse, his eyes unfixed and lifeless. She knew at once it was their son he carried in his arms, though she could not see the boy's face, only the drenched sack that covered it.

The world rippled and swam before her eyes and the earth beneath her feet was all in motion. Frédéric tried to hold her back and yet here she was in the bedroom, seeing Peyre lay their child upon the marriage bed, seeing the dark evidence on his clothes.

She wanted to tear away the sack but many hands restrained her. She struggled and would not be subdued until she saw at last how Peyre was unmanned, trembling and convulsing where he stood like some decrepit ancient.

No one tried to make her return when she ran from the house. They found her later at the house of Isop Noguès, where his wife, Clareta, had taken her in. She sat by the fire pale and still, wrapped in a blanket.

Madame Maurel, who had come to find Frédéric, said, Your husband will need you.

Mathilde made the slightest movement with her head like someone who refuses bitter medicine. Clareta Noguès looked at her own husband and raised her eyebrows.

Make up the cot, he said. She's still shivering.

Mathilde let herself be put to bed. Let herself swallow hot spirits. Let her eyelids close. Hours later, when the house was quiet and she was sure the Noguès were asleep, she set out upon the road, a spectre walking her appointed path.

There was a light still burning in the cottage when she arrived. Its wands shone from the edges of the shutters and fell on the dew-greyed grass beside the path. Someone must have heard her, for Frédéric was at the door. She let him take hold of her and lead her to her husband. Peyre was standing at the kitchen window. If the shutters had been open he would have been staring at the marshes.

She stood beside him and asked her question.

Whose gun was it?

She looked up at him and saw the answer in his face. But she had not meant to wound, only to know.

They took the boy across to Freyzus for the funeral, the sunshine brilliant, the red vines in the fields gay. Frédéric followed behind them, looking as if he walked to the place of his own execution. De Villiers was waiting for them in the churchyard. Those who knew the couple were unsure what to do. Mathilde's father was there, looking grim, but not her stepmother. Guilhem up at Aveyrac had not been informed. His sister, Peyre's aunt, would not venture from her house, but remained inside and wept for all the deaths her life had known. The religious stayed away. In their hierarchy of sins what had happened here was not far behind patricide, that most unspeakable act of all. It was unholy. Others found good reasons of their own to stay away. For some it was respect, the only word they could find to summon the sense of terrible smallness that overcame them in the face of such cosmic misfortune. They were not worthy. For others it was fear, as if a man would have to be touched by some great evil to have done such a thing. For these, evil was always contagious.

De Villiers left immediately after the funeral. He pressed money for the priest into Peyre's hands before he left. Mathilde's father asked her to stay with him in Freyzus.

Mathilde said no. Her duty was with her husband, she said. She would not desert him.

The priest was waiting for his money.

When he had paid him, Peyre helped Mathilde into the trap. He climbed up beside her, nodded to his father-in-law, and sat. Mathilde picked up the reins and clicked the ass forward.

They did not speak. For what, possibly, could be said?

People were not unkind. The ones who came to the cottage outside Gougeac left food at the door in those early days. Some went looking for Giles's dog. Isop Noguès arranged for a boy to take a note to Peyre's uncle. It was written on yellow paper with a hand-drawn line of black ink around the edges. *Peyre's son is dead and buried. Shot by accident by his father's hand. God Rest His Soul.* Guilhem made the boy wait while he considered a reply for him to pencil on the other side: *You are a man alone now. The Lord have mercy on your soul.*

It was Frédéric Maurel who brought the gun back,

Frédéric who once had worked all night to help Peyre finish a commission when he was sick. He held the gun out, trying to hold it clear of accusation, blame, clear of guilt. But the weight of it was insupportable and in the end he had to lower it and quietly lean it against the wall, the front door already closing on him, saying no to friendship, no to all that had occurred and to all that was to come.

The next day a young lad stood at the door, out of breath, pleased with himself for walking the nine miles from his hamlet and grinning with pride to be returning Giles's dog that now ran in circles of joy, now leapt once more in greeting. Peyre hated it for its very life. He sent them both away.

Peyre did not open his door again for days. If, on hearing someone knock, Mathilde moved to open it, he would turn his head and his baleful eyes would forestall her. Together they ignored the tapping, the surreptitious testings of the door. When Alice Maurel thought to come and let them know the gun had been removed, they both heard her trying to be respectfully quiet outside yet still have her words carry through the closed door.

Monsieur Rouff! she called. The gun has been taken away.

Peyre's voice was hollow in response and seemed to carry its own echo. Thank you.

It may have been Alice who sent Frédéric Maurel back two days later. Mathilde opened the door. Frédéric had a broken look about him. It might have been his own son who had lost his life.

He seemed unable to meet Mathilde's eye as he held out

the pheasants. Together they contemplated the grey eyelids of the birds.

Well then. She could hardly bear to say the next words, which would signal acceptance of the fate that had come to her. They would seal the contract for her new role in the world. And she would have this role, bereaved mother, until she herself passed on. That a life could be so long.

Thank you. She put out her hand and took hold of the birds' cold legs. You are very kind. And from this moment, she thought, men and women will know only how to be very kind. For I am the whipped cur, the ass with the broken leg, the bird with the torn wing. And they one day will wish me gone so that they can laugh again freely. *'There was a man who took his life. He meant to shoot a bird and shot his wife.'* Only not his wife. How fine oblivion seemed. A desert place where she could take her flayed soul out of reach of human kindness.

Frédéric put his hand briefly on her arm. She nodded and closed the door.

How heavy the smallest step. She turned.

Peyre had not moved. She went through to the kitchen where he stood, the birds at her side as if they were no more than a switch, a broom. Peyre continued to stare out of the window.

Peyre? Peyre, Frédéric brought these.

She laid them on the table. He did not turn his head.

Something in Mathilde stirred as it must have done in Frédéric when he came to the door. She went to Peyre and leaned against his arm. At once she felt his muscles contract beneath the cloth of his jacket.

Peyre?

His chin lifted sharply as if struck suddenly, her voice a blow.

Please.

Again that flinching beneath the cloth of his sleeve.

She was adrift in a vast sea, fathoms beneath her feet.

A brace of pheasants, she said. Then, under her breath, A brace of damned pheasants.

As she turned she heard his lips part for the air to enter, like a knife. She left him and went to lie down, closed her eyes. But still she could hear that he was not moving. She listened intently and was suddenly overcome with a wave of nausea, and she knew in an instant she was carrying a child. And she was repulsed and wished it to return to oblivion, for no child could be raised in this house, the poor, shattered face of its brother, always at the window, looking in.

In the morning Peyre had gone. She did not know where he had slept. The pheasants too had gone, though their reek lingered. She was ravenous, or the damned child was. She never saw Peyre eating. He was aloof from every worldly need, claiming all grief for himself the way he had once claimed the boy. Her boy. She ate stale bread and cheese, devoured an apple down to the pips. After a while she began to hate even herself and went in search of Peyre. As she had guessed, he was in his workshop. He did not answer when she spoke his name from the doorway. She said it again and from the way that he startled she knew he had only just heard her.

He looked up. The two pheasants lay skinned upon the table. His hands were slippery. She had time only to take a step away before she vomited on the path. Perhaps he did not hear that either for he did not come to her aid.

Peyre no longer worked. He spent his days standing beside his kitchen table, staring in dull incomprehension at the light washing the marshes. No gun to hand. No means of escape. Only the relentless days he had not asked for. He had thought of other means. He had thought of climbing the hill up to the chateau, of crossing the ridge behind, scrambling down to fall forward from the rocks above the gorge. Something kept him from walking up there to complete the thought. It was not his wife. It was his son. In an inversion of all that is just and holy, his son guaranteed his life. He tasted the bitterness every day. If he were to die, the last of his son would die with him. He could not bear the thought that nothing, not even a memory, would remain. Who knew how many memories might exist, afloat in time and lost forever, if no one stood ready to receive them?

And so each day he rose with a sense of duty and went down to the kitchen. A red-and-yellow oil cloth covered the pine boards of the table. A red-and-white curtain, sewn by Mathilde, hung from an iron rod. Even with the shutters closed, light leaked into the room, above, below it, from the sides. The curtain was so thin it might as well not have been there at all. He would hear sparrows outside in the sandy road, where Giles used to throw breadcrumbs before he went to school. The sound of the birds, their chirruping, was scorched into his mind. He did not need to see them. He held the memory of Giles leaning out of the window, eager. Kind.

Kinder than a boy should be. When Peyre opened the shutters, the birds would fly off and then the road would be very quiet, the marshes lying under a flat, colourless light, the mists of autumn starting early.

Bundles of rushes stood untouched in the corner of Peyre's workshop, half-finished frames for the chairs hung from hooks or rested stacked against the wall. And each day Peyre continued his vigil. Those who had visited him in the first weeks no longer came, unable to keep their eyes steady on the vertiginous fall behind his gaze. A man can lose balance on the edge of an abyss, said Frédéric to his friends one night. I can vouch for it. There is nothing there.

The weeks bled into months. The priest from Freyzus sent news of the passing of Peyre's aunt. Peyre took the note from Mathilde and put it in the fire, then he returned to the window. In time the shutters remained open day and night. Even when it was dark, Peyre tried to see again another life taking place beyond them. Life as it was, roaming field and hill, a sky filled with birds, his son at his side. It was a desperate orgy of grief that threatened to shake loose his sternum if ever he were to yield to tears.

How shall we live? Mathilde asked one night as they sat across the table from each other, their meal dismal before them. How shall we live if you refuse work? Though she meant much more, and said it again, How shall we live? He raised his eyes. He too was drowning, her very question the sea that was taking them down. She felt a brief tremor as it took them, a small quivering like that at the fingertips just before they join, like the souls of the two of them brushing, almost, before whirling on, helpless in ancient night. They might have reached out and held each other.

Peyre's chair screeched on the stone as he pushed it back and stood up, and she saw that he was determined to drown alone.

Mathilde thought she might go mad. When she found him in the kitchen next morning, she spoke again. He needed soon to come to his senses, to be a father again when the time came.

We shall starve, you standing at the window, she said.

To starve away — if he could! But it was for Giles that he was keeping himself alive. He stood vigil for memory, that last thread of life. They could return the gun to him now. He would not turn it on himself. Not now. For if he were dead, how would Giles live? Sometimes in the small hours of morning he was overcome with terror at the thought of his own death. The boy dwelt in his memory, existed there, resided unbroken, in sunshine and in shadows, awake or dreaming. To keep him thus, living and whole, was Peyre's sacred and only duty. He would not renege. He stayed awake for Giles. He breathed for Giles.

It was difficult work, more difficult than anyone could know, to keep the moment of loss at bay. To go there was madness and he knew it would destroy him utterly. But the mind has a will of its own and its muscle is tremendous. To fight it is to wrestle a creature of great strength. To keep himself alive and breathing, yet shut the moment of catastrophe from his vision, Peyre summoned order and ritual, actions he performed each day without question, thoughts he assiduously followed. Daily his mental discipline increased until his mind was wholly occupied. His face assumed the vacant gaze of deepest concentration. He compiled mental lists; he recited the qualities of items on his lists in detail most minute. Mathilde could see that he was lost not only to her but to all society. He did not even register the possibility of their coming child. For Peyre the task of keeping Giles alive, and at the same time avoiding the one thing he must never see again, was Herculean. He feared having no more thoughts. His lists were numberless.

In the churchyard the stones over his son's grave began their slow weathering. They were washed with dew and they dried in the morning sun. The rain beat at the letters he carved on the headstone and it ran in the small channels. Peyre went there almost every day, sometimes riding, sometimes on foot. It was a way of using up the day.

WHEN HE SAW the wolf nailed by its forelegs to a board propped upright in the market, Peyre could not ignore it. The seller's price was high. Peyre watched his face carefully as he made his offer. He took the wolf home in the bed of the cart.

Mathilde looked on with revulsion as he carried it inside.

She circled Peyre in the house, loud, insistent, like a dog after its quarry, telling him he had to listen, he had to turn and face her, he had to understand, Peyre turning away, repeating quietly, You'll see. You'll see.

Circling, turning, circling, until Mathilde dropped to her knees. She sobbed like a child. Peyre did not try to help her. He stole away, taking the road to Freyzus, where the stones of the churchyard accepted without reproach all who came to lay down their grief.

He returned late in the day and weary, and went straight to his workshop at the back of the cottage. The work of skinning was difficult because the body of the wolf was so rigid. Though it had been gutted it had begun to reek. He tried to work fast in the lamplight so that he could carry away the carcass, but Mathilde could smell it from their bedroom. She sat on the edge of the bed and covered her mouth.

After Peyre had carried the parts out of the house, he washed himself in the yard and breathed long and deep. The stars showered their light on him, their million points drilling his skin like rain until he felt clean. He could see quite clearly how his wolf would appear.

By the time he went inside again, the bedroom door was shut fast against him.

Sleep somewhere else, Mathilde said.

'Thilde, he said. He leaned his temple against the door.

You can have your bed tomorrow, Mathilde said.

Peyre sat by the cooling stove and dozed. He slept only fitfully. Toward morning he fell into a deep sleep and when he did at last wake to the sound of the door, the first thing he saw was her booted feet as she turned to pick up a second bag.

She asked him to get the gig ready to take her to her father's house. He looked at the bags she held but he made no move.

You will not have your wife walk, surely? All the way to Freyzus?

Peyre didn't answer. At such disadvantage, so unequal, shivering with fatigue, his mouth furred with his sleeping self, while she. While she. Her hat upon her head. Her coat buttoned. He got up and went to open the shutters, stared out at the lifting mist. He heard her open the door but did not turn his head. Heard her shift the bags. Heard the door close behind her. He saw her walk down the track to the road. Saw her turn onto it without looking back. He watched. Then he put on his boots and went out and got the trap ready.

They passed few people on the road, which was a blessing, for how to raise the leaden hand? How smile? They were riders in a tumbrel both.

In Freyzus Madame Maraval, the mother of young Felip, watched as they drove in silence past the cemetery, where she had seen Peyre Rouff only the day before, and on toward the house. Mathilde's father heard them approaching. He came out with his arms open in greeting and he folded his daughter to him while Peyre brought down the bags. Watching from the window, his young wife knew the bags signalled more trouble. Mathilde's father raised his head to see Peyre stepping up into the gig. He called out, perplexed, as Peyre drove away.

On the way back Peyre stopped at the cemetery, but Giles was now within the compass of his wife's grief, not his, and he left feeling like an intruder at his own son's grave.

He went to find the carpenter who sold him wood shavings for his projects. He bought two sacks. He did not think about Mathilde at all.

For days after his return he ate only mouthfuls of soup from the pot when he was hungry. He barely slept, working patiently, his hands like creatures with a mind of their own, sure of their purpose, until at last they caressed a wolf that stood alert, one paw raised in anticipation — while in his mind's eye another stood with stiff forelegs launching a long howl of loss on the night air.

It could not go on, the priest from Freyzus said. He settled comfortably at the red-and-yellow oil cloth, made a gesture with his hands flat on the table. He could have been indicating an end, a finality, or he could have been clearing a space for a little refreshment. Peyre had a wife, a coming child to care for, he said. He said he had responsibilities. He said he had heard he no longer helped his uncle up at Aveyrac. If he continued on this road, he would be destitute. Of course no one would let them starve, but did he want this? To be dependent on the parish? He and his wife no better than indigents? He was hard-pressed to deduce the answer from the unholy blank of Peyre's face. The man was as good as dead. But Peyre suddenly spoke.

My wife has her father, he said. I have these. He gestured to the mounted wolf beside the hearth and to the two pheasants that occupied the dresser. The priest shook his head in despair. The man had lost all reason.

Remarkable. Peyre, quite remarkable. But who will purchase them? People need game to eat, not to look at.

People need all manner of things.

But first, I repeat, they need to eat. Who will purchase?

Someone.

And meanwhile, your wife? And your duty to provide for her?

He would like to have added 'and the child.' The risk of triggering misunderstanding was too high.

She refuses me. She has her father. She does not—

He stopped abruptly and cried out.

I am trying to live. No one knows.

No one knows?

How hard I try to live. Peyre's voice dropped to a whisper. To stay alive.

So that here now, in place of common comfort, was the spectre of the unspeakable, the crime against self, against nature, and against the Holy Spirit, heavy as sin on the air. But the priest had come with only worldly advice to offer. He considered the hour too late to begin work of such vast remediation of the spirit. He returned to matters less unthinkable. Had Peyre noticed the absence of the wild leeks this year? Or perhaps they were delayed?

But Peyre only sat in silence, turned inward like a pregnant wife himself, gestating, nurturing the monster of his grief.

The two of them sat a while longer, the priest floating hopeless topics that were left without response, perhaps, he wondered afterwards, were never even heard—until Peyre seemed suddenly to remember his manners and asked him to stay for supper.

But it was not difficult to deduce the state of Peyre's larder and the priest declined.

The priest rose from the table and was beginning to take his leave when a boy appeared at the door with a sack of songbirds he had netted, the heads pulled through tiny holes in the sacking. For a moment no one spoke. Each waiting on the other.

Goodbye, said Peyre to the priest. He held on to the door frame. His heart had turned over at the sight of the boy. He could barely stand.

The priest hesitated, said, I think...and then abandoned all effort, mounted his horse, and rode away.

The boy at the door was afraid, for now Peyre Rouff was holding the offered bag, yet seemed strangely deprived of speech, and perhaps even sight. The boy's own grandfather had stood in just such a manner before he dropped dead to the ground, never more to stand upright. But Peyre Rouff came back to himself and the boy breathed again. Peyre motioned with his hand for him to wait and then went inside for some coins. The boy said later that Monsieur Rouff had eyes like a church statue—which was not far from the truth, though the boy could not have really seen, for Peyre neither spoke nor smiled as he paid, but only nodded, keeping his eyes on the coins.

It was a while before any other lad had the courage to attempt the same.

MAYOR RAMON PAILHÈS had heard, like everyone else in the village, that Mathilde Rouff and her father had severed all ties with her husband. Nevertheless, when he heard in May about the death of Mathilde's infant, he felt compelled to sit down and write a note to Peyre. It was the right thing to do. Several others in the town thought so too. Madame Maraval and Madame Thibéry badgered their husbands to call on him and take him a honey cake when they went across to the market. They were curious. The priest said he had already decided to deliver the news in person. He rarely saw him anymore on his way to the cemetery.

In her house outside Freyzus, Lizette, Mathilde's young stepmother, was also busy with callers. They came this time not pay their respects to her but to offer their condolences to the unfortunate Mathilde Rouff—and perhaps to see how much damage that small disaster might inflict, following so close upon the heels of the other. Marie Maraval, pregnant with her own child, had baked a honey cake. She was full of sympathy and had made the cake as a simple way of showing it. And a honey cake might be a passport too, or so she thought, allowing her to cross the threshold into some new and complex drama of the blood. She took it in the morning, to the house where Mathilde lay, but it did not get her across the threshold. Mathilde's stepmother took the cake from her at the door, her lips pressing at each other in noisy approval as if she were already devouring it. The mother was sleeping, she said. We know. We know how a mother must sleep. And then she said, Ah, life. And more quietly, Life, and Madame Maraval was forced to go on her way without a glimpse of the mother shedding a complicated tear for her poor infant. No chance to pat the back of her hand in silent sympathy, empathy, and so provoke more tears. No stolen sight of Peyre himself, perhaps come over at last. No chance of a swift sight of him perhaps caught unawares, thinking himself unobserved, with the unholy shame of that greater tragedy darkening his face, so that later she could report it all in detail. Life would indeed be rich if only she could orchestrate it.

The people of Freyzus waited for a glimpse of Peyre—whom they had come to refer to as 'the poor man'—so they could exchange their observations on the state of his well-being—or otherwise. But as time elapsed, their curiosity assumed a certain self-consciousness, and when he did at last come by the village, it was weeks after Mathilde had gone. No one ventured to tell him that his wife had already left—though several people watched him take the road to her father's house.

As he approached the house, Peyre fought the urge to turn back. He did not know what he would say when the door opened. He did not know what he would say when he saw his wife. He felt only his former grief, like a wave long drawn out to sea returning to engulf him at any moment.

But he did not need even to speak. When Mathilde's father came to the door he was brief. He had no time for this spectre of a man who stood on his step, his hat in his hand.

She is gone to Montpellier, he said. To live with my sister there. And then he closed the door.

Peyre stayed at the cemetery for longer than usual, sitting amid the dry grasses and the insects tireless at their work. Then he went back into the village in search of liquor. He sat alone in the tavern. On display, he thought. Mayor Pailhès came in to offer condolences — at which Peyre shrugged in the way of one who has other things, more important things, on his mind. Ramon Pailhès tried again to engage him.

So. Your aunt's house is all closed up now. Is it in good order? he asked.

I wouldn't know, said Peyre — as if to say, Why would I?

The mayor said, Well, then, and rubbed his hands together. Then he said he had best get on with his business. This would not get his work done.

Only Blind Henri was brave enough to sit awhile with Peyre, neither seeing the other's eyes, equally blind.

Peyre finished his drink, took another, and began the journey home, oblivious of the gossip that buzzed now in Henri's tavern. Peyre's father-in-law was reported to have said two nights ago that even Montpellier was too close in his opinion. Everyone had heard it. Or was it Mathilde who had said it before she left? A rumour circulated soon that Peyre's in-laws had let loose unchristian thoughts, uttered in unchristian syllables, and closed their doors to both the daughter and the husband forever. And this time rumour did not lie.

Peyre was accompanied home only by his own imaginings. In his mind he saw a beautiful infant, like an angel in heaven, and it was no consolation at all. It was a robber infant come to usurp the memory of his son. He hated it for the celestial afterlife it had so effortlessly acquired. And the memory of Giles's earthly life so fragile.

Once more he shut the world away and retreated to his workshop. Out of a sense of decency he would open his door to those who came to call. Then they would sit together at the table with the red-and-yellow cloth and share a bowl of indeterminate soup. There was never conversation. In time, not even gifts of honey cakes were sent to his door. The rewards were too meagre.

IN OCTOBER, ONE year after the accident, a note arrived from Martin de Villiers. Despite the letter that Peyre had sent him in the winter announcing his retirement from the hunt, de Villiers declared his intent to host a duck shoot this year. He said he fully understood Peyre's wishes, but all things considered, it really would be best for Peyre to face the world and take up his responsibilities once more. In his opinion the longer he kept from taking the step, the more difficult it would become.

There was no room for dispute. De Villiers arrived at the cottage two days later.

The seigneur's friends, unnaturally quiet as they climbed down from the landau, began to organize themselves, wishing, each one, that he were invisible, that the awkwardness might be over, so that he might freely smile and stride into the splendid morning as they had the year before.

De Villiers was charm itself. I understand, he said. Utterly. There are no words. The year will have been most difficult. Most difficult. Such a fine lad.

Peyre made the slightest movement of acknowledgment, no more than a flinch away from the pain de Villiers was inflicting.

I'll not ask you to accompany us. Just have a trestle ready for our return so that we can fortify ourselves for the journey back. That's all I ask. I have everything with us, all the necessary provisions, that goes without saying.

De Villiers was a generous man. The remnants of his provisions could keep Peyre in food for more than a week. Peyre said he would accompany the party a certain way, although he would not himself participate. The party assembled themselves just as they had the year before, but, out of respect for their guide, they curbed the usual banter. They did not find it hard to imagine Peyre setting out in good spirits on his own hunt, with his own friends, his own son, in ignorance of what was just moments away.

Peyre went into the cottage. He bent down and cupped his hands to the sides of the wolf's head. He looked into the empty eye sockets and longed for their blindness.

He walked for only a short while with the party. The scent of the morning. The tramp of feet, murmured exchanges and whispers. The soft clash of the reeds, faint reek of gun oil. The dogs. He made his excuses and turned back. In his workshop he concentrated on the small form of a mouse until his mind had calmed. When he heard the men's voices in the distance, he went to set out their lunch.

The hunters returned to the cottage with their cheeks flushed and their eyes shining and they laid out their day's work, the lovely plumage bright, the long, soft necks stretched on the ground. So many. De Villiers's cousin had brought down a lone shelduck. He was the envy of them all.

Peyre listened politely as he laid out the dishes.

And Monsieur Rouff—Peyre—would have let you have him, had he been with us, and then he would have taken the one farther off, de Villiers said to his cousin. Peyre never misses, never.

As if stricken by some unimaginably cold wind, the words hung like a dangerous ice crystal in the air. It was astonishing to see the variety of distractions and excuses the hunters found for themselves—their knives, their thumbnails, a sudden itch—in order to avoid a response.

Peyre coughed. I'll leave you then, he said, to your lunch. Bon appétit, seigneur, messieurs.

No, no. You'll stay. Sit with us, eat.

I beg your pardon, mon seigneur, I have work to attend to.

Peyre retreating to his workshop, pulled at the neck of his shirt. If he could breathe. If he could only breathe. Work. Work was the only answer. It always served him when memory threatened. It never failed. He took up the mouse and dusted its fur with a fine sawdust, then he brushed it out and began to work at the fur with a bread crust to restore the gloss. He began to count, purposefully, evenly.

The man should join us, said de Villiers's cousin.

De Villiers made a grand gesture to nobody in particular. Go and fetch him. No, wait. I'll go myself. Then he can't refuse.

He ducked inside the workshop.

Have you had your lunch?

Peyre was concentrating, counting softly as he stroked the fur, keeping thought at bay.

I have, sir.

Well come and join us for some brandy, said de Villiers. He walked closer, smiling. That is astonishingly alive.

Peyre nodded.

Such exacting work. May I see?

Peyre handed him the mouse.

Quite extraordinary. Do you have any others?

Mice?

Mammals?

Peyre got up and went dutifully through to the cottage, where he pulled aside the settle by the hearth.

My God. Monsieur Rouff, this is your best yet.

De Villiers went over to the wolf. He reached to touch the muzzle, stopped short. Remarkable, he said, shaking his head. Get those other fellows in here.

But Peyre was unconscionably slow to respond. De Villiers went to the door himself.

Come and see this.

With their pipes and their half-finished conversations they came, crowding the small room. In no time they were carrying the wolf, like some stiff-legged idol, out into the light. They set it up on the trestle in the midst of the remnants of the feast. One forepaw was lifted delicately. Its blind eyes searched the air it scented.

And then there was only one topic to pursue. Everyone it seemed had had some encounter with a wolf—had been trailed, come face to face, had taken aim, had narrowly missed, had hit, had killed, had collected bounty, smelled its breath.

Peyre did not like to see it there on the table. He began to clear the dishes and pack away those items that had to go back with de Villiers.

De Villiers came to stand beside him. It needs eyes, Peyre.

Peyre nodded.

Will you make them?

He shook his head. Eyes would have to be ordered. They were expensive.

Then what? The creature is magnificent. It must have eyes. They must be purchased.

And then? Will you keep it?

Peyre said quietly, No.

Sell, then? Come. You and I will walk while my guests tell each other lies.

For now the men were reseated, had settled round this totem and progressed to tales of wolves that carried away children, wolves that terrorized whole villages, and wolves they had once, on a special hunt, beaten to death with clubs.

How much do you want? asked de Villiers when they were out of earshot.

Peyre shrugged.

Then shall we say one hundred francs? I shall give you half here, now, and you can order those eyes.

For the first time that day, de Villiers saw some expression on Peyre's face, the dead gaze lifted.

Then shake my hand.

PEYRE ROUFF LAID the wolf, wrapped close in straw and sacking and crated round, in the back of the gig for delivery to Aveyrac.

The ascent took all morning. The road from Gougeac was long, steep in places. The ass was unhappy and made it known. Peyre used a switch of blackthorn. Still the journey was preferable to climbing up through the wild garrigue like an aberrant shepherd with the wolf tied across his shoulders. It was a relief when the road emerged from the last of the evergreen oak onto the wide apron of heath above the valley. The honey-coloured stone of the house seemed all new in the autumn sun.

Peyre had not been up to the chateau since before the accident, nor had his uncle come down. As he drove up between the elms, Guilhem came out to the steps of the terrace. A long-legged dog came hurtling from round the corner of the house at the same time.

The old man had not finished tottering down the steps before the young dog sprang without hesitation for the gig. It missed its footing and fell back.

Tiens! Te voilà! His uncle was trembling. Te voilà, Peyre! He sucked against teeth that were loose in his mouth as he shook his head. His white hair lifted in the breeze.

Already the dog was lining itself up for a more controlled attempt. Peyre braced himself and then the dog was in the trap with him, licking all the accessible skin it could find. The old man did not call it down and Peyre let it continue. It was as if the dog were finding every trace of that other pup, his son's.

When the two men finally stood face to the face, Guilhem frail, Peyre gaunt and absent from his eyes, they did not inquire after each other's health. It was not necessary.

I have brought something for the seigneur, said Peyre.

Peyre pushed the dog out of the way and reached into the gig for the crate.

His uncle watched while he lifted it down.

What have you got?

A wolf.

Guilhem looked askance at his nephew. He might have said a crate of apples for all the interest he conveyed.

The entrance hall had an empty echo. The black and white tiles stretched away to the great staircase. The dark banisters flowed down from the first-floor gallery, the marble stairs cascading silently between them, curving away to right and left at the bottom. A single chair, placed to one side, was the only furniture.

They set the crate down on the left of the stairs. Peyre said they should leave it upright.

The dog flattened itself for an instant, no more, then investigated every part of the crate.

Did it turn out well?

I think it did. It can stay in its case until the seigneur arrives. Peyre had visions of the unruly hound tearing open the crate and chewing his specimen to rags.

Come, then, if we're not to see it. I'll find you something.

Peyre guessed that the refreshment would be liquid. They sat in silence and listened to the demented cooing of the doves. Neither of them felt the need to talk. The old man understood that in the end they were both waiting, that they would be waiting always, all their days, for the same event.

I should go home.

The old man said, Home. He said, People send me news. There's no home for you anymore. You should come here, boy. Come away.

Peyre shook his head.

You've no reason to stay down there.

Peyre looked up at his uncle and the old man saw then his grief deep as the grave and he knew that it was not for the wife who had left him or for the infant who had died, and he knew he did indeed have a reason.

At least tonight, Guilhem said. You can help me here. Go back tomorrow.

And so Peyre stayed on and helped the old man prepare a proper meal, finding dried mushrooms wrapped in old newspaper, and chestnuts, some of them still good. He dug up a giant turnip, all hollow inside, and he took down the remains of the ham that hung over the stove, so dry now he could break pieces away with his thumb.

The old man ate with relish. Peyre saw how scrawny his neck had become, the skin loose there, his uncle disappearing from the inside.

In the morning Peyre walked a little to clear his head, keeping his mind trained on the rooms in the great house, enumerating the features of each, every tile, the least hinge. The long-legged dog came with him. A bottle or two with the old man the night before had been the only way to keep the worst of his thoughts at bay. He had succumbed utterly to the liquor. When he lay down to sleep he remembered briefly the warmth of his wife's thigh, the comfort of her flesh against his, and he had slept without dreams.

Guilhem was watching for his return. He asked him to do some jobs for him before he left, saying he had hurt his arm and he had no more wood for the stove. Peyre nodded and went about the tasks methodically, repairing a broken shutter, cutting neat sections of fallen boughs to fit the stove, stacking them in perfect order near the wall in the courtyard.

Guilhem could not make him stay longer.

I cannot be so far from him, he said, and his uncle knew where it was that Peyre lived behind his sightless eyes.

DE VILLIERS WAS pleased with the wolf. That was clear. In appreciation he sent a gift, a long rectangular applewood box, with an engraved brass inlay: *Les Yeux Assortis—mammifères*

—*oiseaux*—*reptiles. Desjardin et fils PARIS.* When Peyre opened the lid and lifted the velvet cover away, three rows of paired eyes gazed back at him, a dozen in each row. When he removed the top tray, four more rows of eyes stared up from the wooden sockets in their tray. Underneath, five rows. These last, tiny, black and golden and glittering.

A second package arrived a week later. De Villiers had sent a new commission. Peyre recognized it at once. He had always thought the specimen an aberration. It was from the trophy room at the chateau, where guests took their brandy and cigars surrounded by mounted heads projecting from the walls at heights they never attained in life. A mausoleum of slaughter, the living beasts remembered fondly, restored poorly by some hopelessly optimistic novice of years past. He remembered this fox in particular because it must have been regarded well. It had stood under a glass case on a low table. But it craned its neck at an unusual angle. It might have been about to bite its own back. Its lips were set badly and seemed to want to pull back, not in a snarl or in greeting or any expression Peyre could fathom. It would be a kindness to the memory of the creature to reset it.

He agreed to the commission and to the terms of delivery —in person when notified by the seigneur himself.

Two months later Peyre was back at Aveyrac. As before, the long-legged dog came tearing to meet him. It jumped up to sniff at the knapsack where the fox was carefully packed. Peyre knocked it away and it trotted on beside him, forward and back, forward and back, attentive and eager.

There was no one on the steps. He could hear men's voices in the courtyard, the unmistakable loud voices of city men, jovial hunters now, and he realized why de Villiers had waited until now to summon him. His uncle came round the corner, wiping his mouth.

He flailed in Peyre's direction as if shooing a wandering animal away.

He says you are to go round and enter by the front door. He gestured again and went back, and the dog raced ahead.

Peyre did as he was asked and climbed the steps. The front door already stood open. He stepped inside, and there she was, his wolf, just to the right of the bottom step, where the banister made its elegant turn. With one forepaw lifted, poised, she stood, scenting the air, scenting him. The dog lay at her feet, as if it had predicted precisely where Peyre's gaze would go. It watched him closely — and de Villiers watched them both from a doorway to the left.

She looks at home, doesn't she?

It was a poor choice of words, for 'she' was in a foreign country.

Peyre took a while to reply. The smooth cold marble. The stark geometry of tessellation. And the hollow air. Cavernous. The astonishing mirrors on either side. Their dull gleam through the dust. How she would run — ears flattened in terror — from the alien vibrations of capture and confinement.

No. She is not at home.

De Villiers registered a slight disapproving surprise.

Yet Peyre was despite himself seduced by his own art. To see her here on the tiled floor, alert but unafraid. To see her scenting the air as if on any familiar rock or knoll. To see her not destroyed. To see her wildness offered as ornament of the highest order. But he said nothing.

De Villiers suppressed his disappointment. Well, I suppose not, not literally. But what do you think? My visitors, I have to say, have been thrilled by their greeting.

There will come a day, Peyre said, when the hair of her head will be threadbare. So many hands. Everyone brave enough to approach.

De Villiers could not be sure if Peyre was smiling, the eyes of him so hard to read.

And you can see at once what is required, de Villiers said. No.

But a male to stand at the other side!

No. Not that. By herself, she is a surprise. With a mate she becomes a newel post. Furniture.

You speak, Monsieur Rouff, as if your days are consumed with filling orders for mounted hall ornaments. I'm offering work, you understand.

De Villiers waited for an apology. But Rouff was clearly too closed in his own world for that.

Don't worry. De Villiers clapped him on the shoulder. Just think about it, that's all. Now, you have my fox?

But Peyre *had* already begun to think about it. Even then beasts were walking up the terrace steps and slinking in to take up their positions. And he knew now where the fox should go.

He nodded and walked over to the chair that stood by the wall.

De Villiers waited while Peyre put down the knapsack and took out the blanketed fox. The dog stood by and wagged its tail, low with uncertainty. Peyre held out the fox on his forearms. A fox asleep, curled round on itself, its nose tucked under its tail. But, oh, a fox alive.

De Villiers took it, turned it this way and that, and shook his head slowly in admiration.

Here.

Peyre placed it carefully right there between them on the padded chair.

De Villiers stepped back. The thing almost breathed. It was a miracle it did not spring down and run when the dog approached.

The grey toile covering the chair was printed in blue with scenes of the hunt. The fox seemed to rest there naturally. A cushion of russet fur held within the curves of the carved walnut of the chair, it formed an almost perfect circle, its tail sweeping round to hide the folded paws, its nose disappearing under the brush's black tip.

Extraordinary. I can't believe it's the same animal. The others must see it.

Peyre glanced swiftly at him.

You know of course, de Villiers said, that it is no coincidence I have brought you here at the same time as my friends.

Peyre had guessed what he would eventually be asked.

I'll stay to help you, he said, but not with the hunt.

It's just a few close friends. De Villiers laughed. They persuaded me. One last boar hunt in the country before I leave for the Indies.

When he was introduced in the courtyard, Peyre recognized none of them but he sensed from the stiffness of their greeting that they knew all about him. He was a specimen, as clearly as if he were cased in glass. He found himself unable to do more than nod. Conversation, that seconds before had been gaily rolling, seemed to have abruptly hit a patch of gravel.

De Villiers, though manipulative, was not cruel. He saw Peyre's discomfort.

Well, we'll let these gentlemen continue with their preparations, he said. You and I will go to the kitchen.

Guilhem, who had finished chopping turnips for the night's supper, had stepped out to take another look at the fox. He stood in the hall, wiping his hands on a rag.

Well, nephew, he said. It's uncanny what you've done with that beast. Uncanny, lad. You do more than I taught you. Much more. Now, your aunt, he said—my sister, God rest her soul—would have had her own opinion: treachery. A dead thing should look like a dead thing, she always said. Or where would we all be? He laughed, the sound harsh as a rake.

The fox, though it feigned sleep, seemed to be watching him from one open eye.

Martin de Villiers's friends, who were all from Montpellier, said they dreamed of living in such splendid isolation—by which they meant, roughly, that they were glad they did not. They said they relished the wild setting of the house, its authentic charm, and they had forgotten the refreshingly Spartan nature of the days there—by which they meant they wished they had brought their own servants.

To a man they admired the wolf and the strangely appealing fox. One of the guests had a camera and asked Peyre to carry the wolf out to the terrace. The photographer assembled the others in a group behind the wolf. He adjusted the pose of each, seeing to the turn of their heads, the position of their hands, and then he went to his camera. Peyre watched. He saw their faces subtly change while they waited for the photographer to perform his magic beneath the black cloth. Something in them leached away as the seconds ticked by, until only the wolf seemed truly alive. The photographer said it was a shame he could not take a picture with the wolf lying as if shot. He was going to take another with the group, but Peyre had already picked up the wolf and was carrying it back inside.

One or two of the guests exchanged glances. Everything they had heard about the unfortunate man was true. He was no longer quite right in the head. You could tell by his eyes. But they all agreed that he was incomparably skilled.

In the course of the first jovial night, de Villiers's latest acquisition, the fox, was moved to several different locations, including the water closet and de Villiers's bed.

Not surprisingly the next day's hunt was unsuccessful. In the afternoon de Villiers took Peyre on a tour of the estate. His reason for bringing Peyre up to Aveyrac had to do with more than mounted trophies. Aveyrac itself was in disrepair. Even he could not ignore it any longer. He thought that merely pointing out the extent of the work that needed to be done would secure Peyre Rouff's services, for Peyre would surely see for himself that the old man was not managing alone. De Villiers walked Peyre round the grounds, pointed out the missing tiles on the roof of the barn, the rendering fallen away on the north east wall, where frost and rain bit hardest. He showed him the leaves of the red vine piled in drifts in the angles of the walls, a length of lead guttering hanging like the sword of Damocles above the main entrance. The approach to the house was strewn with boughs torn from the great elms in the last gale, months ago.

When they returned to the house, de Villiers showed Peyre into his private study. Over a glass of anise he put his proposition to him. He was leaving soon, he said, for Martinique. He no longer had ties in Montpellier. He wanted Peyre installed in Aveyrac as soon as possible.

You know I can't, Peyre said. I could never leave my son.

A lifetime stipend, Monsieur Rouff.

De Villiers waited.

What would it take to make you reconsider?

Peyre held out his glass for more before he replied.

I would need my son to be buried here.

De Villiers decided that he too needed another drink. The man's grief continued to shock in its intensity — but no, it was not quite that. The shock was in the baldness of it. No attempt to soften or conceal his inhuman resolve.

I am surprised, I have to say. Monsieur Rouff, if you cannot commit to helping me, will you not think of your uncle...?

Peyre stared into his glass. He said, I need to think of my son. No one is more alone than he.

De Villiers got up. There are others to consider, he said. There are the living. You will come to see it.

At the end of three days they had their boar. The photographer then was busy again with his plates and his boxes. Each man had to pose with the beast, then all. And then the wolf was called upon again and the fox too. An unlikely trio was arranged on the terrace, with the fox still sleeping in its chair, the dead boar in the foreground, and the wolf still scenting the air for her mate.

In the afternoon the men packed their belongings for an early departure next day. The boar was divided up, a haunch set aside for the spit that night and the rest packed in salt and shared among the guests, with some of the offal left for Guilhem to make sausage. De Villiers, who was anxious to get away, gave Peyre a list of jobs that he could discretely carry out in preparation for closing the house. He was pleasantly surprised to find in the morning that most of them had already been completed.

On their way home, one or two of the guests discussed the noises they had heard in the night. They came to the conclusion that it was the demented father moving about. One of them said he had heard groaning. They all agreed they would not want Peyre Rouff roaming about the place up there in the dark, not if they were de Villiers.

De Villiers left not long after his guests. He rode down alone, thoughtful. He had left behind a note for Peyre, expressing his wish that he might one day change his mind. To help him, he had folded inside a promissory note made over to the priest at Freyzus, together with the formal request to the mayor, for Peyre to sign, for the exhumation of the remains of the boy Giles Rouff with authority for reinterment at Aveyrac.

Peyre tried not to think about the note. He concentrated on the last of the chores, shaking out the bedsheets, then bringing them inside to cover the furniture once more, closing the last of the shutters.

Although it was not yet midday, Guilhem was already dozing beside the great kitchen hearth when Peyre went to say goodbye. He seemed to barely rouse, and Peyre wondered whether he would remember his going. The dog at least was awake. It watched from the hall as he closed the front door.

Through the closed and silent house the dog roamed, scenting every trace of every guest, tracking the path of the boar parts in their progress toward the table and the town. And then it lay down and dreamed.

That evening Guilhem sat by the fire again. He watched the sparks fly up and vanish and he wondered where his own life had gone, his nights so long and nothing to do but listen to silence, guess the hour.

At his cottage, Peyre began to receive inquiries. With the visits of de Villiers's friends, word of the wolf spread, and with it Peyre's reputation. The little cottage, that he had valued and that his wife had resented for its remoteness, was not so isolated after all. His protracted parley with grief was interrupted often by correspondence from strangers—a letter, a package with a request for mounting, a request to meet. People promised him money. He took the commissions readily. The work was demanding and required concentration. The days when he was occupied with a mount were shorter, the pain less sharp.

Some of the packages contained skins imperfectly cleaned and already spoiled. He could smell them before he opened them. Monsieur Trochet the postman said he was glad it was not summer. He grumbled to his friends about it over a drink. Someone said Peyre was not getting any better.

Once, a crate arrived and Peyre braced himself for what he would find inside, but it was not so bad. A chamois, already mounted, poked from the straw. He could see why the request to remount it had been made. The mouth was set in something suspiciously like the snarl of a dog. The ears were graceless, asinine. It was a form of service to take the commission and set it right.

The chateau itself was suspended in its own wintry dream. Guilhem let the fire die and in the next days he forsook the great hearth for the companionable crackle and spit of the stove in the corner. In the hall the fox slept on, arrested in a comfort denied its maker—who would have settled for a brief forgetting. The fox disturbed Guilhem a little, keeping its face so hidden. Sometimes when the young dog came through the hall, it sniffed at the fox, once or twice nudged it and jumped. Even the dog was uneasy, Guilhem thought. A fox should be running free. Either that or kept under glass respectably. He would have liked to remove it, the wolf too, and not just because it seemed to be taking a liberty with the furniture.

Guilhem, the most practical, the most pragmatic of men, began to feel superstition, like rheumatism, coming upon him. He had been unnerved by his nephew's suggestion of rules to be observed in the treatment of animal remains. He had never heard of such a thing and felt a dangerous lack in his own cavalier approach. He began to wonder if he would be in some way punished. The work of the devil! one of the guests had exclaimed over the fox. And now each day when Guilhem looked at it he had to agree. He just hoped Peyre knew what he was about, that was all. He didn't want any unforeseen consequences. He had not in fact been feeling at all like himself. In truth for a few days he had begun to feel distinctly unwell. But there was as usual much to be done about the place with the end of winter not far off and spring in sight. And fresh air, he knew, would do him good. And so it was that at the end of February on a fine morning threaded with birdsong, Guilhem went out to dig his garden, put his hand to the centre of his chest, and watched darkness fall over the countryside.

A thrush came almost at once to pull worms from the newly turned soil.

One week later news of his death spread through the villages like water. It was a traveller on his way down to Gougeac who discovered the body. He had come onto the hill from the pass above the chateau and was looking for a welcome. Only a skinny, guilty-looking dog came to greet him, trotting away again and coming back. No one came to the door when the traveller knocked. The dog continued its trotting, circling, always in the same direction. The traveller finally followed. When he had recovered from the shock, he took a drink at the pump in the courtyard and hurried on his way, hearing for the first few yards small whimpers of disappointment behind him.

In Gougeac the traveller notified the commissioner and the commissioner notified the priest. The priest went to see Peyre Rouff.

When Peyre opened his door he turned his mind inward at once. The priest from Freyzus had taught him to be wary. Whatever business this one was about, Peyre would not let him disrupt his line of thought. It was a trick he was close to perfecting — if only he concentrated hard enough.

The priest stepped inside without being asked and waited to be invited farther in.

Peyre too waited patiently, and eventually the priest spoke.

Peyre listened. He paused for only a second before he replied.

My uncle does not need me now, he said.

He is your kin, Monsieur Rouff.

Yes, said Peyre, he was.

He turned and went inside, leaving the priest in the doorway.

When he came back he held out two francs. He was staring fixedly ahead. For a mass, he said, and whatever is necessary. The commissioner will know best.

The priest cleared his throat. He had expected this to be difficult.

But Peyre was already taking down his cap from its hook.

Excuse me. The priest would make use of that detail when he recounted later how Peyre Rouff had walked away there and then to the marshes. *Excuse me*, he had said, leaving him standing at the open door.

The commissioner paid for the cheapest labourers he could find to go with the priest up to Aveyrac. They took a mean board coffin and some rope and they buried the steward, rolled in a piece of sacking, in a corner of the little graveyard attached to the de Villiers family chapel.

When it was done, they came straight down, stopping only to bring up some brandy from the cellar and to secure the great front door.

As soon as the party returned, the rumours began. The body of the steward, some said, was strangely preserved. Others said it was half devoured. There was talk of a large wolf in the neighbourhood. But no, the wolf was in the house — *that* wolf.

The men had found only a young dog, it transpired, a long-legged black and tan dog. They encouraged it to accompany them and it rode some way in the cart. But when they stopped to rest, it chewed through its rope and bounded away back up to the house. None of them felt inclined to follow. It would come down soon enough — though, who would undertake to feed such a rangy beast? That was another matter.

By evening, the talk in the town had spread to Freyzus.

Le Boulidou said, That man spreads bad luck.

And what man would that be? Ramon Pailhès sighed at the prospect of the answer.

Peyre Rouff, of course.

Pailhès sighed again. Peyre's uncle was well over eighty, he said. That is more like a stroke of good luck, to die peacefully with your trousers on.

Amid the laughter Blind Henri was still thinking about the dog. He said, Of course Peyre Rouff should take it. The poor man was in a wretched unnatural state. He had felt it in his bones when he sat with him.

The schoolteacher agreed. He said, Monsieur Rouff is all alone now. He sees no one. It would be company of a kind.

The mayor said it was neither here nor there. But Peyre Rouff should decide for himself.

And Peyre did soon enough decide. Some children from Gougeac summoned the courage to knock on his door. It was the uncle's dog they were interested in. They said it was a monster. Black as night, they said, and its head was as large as a burl on an oak. He listened, his gaze tracking their faces one by one until they ran away. The next day he made the journey up to Aveyrac, taking with him a rope and a piece of sausage and one of the bones he had thrown on the dung heap. He hoped the dog had learned to fend for itself, for he was not at all sure how he would provide for it.

The dog heard him coming and ran a considerable distance down the road from the chateau. It flattened itself and waited. Plumes of dust puffed in the air behind it as it beat its tail on the ground. No guard dog, this. Peyre climbed down from the trap and the dog was on its feet at once, its hindquarters swivelling wildly.

It had been a long time since Peyre had felt anything like laughter stir in his belly.

Well, come on, boy, he said, and the dog was on him at once. He looped the rope over the dog's head. It would have followed him in any case.

He led it over to the trap and sat on the footboard and the dog lay at once at his feet. Its eyes fixed on his own, its innocence absolute.

And if I've come to finish you off? The dog's gaze was unwavering. Peyre reached in to his knapsack for the bone. Before it was out, the dog was on its feet. It clamped its teeth round the gift and it settled a little distance off to crack through to the marrow. Peyre watched. He had forgotten what it felt like to eat with such relish.

Peyre decided then that to stay at Aveyrac would not be a bad thing. He began to make plans.

*

The next time he came down from Aveyrac, the dog came with him. He went first to Freyzus to see the mayor. Ramon Pailhès was civil and welcoming, even to the dog, and did his best to tread the difficult path that would raise no memories, provoke no awkwardness. His efforts were lost on Peyre, who without any introduction handed him de Villiers's note and waited. Pailhès read in silence, then he got up and poured each of them a drink before he replied.

You're sure? was all he said. He had not seen such a request in all his years in office. You're sure?

And Peyre said, Yes.

Ramon Pailhès, the colour slowly returning to his face, wondered why this request had landed on his desk. It was the priest's business, after all. But he hesitated, thinking it would be just as well to get involved, now that Peyre Rouff seemed to hold the keys to Aveyrac. It would not hurt his cause to show how cooperative he could be. But Peyre Rouff had no time for displays. He needed only simple assent and an appointed date and when he had them he rose at once, the dog springing to its feet beside him. There was barely time for a handshake and then Peyre was on his way to Gougeac.

In Gougeac he called at the house of Frédéric Maurel and told him he would like to give him his mule once he had moved his belongings up to the chateau. He did not plan on leaving once his son arrived. Deeply unnerved, Frédéric did not ask him what he meant. He tried to be of use. He helped Peyre load his tools and supplies into the trap and he hired a boy to bring the mule back down, for Peyre insisted on going alone up to Aveyrac. Frédéric was more than ready to assist in any way. To do something for Peyre might help alleviate his own nagging need to talk to him, to have the conversation they had never had since the accident — its deferral now become a very want, a lack, a haunting presence all its own. Frédéric Maurel would not be sorry to see the cottage closed up. Perhaps then, with Peyre Rouff comfortably far, he might allow himself to forget — although that night he found it hard to sleep, with memory, as it was, so closely looming.

Like Frédéric Maurel, the people of Gougeac were glad to hear of Peyre Rouff's decision. They had never wished a penitent among their number. They would have preferred Peyre to rise like Lazarus from his sorrow and resume life, plain and simple, break bread, laugh, cry. They had balked at the very idea of an unapproachable. You did not want to encounter a penitent in a hair shirt when you went to post a letter, nor see him coming from a distance on the road out of town and not know how to avoid passing. When a man looked the way Peyre looked, you could not ask, How are you? Even for his friends, perhaps especially for his friends, Peyre was the unwelcome reminder that fate's reversals are without pity, and without limit.

The next day Ramon Pailhès struggled to find volunteers to work with the sexton. He had received instructions, he said — and they had been sanctioned by the priest — to exhume the remains of the boy Giles Rouff and carry them up to

Aveyrac. Peyre Rouff had assumed full stewardship of the estate, and the seigneur, now in Martinique, had agreed to the son's reburial in the de Villiers churchyard at his own expense. It was a condition of Rouff's engagement.

The news confirmed everyone's opinion that Peyre Rouff was now roundly, starkly mad.

Despite the purse, it was difficult to find two men who would take the work. Gustave Thibéry, Thierry Sanis, even le Boulidou, all refused. They had seen Peyre Rouff on his solitary walks to the churchyard, and they had seen him at his son's grave the first time. It was enough. No one needed to see it again. His spare figure leaning above the open grave, as if willing himself to be drawn in, drawn down, his eyes almost closed, his fists, the knuckles white, at his sides. Peyre monumental in the kind of grief no one should have to witness. The thought of it silenced the men while each one occupied himself with some version of the same question: Wasn't it the duty of the bereaved to gamely spare his fellow man the sight of such grief? Wouldn't the merest glimpse of it be enough for it to enter through the eye sockets, burrow into the beholder's heart, and root there, ready always to rise and haunt a man? A change of subject was in order. And at least another drink, or two. After several glasses more, they found they could be kinder, and they could say, and mean it, that it was not for them to determine how the bereaved should live, or where they should bury their dead.

*

Peyre kept the dog chained on the appointed day when the men from Freyzus arrived at Aveyrac. He watched the cart arriving. There was no man there that he knew, nor was there any priest. They had covered the coffin with a white sheet. Two ropes lay coiled on the top. He watched them pass in front of the house and continue up the hill to the chapel behind. He had dug the place himself, carefully removing every stone and root, attentive to the necessary worms. But he did not want Giles in the earth again. He went to find something from the light, the air.

The men waited in the churchyard, wondering who should go and find him. They were ready for something to eat.

He came at last from the house with a small bird, meticulously preserved, in his hands.

He nodded to the men. But he did not speak.

They hesitated and he nodded again.

The coffin went in at an angle. Peyre heard something slide. Each man held the two ends of his rope and eventually the ungainly thing was done. One of them pulled the crumpled paper from his pocket and began as instructed, reciting from heart because he could not read.

Peyre took the paper from him.

> *In the sweat of thy face shalt thou eat bread, till thou return unto the ground; for out of it wast thou taken: for dust thou art, and unto dust shalt thou return.*

Though neither was he reading. The words came from his mouth as if from the priest and he paid them no heed. They were in Latin and would have remained foreign to him even in his own tongue. He listened instead to the words that formed in his heart and were carried away under the spoken words unheard.

One of the men pulled away the linen sheet, for it had to be returned to Madame Pailhès. Peyre saw how the pine was not yet blackened by the earth. He threw the bird onto it. The men were waiting for him to walk away. Instead he took up one of the shovels.

Go to the house, he said. You will be hungry. And while they dithered, he began to fill the hole. He did not look up when they walked away.

In the kitchen, the men helped themselves to what they could find. They sat at the great table and shook their heads while they soaked the obstinate bread in Peyre's cold soup. And poured themselves another glass of wine.

When they left, they caught sight of him coming down from the hill behind the churchyard and someone voiced the thought that the sooner he put an end to everything once and for all, the better.

Peyre Rouff had no intention of harming any life, least of all his own. When he left this earth who would assume the sacred duty of living, of witnessing the world in place of his son? He walked miles each day, walking into the world to absorb all it had to offer. For his son he learned to love the deep shade of the chestnut woods and the sun-baked heaths and limestone pavements of the high garrigue. At Aveyrac he could embrace his grief like a lover.

He walked in all weathers, seeing the blossom cover the valley sides like heavenly snow, breathing the perfume. For his son, always for his son. He walked in summer storms, flinching under the thunder, catching from the corner of his eye a lightning bolt striking earth above him, somewhere on the path he had just descended. He saw cypress trees bend like grasses under the mistral. He saw flocks of tiny finches like a flung net across the sky, gathering themselves in a tight vortex and ballooning out again until they disappeared against the blue.

He tended the animals at the house with special care, loving them for Giles — the hens and the goat, the cats who mewed for milk, and the dog. Always the dog, which, though he did not see it, performed its own duty, keeping Peyre always from straying too far from life. As soon as he put his feet to the floor in the morning, he would hear its answering yawn from the courtyard, its comic vowels greeting the day. By the time he reached the kitchen, it would, with the bad manners of the young, be clawing at the door. The scrabbling would stop the moment his hand touched the latch, and when he opened the door the dog would be waiting, its eyes upon him, long limbs frozen, tail waving furiously behind, and every inch of its skin alive in expectation. And each day the same paroxysm of joy at the sight of food. It searched Peyre's eyes often. Sometimes Peyre looked right back, looked deep into the dog's foreign heart, and recognized something he had lost.

After the animals, Peyre looked after himself. It was not difficult. A pot of soup or beans lasted several days, usually a week. Most days all he had to do was set the pot upon the fire.

Isolation. The absence of any eye that might accuse. He welcomed it. Life, what there was of it, smooth like a waveless sea, though the knowledge, the fact of the event, was there forever, a giant swell beneath the smooth surface, and Giles now so near. At each day's waning Peyre felt the pull, like the drag of a strong tide, calling him to his son's grave. It was not good to stand there, to kneel there, sometimes to lie there vacantly staring, helpless. He knew that. Yet fighting the need was exhausting and too often he succumbed. Always when he had been drinking.

He was forced once to make a visit to the town. He did not relish it, the hiring of the mule again and the boy who would accompany it to bring the supplies back up, the negotiations with Frédéric, who seemed always to behave as if he was shocked to see him. It required fortitude, resilience. When he entered Gougeac, his skin remembered the stares, his ears the whispered pity. The look of surprise and—what was it?—panic on Madame Maurel's face when she saw him. She asked him to come in and eat with them, and Frédéric, when he came in and saw Peyre, had the same expression. He told him how a vagrant had broken into his cottage and been found living there, discovered by the smoke, for he had started burning chairs. Peyre was not perturbed. He wished he, like his house, could simply loosen and crumble away. Go up in smoke.

Climbing back up to the chateau with the boy who had come to help was a trial. He let the boy talk—but he tried not to listen. To endure was everything. The boy on his way back down again with the mule thought he had done something wrong, Monsieur Rouff so fierce and silent.

When the boy had gone, Peyre breathed more deeply. The chatter of the town fell away, gravel skittering into a ravine. Silence of the broad sky. Fine emptiness of air. Lungfuls of it were good. The wind peeled the harshness of human contact from his skin.

RAMON PAILHÈS HAD a particular interest in the management of Aveyrac. He was a shrewd man. He guessed that Martin de Villiers would not be returning any time soon to hunt for boar or anything else. Peyre Rouff, given the right encouragement and plenty of time on his hands, might be ready to entertain a suggestion regarding the restoration of the mill. Freyzus had been prosperous in former times, bustling with the business the mill attracted. Even when the original comte built his great house and began to harness the waters of the hill for himself, there had existed a system of conduits and sluice gates to redirect them to the mill on demand. But de Villiers's grandfather, the merchant who had purchased the property when it was held in trust by the town of Gougeac, had not been so accommodating. He diverted the stream that had once leapt and tumbled down from the high bluffs in the east before it disappeared underground. The redirected waters supplied his trout pond farther upstream on the eastern hill, while the outflow irrigated his land as it made its way down in a new direction toward the river Vaz. The drained reservoir was the perfect site for an orangerie. He did not listen to the people of Freyzus when they complained. And nor did his son, de Villiers's father. He built terraces, diverted water yet again, and planted vines, and for a while they thrived. Whenever a contingent of men came from Freyzus to ask for the water to be restored to the millrace, he said it was out of the question. It did not matter how many times they asked. He did not understand how he could possibly be responsible for their water supply. They did not even live within sight of his house, but down in the gorge behind the great ridge at its back. De Villiers's father was never kept awake with worry for their plight, and though he had made so many people miserable, he died at last a happy man — spared the knowledge of the fearful blight that several years later withered the grapes on his vines and spoiled his land forever. Martin de Villiers, unlike his father, had no wish to spend his life contesting nature, or even working. He left the draughty chateau to the elements. But he too refused all requests from the town of Freyzus to look into the question of the mill. It was far too much trouble.

Pailhès knew an interesting opportunity when he saw one. He had already cooperated with Peyre Rouff and now, hoping to underline the fact, he took the time to make the journey across to Aveyrac in a show of friendship. He did not meet with much success. Peyre Rouff's manner was civil but—Pailhès could only call it absent. Rouff did not apologize when he refused permission for any workman from Freyzus to come on to de Villiers's property. He made it clear that he did not wish to be disturbed and his answer did not vary when Pailhès came again some months later. Nevertheless, the mayor was persistent. As one year rolled into the next, he kept up the unproductive visits. Madame Maraval said uncharitably that he liked a nice leisurely ride on his ass and did anyone notice he only went up to Aveyrac in the most clement weather? What if she could afford to go lolloping around the countryside when the wild thyme was in bloom? How would the work get done then? Well, how would it?

For five years Pailhès kept up his attempts, but his visits grew progressively shorter and the intervals between them gradually longer. The last time he made the six-hour journey, he knocked and waited. And this time Peyre did not ask him in. Instead he called through the heavy oak of the door, saying he did not wish to be disturbed. Pailhès could hear the dog on the other side whimpering in frustration. The dog would have let him in.

I have no wish to be a distur—

But you are. I am already disturbed. There is water at the pump in the courtyard if you are thirsty. And there is a fine patch of spring grass for your mount. Good day.

The mayor felt a thoroughly unchristian anger rising. He did not take a drink but filled his flask at the pump and set off again, parched and bitter, deciding he would rest his horse farther down.

*

The house at last was left in peace, closed and shuttered, the furniture marshalled under grey dustsheets. Sometimes the tramontane tore another limb from one of the elms along the drive, and once it took down an entire tree that lay then like a combatant fallen. The winter gales lifted tiles regularly from the roof and occasionally a piece of ironwork that had held its place for a century or two gave out. Then Peyre would spend a day or more forging a new piece. Anything to avoid making the descent to the village again.

Ramon Pailhès was right: de Villiers never did come back. There was talk of him being wed, a suggestion that the wife was not a Frenchwoman. Once a year he sent a banker's draft. Peyre Rouff took one of them once to the mayor. He gave it to him and asked him to pay his debts. Pailhès imagined that the poor man was planning finally to take his life. He thought it best, but, being an honest man, he paid the tanner and the vigneron anyway. There was no one else.

Peyre continued as before, bearing his pain like an aching limb, or a failing heart, through the rotation of the years to till the soil, to sow the leeks, to beat down the almonds, to make some small repair. No one was in need of the fruit of his labours. Himself, he would have been content to eat dirt, so indifferent was he to appetite — though not to thirst. His only visitor now was the postman, who came up from time to time with a new commission. Work was as effective as alcohol. When he was sober, he devised new projects for himself and began to prepare fresh specimens for mounting.

And always, when this work was done, he dreamed up more creations and yet more.

His work became his purpose. Though his hands shook sometimes in the morning, when he set his traps his fingers were steady. He handled the traps and the animals alike with precision and care. In his workshop he made his cuts clean, his moves precise so the skin would slip easily away. He steadied himself with the words: For Giles. Always for Giles. And when he had the pelt he wanted, he was immune to the naked finality of the carcass. He put it aside to cook and share with the dog — just as he would share his repast with a wife and child.

His work grew in importance and came to mean for him not just restoration of the life that he had taken — or why then take it? — but some kind of immortality achieved, or perhaps bestowed, where before there was no hope. The house began to fill. He placed the small birds, the voles and the rabbits, and the quail and the snipe strategically on ledges and on chair backs, in the corner of the stairs. In the afternoons he took to walking out with a small axe and a sturdy knife, returning with branches and cuttings for the creation of an impossible garden. He decided he would build for them an Eden, where his birds would live in groves of delight and where every creature would find its eternity.

In his wooden house on Martinique, de Villiers sometimes tells the sad story of his steward who lives all alone in his chateau in the mountains. Though not quite alone. He tells how he tried to secure the man's services in perpetuity, asked him to name his price. And he tells how the response he received was not what he expected.

—I would need my son to be buried here.

When he tells this story in his island house, under the rattling palms, the night wind warm like his wife's skin, de Villiers will say, raising his eyebrows a little at the memory, that he had never been so unnerved by a single sentence, or so unable to refuse a request.

OUT OF SIGHT, beyond easy reach, Peyre was lost to society. Since he did not come down, it was easy to imagine him dead. In fourteen years gossip might be expected to starve for want of nourishment, but occasional reports from travellers—always disgruntled by the lack of hospitality they met up there—kept rumour alive during that time. And because it was so close to Saint Hubert's day that the fatal shot was fired, each anniversary of the saint recalled the accident and breathed life again into the story of Peyre Rouff, unlucky man, now mad in the head. The story shifted its shape according to the circumstances of the telling. He appeared sometimes as the crazed recluse who let dogs loose if a visitor came near, sometimes as a diabolically clever man, dangerous and unpredictable. In Freyzus, they spoke of Poor Peyre Rouff and sometimes of the madman over the gorge. And in Gougeac, the children knew, every one of them, the story of the son sent to his Maker.

At Gustave Thibéry's house in Freyzus, on the twelfth anniversary, they wondered aloud how Peyre Rouff had gone on all these years. They wondered what sustained him. And literally too, since he had long ago given up hunting (who wouldn't?). He did not come over to the village at all and they said he no longer went down to the market in Gougeac.

Gabriel suggested that efforts to reach him should be renewed. And Clarius Pech, always sardonic, said, Yes, why not. It's time for some more good stories.

There is no guarantee the stories would please you. Gabriel spoke quietly. They might, he said, be as terrible as the first.

And then we would have the Lunatic of Aveyrac on our hands?

Exactly.

Le Boulidou voiced what several others thought—that he would be better dead. Imagine..., he said.

But others had had enough of imagining. They had done it too many times, imagined their *own* offspring lying stone cold on the ground.

The women had their own conversations. They asked each other if there had been news of the wife all these years. They were divided on the subject of whether or not she ever should have been sent away, and on whether or not the second son would have died as it did that year if she had not been so miserable. *As it did.* Some of the women smiled knowingly at that. Others were prepared to be more charitable and expressed a dutiful pity. Thibéry's wife said it was Mathilde's father who had insisted on her going. Or was it was the stepmother?

They all agreed the tragedy would have killed Mathilde's own mother if she hadn't already been dead these twenty years.

Each year those who attended mass heard the priest offer up prayers for the soul of Giles Rouff and for the father too. And perhaps there was power in the words, for it was then that the people remembered true pity, and in the course of their prayers Peyre was transformed: no longer Peyre Rouff to be shunned or feared but Peyre to be forgiven. As if in the cold and vaulted church they, the townspeople, could perform the miracle of forgiveness that Peyre Rouff denied himself.

For there were times, times in winter especially, when Peyre looked out on the world and saw there his own soul displayed, laid bare upon the leaden and liverish firmament; when late in the afternoon the grey sky bruised to dark plum, and ill-defined clouds heavy with puce merged with infinity, leaving the mind to guess at their contour. It was his future, this skyscape of dread with its ominous light, that might discover and expose yet deeper chasms within. And when he saw this augury of his life to come, the impulse to pre-empt it rose again and he retreated to his work, or to his mind-erasing lists, finding salvation from his torment.

In his workshop, the skins of woodcock, partridge, and snipe hung alongside the skins of small mammals, a snake, whatever Peyre could come by, all dusted with arsenic and borax and ready for mounting. It was no longer enough to create or to recreate a life. The work now was to recreate Life, all of it. In the orangerie Peyre was creating Eden. When he was eating, or walking, when he was about his chores, even when he lay down to sleep, his mind was consumed by the work. The hours he spent in the construction of his diorama could not be counted. For the illusion to succeed, all had to be suspended between death and life, each leaf of the chestnut limb removed and preserved with wax and glycerin before being carefully reattached with glue, every small plant painstakingly treated the same. His birds lived in copses as if Eden had never emptied. The impossible garden grew up around them until the interior of the orangerie was transformed. To open the door and look inside was to stand on the border of a country without pain, where the lark endlessly ascends and the hare lifts an ear to listen to the echo of infinity. When Peyre entered that country he sat in perfect stillness on the bench in the corner as if observing his creatures at their business. Sometimes he was reluctant to rise and step outside the charmed circle of their silent presence. To leave was to cast himself again on the mercy of the world.

Peyre made sure the work was never finished. When almost every bird and animal was represented in his silent Eden, Peyre turned to fancy and his creations became ever more outlandish, the work of one at odds, the priest would have said, with his Maker.

Three

SOMETIME BEFORE MORNING on the fourth day after her arrival, the temperature suddenly drops, frosting every roof and wall, limning every leaf of the dark ivy.

The stones glitter underfoot as Peyre crosses the yard with his lamp to check on the girl.

When he opens the door, she looks up from where she is kneeling. She is shivering. He puts down the lamp and the water he has brought for her in a pail and goes to pick up the smock. She gets to it first and clutches it to her, shrinking back when he reaches for it, hollowing her chest, not taking her eyes from him. He can see he will have to tear it from her, engage them both again in an ugly tussle. And then suddenly it is free in his hands. He pulls it in one motion over her head and her face emerges startled, as if she has been suddenly born. He tries to straighten it while she is still surprised. Or perhaps she allows it. For just a moment she leans into him, against him, sensing warmth perhaps, perhaps enjoying it, before she makes a dash for the door. He has to block her so that he can get out again.

In his kitchen he makes a decision. He has done what was asked of him when he found her under the furze bush. He has nursed her back to health. He has clothed her. He is not accountable for more. Last night was so cold she could have frozen to death in the shed. He will give her some warm mash; he will give her a blanket against the cold; and he will take her down the hill to Gougeac. The commissioner can decide what to do with her.

He packs a haversack for himself and warms the mash. He finds an old brown blanket for her and makes a slit in the centre, then he puts on his hat and his coat and takes everything to the shed.

When she sees him put the breakfast pail down, she darts forward. He lets her eat. She gives the meal her complete, her fierce, attention, oblivious of his presence until the food is finished. She seems then to submit when he puts the rope around her waist. Or is he imagining it?

Outside she stops and turns her head from side to side, confirming the evidence of her eyes: the roofs glittering, the trees in the drive imprisoned in clouds of ice.

Standing there, with her bare limbs, the smock all askew, the rope at her waist, she might be some devilish doll brought to life. But at least she is dressed. When she squats Peyre turns away, but he notes it for the second advance this day, for the floor of the shed was unsoiled.

The girl will have nothing to do with the blanket, though her knees and her elbows are blue, but she does let herself be led. At first on her way out of the grounds, she is docile and curious, stepping wide-eyed after him, but keeping the tension on the leash, ready, he thinks, to fight her way free if she has to.

Once they have passed through the gate, she tenses. Her breathing quickens and she begins to pull, looking wildly about her. Peyre finds it necessary to repeatedly shorten the leash as he starts the climb up the slope behind the house, taking the harder but shorter route to the other side of the high ridge.

Though the cold is an unforgiving razor this bright morning, she shows no more sign of feeling it. She is so exhilarated by the open mountain that he has trouble holding her back. She is a creature now with at least a dozen limbs and all wanting to go their own way. The only way to control her direction is to keep the rope short, yet the closer he walks to her the more she pulls away, thrashing and flailing. Sometimes she pulls so hard and so unexpectedly she throws him off balance. He sits down, leaving her to prowl and pull and roll on the cold ground. He sees the grey soles of her feet, thick like the pads of a dog. He has four hours' walking ahead of him. When he regains his breath, he takes her to a stunted juniper, ties her there, and sits down. The girl attacks the rope, wrenching and twisting. She bites it. She tries slowly, smoothly, backing away from the tree. When the rope arrests her she leans back, giving all her weight to it. She lets her head fall back and she wails. It is what Peyre himself would like to do. He laughs out loud. At that, she resumes her wrenching and writhing—while Peyre sits in quiet shock at the sound he has not heard from himself for more than fourteen years.

He is getting cold. When it is clear that the tantrum is not going to subside, he puts the blanket he has been carrying for her over his own shoulders. Like a mechanical toy, she stops. She stares at him and then, just as if she had not broken off, she resumes her crazy dance. He waits perhaps twenty minutes more for her to tire, then he gets up stiffly and goes over to her. He has lost at least an hour of good walking already.

He unties the rope from the tree. It has rubbed a pale scar in the bark. He tries to look her in the eye, but she turns angrily away, blood smeared on her lip where she has been chewing. Peyre takes the blanket from his shoulders and struggles to get it over her head, but she flings herself on the ground. He keeps a hold on the rope but turns his back on her. There is no time to waste on these shenanigans. He can hear her get up, senses that she is staring at him. That at least is a kind of connection. It is something.

Walking on is no easier than before. Her stamina is boundless. Their pace is half what he hoped for. He has not brought enough food with him. Not only that, it is colder now than when they set out. He makes another attempt to get the blanket over her head, but she continues to fight and he gives up. Gradually he steers their course in a wide circle so that they are eventually beginning to descend the slope for home. When the chateau comes in sight, he feels the rope slacken as he had hoped, but in only minutes she has resumed her antics and it is with the utmost effort on both sides that they reach the house.

He throws the blanket into the corner of the shed, struggles to loosen the knot, and untie the rope from her waist, cursing her under his breath. Perversely she springs for the blanket and burrows. He goes out and slams the door shut, bars it behind him.

At the house he makes a mash of broth and bread, puts in an uncooked potato and a carrot, then carries the pot and a flagon of water outside.

From across the yard he already sees the door of the shed standing open. The bar is lying on the ground, its socket hanging from one rusted nail in the jamb. The smock lies discarded just inside the shed. He turns in every direction but can see no sign of her. He leaves the pail and goes round to the front of the house to survey the hillside below. Massing clouds signal a storm. He watches for some sign of her, birds flying up, anything. She could be anywhere. If he had a dog. Damned girl. Damned girl.

He goes to take the food back to the house, thinking how now he has what he wanted, his peace restored. But when he bends to pick up the pail, he has another thought and he simply moves it, repositioning it directly in front of the open door of the shed, fully visible.

His own meal is as tasteless as the mash that he left outside. He scrapes the remains into a basin for his chickens, remembering that now he will have to padlock their barn again.

In the night, it snows. Behind a lip of rock the girl sleeps, curled in a tight ball under a furze bush. The snowflakes catch in the intricate structure of the bush, lofting flake by flake to a blanket above her. When she opens her eyes, the world outside is obscured by whatever thick cocoon contains her. She stays without moving. Not hearing it at first for what it is, she has only a sense of something half remembered, a minute sound like the points of distant dry leaves touching stone. Unfathomable specks. And then she recognizes it. Not the word of course—words are not the currency of her mind—but the thing itself, the cold of it, the curious wet-dryness of it, the dazzle. Air made visible. She stays until it is light, watching her blind white world appear, then she wriggles out to stand and gaze at the brilliance before flinging herself down to roll in it, gasping with the shock, standing, shaking out her hair, and doing it all again. She runs to the bushes and shakes the snow from them, falls on her knees, and pushes her face into it, blowing, spitting. She sweeps it into the air with her hands, kicks it into sprays with her feet and there, while the early morning sun casts a glitter on every surface, she knows ecstasy.

Peyre too wakes before it is light and senses the change. He stays awake until dawn, thinking about the girl.

Even through the shutters, the light is new. He feels the chill as he goes to throw them open, thinks better of it, and leaves them closed.

Passing the barn, he hopes his chickens have survived the cold. He does not stop to check but goes on down to the shed. Snow has blown in through the open door. The pail is untouched, the snow all around unmarked.

He passes Berzélius's burial place and sees how the snow seems to make the disturbed earth whole again, covering it over as if no darkness lies beneath. He walks up to the churchyard and he does not need a list to occupy his mind, concentrating as he is, looking all the time for footprints, imagining her feet bony and blue in the new snow. He stops before he reaches his son's grave. He stands a little way off looking at the perfection of the snow. He thinks heaven to be this. Obliteration. No mark or blemish, no feeling. The snow so untouched. He does not want to disturb its purity with his footsteps.

For an hour he walks out in several directions looking for the girl, but he does not go up over the lip of rock where he would have seen her traces, the snow there flurried as if by some great raptor come to flail and thrash in the immaculate.

He goes to his workshop, where, if he were not so uneasy, it would be a fine thing to settle down to work, the room filled as it is with reflected snowlight, the little pipe stove ticking in the corner, keeping the temperature steady. Would there be winter in his Eden? Perhaps his diorama can circle the space in the orangerie completely so that it represents the year's round, the seasons cycling eternally before the eye of the spectator as the spectator turns in the room. Without winter, without spring. There will have to be winter. He does not know how he will manufacture snow. A detail. He can solve it when the time comes.

After a while he cannot resist. He goes back again to the shed. The lid is off the food pail. And there she is, just inside the door.

She springs and is past him in two bounds, vanishing into the lightly falling snow.

Peyre is at a loss. If she wants only food, why hasn't she run off with it? If it is the shelter she craved, why doesn't she stay? He takes the pail back to the kitchen to replenish it, thinks he might bring another blanket so that she can burrow deeper. This is an extra animal he is caring for — though she is no replacement for his dog. And more trouble.

In the days to follow, as the thaw sets in, Peyre goes often to the shed. It becomes clear that the girl wishes to escape only when the door is locked against her. When the door is open she has no inclination to disappear into the garrigue. He begins to understand that food and shelter are not her only needs. He decides to show her she is still at liberty and then let things run their course. Once she becomes tractable enough, he will try again to take her to Gougeac, for she will in the end have to be given some official protection. He is not the one to take it on. Meanwhile, he continues to put the food down whether she is there or not. Most afternoons it is gone.

He acknowledges a certain disappointment on the days when she does not appear. He goes back to the shed once or twice to check, then he laces up his boots, takes up his stick, and strikes out on a walk. But as the pattern continues, he comes to accept that she will eventually return. He does not have to go and scour the country. Sometimes he does not see her for days. She can always surprise him. He is one day in the very process of lacing his boots when he hears a noise in the courtyard. He goes outside, carrying the second boot. There is no one. As he bends to put on the boot a shadow falls across it, and he turns to see her standing in the low afternoon light, her arms akimbo, her head cocked to one side. She is against the light, but he imagines she is smiling. She has been away for a week. He thought she was gone for good.

You, he says, and she flinches as she always does at the first sound of his voice.

You. Isn't it time you ate something?

Her hand goes to her mouth. He wants to think she understands and that there might be hope for her after all. If she can be pulled just clear of feral. If she can be taught to understand language, perhaps to speak a word, then perhaps she can be taught to cooperate — and with the right help might one day find a home.

Well, but you will be clothed first, he says aloud. They won't take you in like that. They'll lock you up for certain.

She watches him straighten up and turn to the door. He can feel her eyes on him.

He goes inside, glancing back to see if she will follow, or if she is even interested. She is still standing in the same spot. When he comes out again, she is crouched down and hugging her knees.

He holds out the smock and she leans away, bracing against even the memory of its contact. Matching her pose, he drops to his haunches and tosses the smock down between them. It is clear to him that she knows exactly what he wants because she jams her lower jaw shut and turns her face away, her chin jutting, her eyelids almost closed. It is language and he understands.

He gets up and kicks at the ground in frustration, sending a spray of gravel across the shirt. Before it has settled she has sprung to her feet and is mimicking the action perfectly. It is an advance. He holds out the piece of potato he has brought for a reward. She is already drooling as she snatches it from him. Yet she does not run off with it. Instead she stands chewing, her eyes fixed on his. He knows enough about animals to understand the significance. He has the key to her cooperation. He will be patient.

Ten days pass before she comes back. Peyre never doubted that she would. When next he sees her, over by the woodpile, he begins exactly where they ended. The smock hangs ready by the door. Beside it is a shirt of his own. He carries them both outside with a handful of things he knows she likes to eat and he spreads the shirts on the ground.

She comes and stands before him in her nakedness. So still she is, so resolute. He stares at her without blinking and knows a kind of reverence then for her holy autonomy, her solitary survival, no other protection but her wits, her wiry strength. He crosses his arms and waits.

From her blaze of innocence she looks back at him. And then she too crosses her arms.

Now, looking for reward, she is opening and closing her mouth like a bird. He holds out a piece of dried fig. She grabs it and wolfs it down. For the first time in years he wants someone by his side. He wants to turn and smile and say, Look. Is this not astonishing?

She looks to him for more fig. Instead, he reaches for his shirt and gathers it to his chest. And there she is at once, holding his son's smock against her bony chest but with only one hand. She is ahead of her teacher, for her other hand is already extended for her reward. Yes, a bird. She has her mouth open, her neck craning. Soon she will be clothed.

The process takes several days more and tests the limits of his patience. Once when in frustration he throws down the shirt he is using, she kicks sand over it, mimicking exactly his gesture of days before. He smiles broadly and starts over.

By the time the spring days begin to lengthen into summer, the girl has learned to clothe herself. Her actions are predictable. As soon as she arrives, she finds the shirt—lying wherever she has last thrown it down—and drags it over her head, putting her arms through the wide sleeves to go and stand before him, or before the door if he is in the house, her mouth watering. Sometimes, if she does not see him working outside, she lifts the latch of the door and steps into the house. Then comes the morning he returns from his chickens to find her in his kitchen eating potatoes from the pot.

Though she has made such progress, still Peyre finds excuses to delay taking her into Gougeac. Her motivation is ever the same: food her sole interest, hunger the engine that impels her. To watch her eat is to see the beast uncontained. He does not like the thought of other eyes witnessing her savagery. If she behaves like a beast, she may well be treated like one. Who knows where she will be taken after he delivers her, what obstacles she will encounter, what impossible tasks she will be expected to perform?

For several mornings he waits for her from the hour of dawn. The next time she appears, he is working in his garden setting string for the beans he will plant. He sees her from the corner of his eye and waits until she comes near. He does not look up. She leans in closer and without warning he grabs her arm. She makes no sound, but had she been a cat she could not be more wild. She kicks at his legs and bites down hard on his thumb, continuing her struggles, then, as suddenly as she began, she stops her efforts and stares at the blood running down her arm. And now she finds her voice and begins to whimper, making a small stifled sound in the back of her throat, like a cry coming from a great distance. She turns her head to lick at his blood, perhaps thinking it her own. He has the rope around her waist at once. She looks at him and her gaze burns with a fierce understanding of what he is about. She turns and looks in the direction of the shed where he kept her in the first days.

The house, he says. We're going to the house.

He pauses at the door to the kitchen, expecting some show of resistance, but the wild girl has left. She is compliant now, keen. This is where she found food. It is no trouble to lead her inside, though she wants to stay and he has to force her to continue, shoving her on out of the room and into the passage on the other side, steering her to the back stairs, murmuring, encouraging. If she could speak, if she could understand, it would be easy. She hangs back, looking over her shoulder at the main hall where she can see the black-and-white tiles. He takes the first step on the stairs, and the second. He tugs on the rope. She hesitates, then all at once she is ahead of him, using her hands to scramble up, and stopping abruptly at the top, holding her breath as she catches sight of the motionless rabbits posed along the base of the wall at the far end of the corridor. With difficulty he turns her in the opposite direction and leads her to the small bedroom he has chosen for its barred window. He closes the door behind them and locks it. The room contains a bed, a washstand, a table and a chair, everything she might require, yet her face shows not a flicker of interest as he unties the rope. Her eyes are focused intently on the blue panes of the window. The tops of an elm show green in the lower half, a small white cloud rising behind them.

He opens the window and she pushes past him to thrust her hands through the bars. Out in the air her hands open and close on the sunlight. He tries to draw them inside, but she holds tight to one of the bars, the fingers of her free hand still opening and closing.

He leaves her and sits on the edge of the bed to wait. She remains in the same position, swaying slightly as she rocks from foot to foot. Once, a bird passes by low and she thrusts her arms out farther, stands motionless for a moment, and then resumes her rocking.

In the end he entices her from the window with water. But it is a short-lived experiment. She rushes to him at the sound of water being poured into the basin. Her hands splash in the bowl, scoop the water to her open mouth, to her eyes. She plunges her face in it and turns her head from side to side. When she lifts her head, she is gasping and coughing—and already returning, dripping to the window.

He has a tumbler on the table and had thought to teach her some of the things that might be required of her. She does return when she hears him pouring water again, and she does watch when he drinks, but when he gives her the tumbler and she has drunk her fill, soaking her neck and chest, she lets it fall without a glance in its direction as it hits the floor, and then walks unflinching over the broken glass to stand at the window as before.

Peyre tries to inspect her feet and is kicked violently on the chin for his pains. He collects the pieces of glass in his handkerchief, cutting himself in the process, and carries them from the room without a word, locking the door behind him.

In the afternoon he tries coming back with food. She is still there at the window and turns to look at him only briefly when he comes in, but the smell of broth draws her when he unhinges the lid of the pail. He has brought bowls and a potato hot from the fire. Instinct tells him to set out the meal on the floor.

It is a painstaking lesson in eating from dishes, and at the end of it the broth is distributed in many places. Some of it at least is inside the girl and he settles for that.

She watches him pack the items in the pail, then, seeing he is going, she follows him to the door. He has to fend her off, forcing her back into the room so that he can get out. He does not look at her face. He knows what he would see. He imagines her on the other side of the door listening to the small sound of the key in the lock. Even to save her from a feral existence, none of what he is doing seems right.

Through the window the girl sees the tops of the elm trees tossing in the wind. They roil and lift, roll, fall back and roil again. And every leaf shivers and flashes in the dance. A sense of water returns to her. She closes her eyes to feel it, but opens them almost straight away, not wanting to lose sight of the dancing, rolling treetops. She can hear their distant rushing. She knows the sound. She moves closer to the window, stretches her neck, and turns her head to lay her ear against the sight of them. She raises her arms high and sways to their dance, holding the bars. Then she slips her hands through again. O, the waving of them. And the ache begins, a long, slow pull like something being drawn out of her core but never coming free. An aching and a drawing she has known before. Something she knew when the man was with his dog. A cataclysm of loss.

When Peyre comes in again, she is at the window perfectly still, her hands on the bars. He goes to stand beside her and she does not move. And he has come to pursue his lesson — in the art of drinking from a cup. As if it is the remedy for her untamed state. He backs out of the room again and quietly turns the key.

That night, rinsing the soup from his plate, he does not have to battle demons. His son is far from his mind. Watching the light fade, Peyre imagines the girl still standing at the window. He knows what draws her there, what she is longing for, what she is mourning. He imagines she still will not have moved, her grieving so absolute, her need to honour it so serious. He had intended the room would become for her both haven and schoolroom. That she would grow accustomed to living inside, that she would learn new skills, perhaps one day would speak. And he would take her down trained and civilized to the authorities and she would be ready to be taken in.

He thinks about the light pouring out of the elms, their leaves darkening, their tops filling with dusk, becoming heavy and massed as rain clouds until they merge with night. He thinks about the girl grieving the loss of her liberty. He thinks about the sense of loss. He always thought he held sole title to loss.

In the morning he opens the front door of the house in readiness. When he goes upstairs and enters the girl's room, he can see she has slept under the window. She is scrambling to her feet as he comes in. Her eyes are quick and uncomprehending until her waking mind catches up.

She sees the leash in his hand and surprises him by coming at once to stand before him, her arms lifted. The gesture fills him with a boundless satisfaction and he smiles as he ties it round her waist. She learns anyway. She learns whether he teaches her or not.

At the stairs they almost fall together from the top. Where he expects her to turn and descend on all fours she leaps and takes them two at a time, swinging hand over hand on the banister. He clings to the rail with one hand as he follows her down, the rope jerking taut between them. She makes straight for the wolf and drops into a crouch to look it in the eye, her head moving from side to side as she sniffs the air at its muzzle. And then she is up again and pulling for the front door where she first entered the house. Through the open door and down the steps of the terrace she pulls him, leading him, and he lets her. When they come to the elms she stops and looks up to the hushing crowns. Her upper body sways gently. He takes off the leash and steps away. Her face is still raised to the treetops. She lifts her arms to them, and he sees her face is transformed. In the midst of some airy heaven of her own she breathes deeply, quietly. And he believed too he had a unique claim on love, on life. He walks away.

LIKE ANY STRAY, the girl appeared always on her own terms and at the time and place of her own choosing. She came sometimes with the first light of day, but she came most regularly at dusk. Once, he saw her shadow pass across his workshop wall and when he looked out she was drinking from the pail he had left at the pump. She was using the tin cup he had left hanging on the side of the pail. He did not disturb her. But the next day he set a little food there. That summer, he knew more ease than he had known for many years. Her presence simply. The mere knowledge of her existence. It was a wordless comfort to know her out there.

One morning, later than usual, she came when he was outside repairing a low wall. He kept her waiting while he selected a stone from the pile and turned it in his hands before he set it in place. Her dusty feet appeared beside him, her scarred ankles. He sought out another stone, examined it from every angle, and set it beside the first. With a swiftness that took his breath away, she reached for a stone and set it beside his. When it toppled from the wall, she stared at him, starting to rock slightly back and forth, her body tense. He knew she was waiting only for food. And suddenly she was picking up the stone again, turning it in her hands and setting it on the wall, where it stayed in place. She stepped back as if to say, Now will you feed me? Her teeth were clenched, her eyes anxious. She reached forward and jigged the stone before staring the same question at him: *Now* will you?

Why not, he thought. She had met his first condition months ago when she allowed herself to be clothed. Why should she be taught more? Whose purpose would it serve? He gave her all the figs he had brought outside. His pleasure was to see her pleasure as she swallowed down the food he offered. To see desperation dissolve and melt away into relief, into satisfaction. Like Berzélius, she hid nothing, and he warmed himself at the glow of her vitality.

He got up and went to the pump and, yes, like a dog, she ran ahead. Bending, she put her face beneath the spout. At the first gush, he saw her eyes close. He watched her gulping pleasure, drowning in it. Then she stood and with her eyes still closed, with water running down her chin, she smiled. And was building walls a more worthwhile way to spend one's days on earth?

He bent to take a drink himself, already contradicting himself; thinking, Yes, but building walls was necessary, or who would have shelter? Man must have skills, knowledge, to survive. And yes, she would have to be taught many things; and yes, she perhaps one day would have to join society. For a girl alone, at large…? And then one day to die alone of cold, or hunger, or some accident unforeseen? It was as if she had heard him thinking, for when he straightened up, she was gone. As if she had never been there at all.

His days were changed by the girl. He felt it. The day he left her under the elms, he had watched her from the terrace. She had stood awhile longer at her holy devotions until she let her arms fall and from a standstill set off running at full tilt down across the sunlit slope of the hill. He had watched her figure diminish. She did not slow down before she disappeared from view. She was out there still, a possibility where none had existed, and he took pleasure in the thought of her tough bony feet on the sandy soil, the white rocks. It was as if in a barren desert on a vast and empty night a flower had sprung into existence and bravely bloomed.

He worked in the orangerie that summer more for the pleasure of the creation than for the oblivion it brought.

He would have liked to have her in his Eden. She belonged with the rest. But if she could not be there in the flesh, she could at least be represented. A glimpse of her. A memory. He began to spend whole days and nights studying the equipment in de Villiers's photographic laboratory. There were notes de Villiers had written to himself, numerical lists of the steps to take. Peyre liked the orderliness. He could not pronounce some of the words, but he could match them easily with the labels on the glass bottles. After two weeks of trial and error he watched an image — of a guêpier he had mounted with a wasp in its beak — appear like a dream, floating into sight.

He set up the camera at the open window of the scullery and trained its lens on the pump in the courtyard. She was like an animal that comes regularly to the watering hole. Except that she used the cup. He was not sure anymore if that was a useful skill.

Capturing her image was not as easy as he had hoped. He waited several days with a prepared plate in the camera. Each day the gelatin hardened and dried before she appeared. His reward came on a day when the light was perfect. She appeared while the sun was fully shining on the spot. She dipped the cup in the pail and raised it with both hands to drink. He took away the lens cover and counted as she gulped...three...four ...five, but she held her head tilted still, savouring...six...seven...eight. She began to sway. Reluctantly he put back the cover. He could not be sure he had her.

In the laboratory he watched her ghost appear on the plate as he rinsed away the gelatin. He held it up. There she was at some sacred libation...and there, beside her, the pump, inert and clear, competing for attention. It had no place in his Eden.

He had tried for a time to keep her clothed when she appeared about the place, and then he could no longer see the point. When he succeeded in capturing her in front of the camera again, it was from the terrace in front of the house and she was not clothed. She had been standing, listening perhaps, under the elms. He did not mind the sight of her grubby limbs, her torso lean as a goat's. While the lens cover was still off, he was distracted by a commotion of small birds. They swooped and parried overhead, driving off a hawk. When he looked back, she was running.

He carried the plate back without much hope of success, but when he developed the flawed image, he knew he had what he wanted. The image was blurred, could not be grasped and held. It was fleet as life.

Sometimes she stayed for hours even after she had taken the food. He would watch her, trying to fathom her intentions, but came to see she had none. When she was not hungry she lived without aim — brushing her forearm against the long tines of rosemary and inhaling its scent, rubbing her shoulder gently on warmed stone, like one of the cats. Sometimes she would crouch for an hour or more, in a spot of dappled sun, hugging her knees, rocking, perhaps listening. Once, he saw her standing a long while with her forehead pressed against the bark of the elm, assuaging pain, he guessed. He did not intrude. She was there not many days later, standing in the same spot, her arms loose at her sides, her fingers moving as if plucking invisible strings to extract a melody from the air. He approached her and bent to see her face. She made no sign that she had registered his presence but put her arms around the trunk as if it were the body of a giant standing there. And she seemed content.

She was at other times infused with some relentless energy that drove her to dart from place to place, picking up objects—a stone, a rake—and flinging them down. At these times she remained in constant capricious movement, circling a bush, loping repeatedly the length of a hedge or a wall, brushing its surface with her hand. He saw her climb the pear tree and spread her length along a limb, as if trying to take its measure with her body or fuse her being with the tree's. But he had seen her, too, stop whatever she was at and simply sit. He did not think it was fatigue that made her stop. She sat in contemplation, or perhaps it was wonder. He could fathom no pattern to her behaviour, this pendulum swing between motion and stillness, the way she was sometimes there behind her eyes—and sometimes in a place he could not know.

The day she climbed the tree he thought of his son, how could he not? She climbed with that strange oblivious focus of the child, stretching herself against the limbs, laying her cheek against a branch—and he saw his son, agile and alive. His son so competent, so purposeful. He was wearing the very smock that had been the cause of so much strife. He hauled himself up with a rocking rhythm, placing a foot high, pulling up with an outward swing to place the next foot higher still.

Peyre had watched him rise until his upper torso disappeared into the leafy green. And then he had seen both feet lift from the branch on which they stood. His son, sitting on top of the world, surveying all the lesser mortals down below. And Peyre, remembering, smiles, all unaware how memory has at last wriggled clear of its own appalling trap.

THAT AUTUMN AT the school in Freyzus, the talk centred on Raoul's latest scheme. Hunting season had begun. The two classes were rarely fully attended. Many of the older boys went with their fathers into the thickets of green oak after squirrel or wild boar. The younger ones were recruited often by their mothers to help look for morels or for acorns, or hazelnuts. The practice was not condoned by Gabriel, their teacher, was in fact expressly forbidden, but everyone knew it would continue. In the mornings those who did attend school gathered at the twisted olive tree that served as their meeting place until the season was cold enough for the stove to be lighted and the doors to the little cloakroom opened early.

At sixteen Raoul easily attracted a following. His schemes were not always a success—at least not for his entourage—but they were always interesting. Last year the boys who sold mushrooms for him had attracted the wrath of half the village when their mushrooms thrown to sizzle in the pan had yielded lively maggots trying to escape the heat. This morning Raoul had sketched out something new. He had found out, he said, at no small cost and trouble to himself (when what he meant was that he had overheard one of the hunters talking) that the Lunatic of Aveyrac still had an insatiable appetite for small mammals and even reptiles.

He eats them?

There was always one naive idiot in the group. Raoul was impatient.

No. He does not. Will you listen? I have found out, *in addition*, that this same man, Mad Peyre, will pay good money for them provided they're in the right condition. *Moreover and furthermore* (which was what the schoolmaster always said when he had lost his train of thought), I have gone to considerable pains to *ascertain* exactly what that condition might be. He paused for effect, losing the attention of at least one young fellow, busy with the lining of his nostril.

That condition, Raoul continued, would be 'fresh,' as in dead just a few hours. Now for an animal in the said condition — 'fresh' — Mad Peyre is prepared to pay a certain sum of money. And what does this mean to all you short-legged bastards who lack permission to stray on the other side of the gorge? Does it mean all hope of profit is lost? *Quite the contrary.* It means you have an opportunity of making money. You give your small game to me and I undertake to see that it reaches Mad Peyre. I then return with the payment, having taken only ten centimes a piece for myself.

You will have to tell us first what he will pay, said one bright spark.

Well, I shan't know that until I've been there, stupid.

The bright spark dimmed visibly.

And so it was arranged — though as Raoul pointed out, the hunt would have to be extremely well coordinated and would require the complete cooperation of all.

It was set for the following Thursday, a holiday.

Felip woke up early. He tried to be as quiet as possible as he dressed. His brother turned over and slept on. Madame Maraval was already awake and called to him from the kitchen.

Felip? No school today, remember?

He decided to remain neutral and answered only with, Oui, maman.

He went downstairs with his sabots in his hand. At the door he put on his wool jacket and his cap and grabbed a heavy muffler. He had the door open before his mother called again.

M'entends, toi?

Oui, maman, he said quietly and slipped out, racing away down the quiet street with sabots clacking and the muffler flying, his slingshot in his pocket and a sack in his hand. The early morning was raw. A chill mist numbed the edges of things and blurred the outlines of roofs and walls. He left the village for the descent to the bridge and walked beside cliffs glowing rose and gold in the sunrise.

He thought he knew a place on the other side where hare might still be found at this time of year. When he was over the bridge he made his way down to the water and filled his pockets with stones of the right size and weight, looking for those hefty enough to fell at least a rabbit if not a hare. He picked up pebbles for any birds that might come his way. Then he climbed on up.

The slope eventually levelled out at the base of a giant boulder. Behind the boulder, between it and the continuing rise of the hill, was a second plateau where a few trees grew happily in the protection from the wind, replenishing the soil each year with their leaves. It was like a piece of the valley floor lifted to this mountainside and the animals found it to their liking.

One of the other boys, Maillet, was already there. The two eyed each other jealously, trying to maintain an air of nonchalance in the face of the calamity. With a stroke of brilliance Maillet spoke.

So the two of us will surpass all the rest with our teamwork, uh?

Felip smiled and nodded and took out his slingshot. And so the situation was saved, although the morning's rewards were not what either of them had hoped. And yet it was good to lie in the early sun on the still damp grass, to see the blades part as a beetle, lost in deepest forest, trundled through. It was good especially to see the first hare of the morning stretching up on its hind legs, chest and forepaws lifted, one ear vertical as a church steeple, the other turned to catch the sound of their own breath. It leapt away, shooting waist-high into air before it landed and was gone. They caught another that must surely have been deaf. Its bones stuck out from its haunches.

At the olive tree, at the appointed hour, they handed over their single, rather aged hare to Raoul. The combined haul was mediocre. There was the mangy hare. There was part of a weasel and there was a nice-looking finch, but other than that there were sparrows and pigeons and a cat that everyone recognized as Madame Bourbillière's. Cédric said he had found it lying in a ditch, but no one believed him. Raoul refused to take it—though he was tempted. He began to wonder if this venture would ever be worth repeating, but he had no time right now to consider, for it would take many hours to reach the chateau and return before dark. He loaded his knapsack and set off, some of the smaller boys trotting beside him until he reached the bridge.

Felip watched Raoul's figure recede. To go as Raoul was going across the gorge. Over the far side of the ridge. Such a fierce longing, and so sudden. The day seemed endless.

Raoul stood with his hands in his pockets, waiting for his payment. He had calmed down a little. Here at Peyre Rouff's kitchen door, he could breathe more easily than before. He had not had a care on the way up to Aveyrac, but when the chateau came in sight, so quiet, so still, he had begun to remember every rumour. The mad dogs, the wild-eyed owner with hair down to his waist. By the time he reached the front door, he was prepared to believe them all, especially the report that the wolf of Aveyrac was a live one. Raoul did not like the look of it at all when Monsieur Rouff opened the door. It was a relief to be asked to go round to the back and wait. He did not want to be asked inside.

He heard footsteps and Peyre Rouff returned with his money. He looked, thought Raoul, as ragged and as hungry as a peasant. Monsieur Rouff did not make eye contact. Raoul stared him up and down as he would not dare to do with another man. He was looking for lunacy. Bolder now, without the awful vision of the wolf, Raoul peered through to the kitchen, where a magpie was perched on a chair back. Monsieur Rouff kept his eyes on the coins. He seemed to be counting them several times over, and Raoul believed him afraid of making a mistake, afraid he, Raoul, would challenge him with his youthful vigour, his strong bones. And then as Peyre Rouff raised his eyes, something Raoul saw there—a flicker of recognition as the man looked past him into the courtyard behind—something made him turn and look over his shoulder in the same direction, so that he just caught it: the flash of limbs, a naked body, spinning to disappear in two bounds behind a shed. He turned back and knew from the direction of Monsieur Rouff's gaze that he most certainly saw it too.

What—? Raoul began.

What? Peyre's abruptness left no doubt that the question should not be asked. Raoul took his money quickly and tried to quell the sudden unease that was filling him. Something about Peyre living in such isolation and about the remoteness of this place. Something about tales told at night and about the deportment of ogres and the general disposition of men who were not what they seemed. He began to run. It is only when he was halfway back down the hill that the thought of the wild girl came to him. And how stupid he had been not to have gone exploring. A wild naked girl! Imagine that as a trophy to take back to town!

It took him longer than he had hoped to get back. His suppliers had all been sent to bed. He wrapped half of the money in a sock and hid it behind the broken stone under the window of his room. His parents were not impressed with the money he showed them. His mother said he should keep two-thirds of it for himself and his efforts. His father said if he tried to keep two-thirds, he would personally take it all. He was to hand over one-half of what he had immediately. He could keep the other half to divide with his friends. They listened skeptically to his account of the chateau. They had heard Peyre was eccentric and quite possibly mad by now. But Raoul's tales of stuffed animals inhabiting every part of the house seemed preposterous.

And little fairy folk, said his father. I suppose there were little fairy folk too to open the door for you.

Raoul decided he could not tell them what else he had seen. It kept him lying awake in the dark that night, stroking himself to a fever.

He left late for school the next morning. It suited him to have only minutes to spare for the partition of the profits. The boys were waiting in a tight cluster at the door. They broke apart a little to let Raoul in to the centre, then closed again round him as if to block any means of escape.

Give me some air. I have it. I have your money.

Then give it to us. You kept us waiting a whole night.

Raoul cuffed the complainer on the ear.

And I walked a whole day for you. Would you prefer we changed places? Now give me some air.

He dug in his pocket and brought out the coins. He had rehearsed his script several times on the way.

So. For you, Felip, a hare, wasn't it? With Maillet there. Monsieur Rouff's price was seventy centimes, therefore twenty for you and twenty for Maillet and twenty for me and ten. Voilà.

He put twenty centimes in Maillet's hand. Maillet's relief at the feel of the coins made him smile, until he realized how few he had.

And little Toady. What was it you had? Raoul liked that touch, asking a question if he was working it all out for them on the spot.

A weasel. Almost a weasel.

Right. Almost a payment then.

Little Toady held out his hand and received ten centimes. By the time the other boys had been paid the air was turning sour with their resentment, but Raoul had thought of everything.

And now a bonus for each one of you.

They snatched the coins and pocketed them, but they did not look as impressed as he had hoped. He asked them if they were prepared to go out again in two weeks' time. They hesitated, looked away as if suddenly hearing someone calling from their houses, and Raoul wished he had left the question until after they had spent their earnings.

You'd be crazy if you walk away now, he said. From this *enterprise*. He gave the word emphasis and hoped some of its gravitas would rub off on him. This is just the beginning of something much bigger, much more interesting.

Right! You'll take even more off of us. Little Toady stuck out his chin.

You don't have to listen, you. Why don't you just bugger off right now, you little runt.

Little Toady lowered his eyes, as if the smear of clay he had just found on his boot was suddenly engrossing.

Swear to keep a secret?

Their word did not seem to be enough for Raoul, who wanted guarantees. Fists were offered, stacked in the centre. Raoul lowered his voice.

She's up there.

For all they knew, Raoul might as well have been talking about the Virgin Mary. They were bemused, all of them — with the exception of Felip, who felt his insides slip as if he had just fallen from a cliff. He found it hard to breathe normally.

The girl, dumbheads. The wild girl who jumped in the river. She's up there.

One tentative murmur was all it took to provoke a chorus of dissent.

I'm telling you. She's up there, and I have a plan. If you want to know how it turns out you'll have to keep giving me a reason to go back. But I'm telling you, she's there. He giggled.

Naked as the day she was born. Hey, what's wrong with you, 'Lipi? Where're you going?

Home, said Felip. I have to go home.

—Embarrassing you? I thought you liked all that stuff about girls.

Felip didn't reply.

His mother missed nothing. You're thoughtful this evening.

Am I? Felip tried to look thoughtless. In fact, his only thought as he began his supper was, *What if?*

What if it were true? What if she were up there? What if Peyre found her? What if Raoul found her? What if she were taken?

His supper tasted like sawdust. He went to bed before his usual hour. It was all wrong, all of it. None of them could feel about her the way he did. They thought she was a savage and an animal. They laughed about her. He could not. She was his secret and his dream. She was his, and they had no right to her.

The next day at school, he told Raoul he could count him out of the next expedition. He made sure to tell him while there were others in earshot. They might follow. With luck Raoul's enterprise would fall apart. But as the day wore on it became clear that the others were intrigued and wanted Raoul to return.

Felip began to worry. If someone gave away Raoul's secret, they would send men up there surely. The girl would be captured. They would lock her up somewhere dark, somewhere with bars.

When it was clear that the second expedition would go ahead, Felip decided to take action. He was sure Raoul had cheated them all of some of their earnings, and though he had no proof and though what he was about to do was a risk, he went to Raoul Castres's parents and told them he had been cheated, and younger boys than him too.

The side of Raoul's father's hand came up like the edge of a sword at the perfect angle for taking off the top of his head, then Monsieur Castres told him to get away, get away from his house with his pack of lies and calumny. The raised hand fell later on the side of Raoul's head—and Felip had a sworn enemy.

And on the second Thursday, despite his efforts, the boys were there again at the olive tree with their furred and feathered offerings.

Felip in his house watched them from the little window at the turn of the stairs. He saw Raoul swing the full bag over his back and set off at a splendid striding pace, the smaller boys running along as before.

Felip was at a loss all day, seeing in his mind's eye Raoul encountering the girl in the dappled chestnut woods, the girl running half glimpsed beside a stream, the girl caught unawares, turning, naked, to see Raoul creeping up on her. He saw the chateau, remote and exotic like a castle in a dream. He saw Raoul marching the girl to a massive studded door, her hands tied with a rope. There was no stopping the story unfolding in his head. By suppertime he saw Raoul with a bag of gold and the girl—his wild apparition—lost forever, dressed now in the grey serge of a servant drawing water for Peyre's table. Her hair was caught in a cap and she looked like any other poor girl of the village.

On Friday at the start of school, boys gathered at the door as before, but Felip excluded himself from the group. He tried furtively to read the expressions of their faces and the gestures of their bodies, scrutinizing them as best he could from a distance, looking for signs of intrigue, a secret given and received. Nothing he saw suggested it.

Throughout the day he tried to place himself within earshot of the sillier boys, the ones most likely to repeat sworn secrets. He heard not a whisper of the girl until the hour when the boys surged through the gate of the school like a gush of dirty water. Two of them lingered, arguing stubbornly and unimaginatively.

You did.

I didn't.

You did. You said you would go up and see for yourself if he didn't come back with her.

That doesn't count. Of course I won't go if he's already searched the place. You heard him.

He *said* he'd looked everywhere. Number one: she could be hiding. Number two: he could be lying.

There was no disputing such bald statements.

Well, I'm still not going, the boy said, aware that though he had stood his ground it felt like defeat.

Felip had heard what he needed to know. But the fact that Raoul had not seen the girl again did not mean that she was not still up there. He wanted suddenly to find himself three years older, to be able with a casual word to say, I'm off, to shoulder a knapsack with a nonchalant shrug, and be accountable to no one. He could not wait for night and the possibility of glimpsing the girl again — if only in dreams.

But dreams will not be bidden and none came to him, or none that he remembered—though he could not forget the girl and her troubling existence in the world.

RAOUL'S SECRET SOON became healthy rumour—believed by no one over the age of sixteen until the following month. In mid-November, a government surveyor, travelling through the region for the Geometric Offices of the Department of Highways and Bridges, rode from Bresailles through the narrow pass up above Aveyrac. The girl, peering cautiously from behind the trunk of an elm, watched the horse pick its way down the hill toward the chateau. Horse and rider stopped once and the horse stretched a foreleg and put its head down to rub at it, then the man urged it on down the slope. They wove across and back, so that as he drew near it seemed that he would pass the chateau, but he turned abruptly, and the girl made her move too late.

The surveyor, almost as tired as his horse, looked up just in time to see someone—a child?—disappearing through a gap in the hedge that ran at a right angle to the tall trees that lined the drive. He pressed the horse forward and kept his eye on the place where she had vanished.

Heh, bonjour!

He dismounted and walked over to the hedge.

Heh! You!

But no one answered and the child had clearly made off. Well, but a child all naked would be reluctant to talk. He could see that.

He picked up the reins and continued to the chateau.

Peyre had heard his approach and was waiting on the top step of the terrace.

Bonjour, monsieur! The surveyor took off his hat and waved a cheery salutation as he came through the gates.

Peyre waited until he was at the steps before he replied.

What can I do for you?

A little water for us both, if you please, monsieur. The surveyor put out his hand. Matthieu Laurens, he said. It's thirsty work, riding. No matter the time of year.

Peyre nodded, but when he came down the steps he did not extend his hand.

Follow me, he said. He led the way through to the courtyard. The surveyor looked around, hoping for someone more genial. He coughed.

You are the master here.

Peyre shook his head.

Is the master home?

No. Peyre pointed to the pump where the pail and the cup stood ready.

Matthieu Laurens began to modify his plan of staying the night. His host stood by silently while he drank from the cup and his horse drank noisily from the pail. He wiped his mouth.

So it's just you and your wife and child?

There is no family here, monsieur.

But the child.

There is no child.

But—

But Peyre was already walking away.

Laurens watched him go back to the front of the house. Accustomed to all manner of rude receptions, he did not waste time on this one, though on his way down and round to the bridge the vision of the naked figure returned unbidden several times, a wraith dogging his steps through the dense garrigue.

When his horse shied at an item of clothing lying by the path, he dismounted and picked it up. Though it was faded and torn he put it in his satchel.

When he went to bed late that night in a room above Henri's tavern, the surveyor, if he had not been a man of science, could have convinced himself he had seen a ghost. He had made inquiries in the evening, turning the conversation in the tavern downstairs to the subject of the remote chateau.

And who exactly lives up there, apart from the steward?

No one. Peyre Rouff likes to be alone.

With his son.

His words caused a hush.

Not with his son, no. That would be difficult, to say the least. Le Boulidou, who was a little drunk as always, laughed. There was no other sound.

Well, his daughter, then. I saw a child.

No, you could see many strange sights up there, but no child.

The silence was glassy. It was evident to everyone that Peyre's history was about to appear in the room in all its horrid detail.

He's a very fine taxidermist, is Peyre Rouff, said the mayor, hoping to deflect attention. Yes, quite well known. People send him orders from all over. Paris quite often.

But the surveyor knew something had been about to be revealed and he wanted to hear it.

But definitely no child?

How intent now every man on examining some spot, any spot, far from the surveyor's face. Gustave Thibéry spoke.

Peyre had only one son. He died.

So this — the young man rummaged in is satchel — so this might have belonged to his son. He held up a schoolboy's smock, faded and torn.

Such discomfort for a thing so commonplace? Laurens inclined his head for more.

In an accident in Gougeac. He's buried up at the chateau.

One or two picked up their glasses self-consciously. Everyone loved a good story. Rumour was the fuel. But in this case to summon Giles Rouff to the room on the heels of a substantiated sighting of a child, whether of a boy or a girl, seemed to strongly suggest a ghost — and Aveyrac, in the realm of ghosts, was far too close for comfort.

I doubt this was his, Thibéry said. Trying to be matter of fact, he took the garment and turned it over. But I could use it for drying my dog, if no one wants it.

Now, another drink? The mayor rubbed his hands to-gether. Monsieur Pech? It's up to you, I believe.

The next morning, when Ramon Pailhès went to open his office, he was surprised to see the surveyor again.

The carter will be leaving from the church, he said. You have about twenty minutes still.

I'm here to see you, Monsieur le Maire.

Ramon Pailhès had feared as much. He enjoyed his quiet five minutes with a small glass of wine before he started work.

The young man, this Matthieu Laurens, could not have been more than twenty. He sat before him on the other side of the table like an overgrown schoolboy with his cap in lap, and he spoke — almost as if to his confessor — of the sight he had seen at the chateau.

When I look back at my conversation with Monsieur Rouff, I can't help feeling sure he knew there was someone about the place. Is it true he has no child at all there? If it is, then what I saw is something of a mystery.

The mayor straightened up and drew a breath.

Peyre Rouff lives in isolation. He chooses to. Some years ago, fourteen or so by now, he was involved in a sorry accident. The mayor adjusted his blotter, let his forefingers and his thumbs rest at the corners in a perfect right angle. In an unhappy contrivance of circumstance, he said, while hunting, he shot his own son. He was a particularly fine hunter, Peyre Rouff, which is what makes this turn of fate particularly cruel. It is why he lives alone — and why he most certainly has no child at the house.

The surveyor examined the seam of his cap.

But I know what I saw, he said, looking up.

I understand. And I've thought about what you told us last night. There was a recent rumour that started at the school. It has some similarities. The mayor turned the blotter on his desk diagonally, turned it back again, considering, traced its border with his finger before he continued.

About a year ago a feral child came out of the hills here. She ran away and was never captured. We tried. We sent out several parties but none was successful. She may still be about, if what you're telling me proves true. You may indeed have surprised her, for—as you say—she ran off. I should think it quite possible myself. If I were you I'd think no more about it. If she is in the vicinity and if she returns here, she'll be taken into custody. We shall take all the proper steps. He straightened the blotter on his desk, adjusted the angle of his pen. But really it's of no consequence at all, and nothing can be done until and unless she does reappear, which is unlikely. She's probably miles away by now. He coughed sharply.

Now, you have everything you require for your journey? The post leaves at twelve from Soulières. It's never late.

On his way back to Paris, Matthieu Laurens felt that his real question had been cleverly avoided. The mayor had not responded in any way to his suggestion that Peyre knew about the presence of the child. And if he did—what then did that imply? It was altogether an unsavoury thought he had: an eccentric recluse, far from society and at liberty to do as he willed with a feral child?

LAURENS WAS GLAD to be back in Paris after his travels. The day after he arrived, the surveyor took himself to his favourite bar and was treated by four of his friends as if he had just returned from the heart of the Congo.

But you would hardly believe these villages. He shook his head. The isolation! And they are isolated in time too. My friends, they live in another century.

And he told them tales of the women he had seen doing the work of labourers, constructing walls of a village where, when the source dried up, the inhabitants took a cart loaded with empty barrels to the neighbouring village ten miles away. And they had been doing that for fifteen years! And ignorant? Their ignorance was limitless. He passed through one place where they seriously considered Paris to be a foreign country.

He shook his head again, laughing, raised his hands to point out the gilded mirror behind the bar, the newspapers hanging on their rack in the corner, the cabs waiting outside —

And it is! It truly is!

Well, a good thing you didn't get lost somewhere down there, Matthieu.

With the troglodytes!

Not to mention the wolves. Did you come across them?

No, but it would not have surprised me. Not at all. There could be hundreds in there, thousands, the maquis is so dense there you would not believe.

If I recall, said his friend Antoine, there was a report last year of an enfant sauvage living in that very area. But these stories can't always be believed.

Antoine Rochas wrote for the *Gazette de France*. He took pride in the integrity of his own articles.

The memory of the girl passed through the surveyor with that same fleeting quality she herself had possessed that day.

That's right, he said. I heard about her in Freyzus. In those same mountains. She went right into the village apparently, but they couldn't catch her. Matthieu Laurens could not bring himself to say just then that he thought he had seen the very child at Aveyrac. It would sound too much like fabrication. And he could never admit to the impression he had that day of the wraith who seemed to be haunting his path down the mountainside. It would have made him seem too naive beside his friend Rochas, and the other three were far too cynical. Like wolves, they would only tear her to shreds.

Then, not like the boy they caught at Saint-Sernin?

No. Perhaps wilder. She was supposed to have thrown herself into the gorge. The carter there showed me the place.

Don't you wonder if they invent these stories for their amusement? So isolated like that—

No, Matthieu said. It's entirely believable. If you saw the density of the vegetation. This isn't the countryside we know: a pleasant wood, a few fields, a pasture, a canal or a winding stream. It's rugged, most of it, just rocks and scrub. But other places . . . He shook his head. Whole hillsides entirely covered with a thick green blanket, coarse and spiny. Not a space between. Anything could live there for a lifetime and never be found.

One of the men raised a glass, keen to get on with the rest of the evening.

Then we're glad you're back, he said. And just in time for the new billiards table at Latour's!

And so it was as if they had passed the girl by, swerved to take another road altogether, and left her standing beside the one they had been on. Only later, as they were on their way out of Latour's and saying goodbye, did she make a reappearance. Rochas took the surveyor aside from the group and quietly invited him to dine next day. Neither man mentioned the girl but she stood like a waif, small and pale in the minds of both. Rochas was always searching for a good story.

They went to a small restaurant off St. Michel, where it was not too noisy.

I'll tell you straight away, Rochas said. It's not your genial company I'm after.

I know, I know. It's the Enfant Sauvage.

Exactly. Tell me her story again.

There's not really much to tell. She appeared out of nowhere. She ran stark naked through the village and then when the dogs began to chase her she jumped into the gorge. I've seen the place. It's a long way down...

So she drowned.

Matthieu shrugged. Possibly she did. Why?

You know, you wouldn't be asking that unless you were keeping something back. You would have said, Of course!

You'd have said, Certainly! No one could survive such a drop. Rochas swirled his glass, seemed to contemplate the quality of the wine. *Possibly* implies a measure of doubt. What makes you think she might have survived?

The surveyor drew a breath and considered.

I *think* I saw her. Remember me, Rochas, if you get rich on this story. He smiled. I was on my way across to Freyzus.

Rochas listened. There wasn't much to Matthieu's story. A flash of something, someone, nothing confirmed.

I wasn't so sure any longer that I wanted to visit. You have to ask yourself what kind of occupants let their half-grown children run naked. But the place, you know, is isolated. Not many people pass that way. I think it was built purely as a hunting lodge. The wealth that must have been at their disposal.

And who are the occupants?

Well, there is only one — or so he insisted. He came out. I thought it was a groundsman of some sort — he looked so rough — but he introduced himself as the steward. And he, it turns out, was the man I found out later had a history. I made a reference to his family and he corrected me at once, saying he lived there all by himself. When I mentioned a child he walked off on me. But you know, Rochas, I know what I saw there. And what I heard in the village. It had to be the wild girl lurking up there — with or without his knowledge, though, personally, I think he knew.

Because?

I don't know. I just think he did.

Not much to go on.

I know. And I might be wrong. But if I'm not...

If you're not?

That's your story, right there. Think about it. It's months since she was last seen. If she's been up there all this time. *With* his knowledge. And if he's never done anything about it. *There's* your real story — in the fact that he *knew*. He has a history, this man.

ANTOINE ROCHAS WATCHED the countryside roll away from the train like water from the bow of a boat, pasture land ceding to the rugged mountains of the massif. He was long overdue for a holiday — and long overdue for a story that was all his own. He shook out his travelling rug and put his feet up on the seat opposite. Change. Anticipation of the unknown. New rhythms. A dose of winter sunshine in place of grey Parisian rain. He let himself be lulled into sleep. When he woke, the mountain ranges had sunk and given way to vines, regular sets of twiggy rows were unfurling in waves past his window, opening like a fan.

From Montpellier it was a six-hour journey by coach through Ceresc, watching the mountains reappear, and then down to Soulières, another hour or more by hired vehicle to Gougeac. The town was in deep mountain shadow by the time he arrived. He stayed the night there and set out in the morning, hiring a donkey for his purpose, loading the panniers with the small amount of luggage he had brought and the parcel for Peyre Rouff. He did not want to talk with any of the local people until he had seen the chateau for himself.

The direction was pointed out to him by the innkeeper. He could not believe he was going to ride so high — or that the donkey would want to. The path took him up between rough stone walls that opened now and then to a balcon overlooking the valley and showing him how high he had climbed. He passed through a forest of evergreen oak and saw when he looked out at a turn in the road mile after mile of massed box and juniper. His eye could pick out no land, no earth at all between the billows of green. The river could only be guessed at. Yes, a person could get lost — or hide.

He was just beginning to think he had taken the wrong path in this wilderness when the road widened again onto an open scrubland of heather and fragrant herbs. And there above a broad apron of land, bucolic as a meadow, he saw the tips of impossibly refined turrets above an incongruous avenue of elms.

What a treat Matthieu had missed when he decided not to stay! The chance to poke around this isolated estate, this palace from some antique realm. Rochas was ready, as he entered the long driveway, for the owner's eccentricity. At once he could see that even without evidence of the wild girl his journey would not be wasted. Here, even if he did not find what he was looking for, he could concoct more than one story around the remoteness of this secluded monument to wealth. *Testament to Former Excess. Forlorn Grandeur.* He imagined that inside little would have changed, except to age and fade. The walls would be hung with heavy tapestries, the ceilings painted to resemble open skies, and everywhere gilding, around the mirrors, the chandeliers, the candelabra, the picture frames. Across the country a thousand such chateaux had been left to rot, their doors open to rodents and their roofs to the winds and rains.

His friend had told him that, according to the mayor over at Freyzus, the proprietor's only passion was his taxidermy. He paid good money to the boys in the town for the birds and small mammals they brought him. And every so often the postman would have to make the journey with a packet that contained supplies sent all the way from a shop in Paris. Antoine Rochas was ready with a story of his own. He arrived at the door with a badly preserved ermine, grinning its inane grin in the darkness of his travelling bag.

A man came out of the chateau and gestured to the side of the house.

There is water in the courtyard, he said, and went back inside.

Rochas found the man's tone unsettlingly indifferent. He had shown no sign of interest in his arrival. He waited for the donkey to finish drinking and then led it round to the front of the house again where it could graze beneath one of the elms.

The front door was closed now. Rochas rang the bell.

Rouff's expression when he answered was as inscrutable as before.

Antoine Rochas held out his hand. Antoine Rochas, monsieur. I take it you are the taxidermist.

The taxidermist?

Wary now, thought Rochas. But at least a flicker of interest. The celebrated taxidermist.

At the word 'celebrated,' some veil fell between them. Peyre Rouff blinked and his unnerving neutrality returned.

The sought-after taxidermist whose skills are legendary— so I've heard. Rochas was already hauling out the moth-eaten specimen from his bag and unwrapping it. He had Rouff's interest back. He was careful not to look him in the eye again as he went on unwrapping.

I've heard you're good, very good, and I'm hoping you might be able to rectify this sorry little disaster. He held the ermine to face the steward. Peyre Rouff looked briefly at it and took it from him.

Follow me.

Rochas was at first taken aback by the wolf that greeted him, but he considered it only a variation of the stag's head that would routinely survey the entrance of such a house, the trophies that might grace the gun room. The curled fox startled him more—its placement on the chair, like a domestic cat stealing a nap. The sight of it ruffled all sense of reason.

Without ceremony, Peyre led the way to the kitchen, where he set the ermine on the table. It did not stand quite straight and the magpie on the chair back seemed to view it quizzically. Peyre drew a pitcher close to support it. Rochas waited for some expression of wry amusement, but Rouff remained impassive.

Well? There's my problem. Do you think you can rectify it?

Yes.

Can you show me samples of your work?

You've seen the wolf. The fox.

All right. I'll be frank. I've heard the young lads from Freyzus bring you many subjects — birds, small animals. I have a collection of my own. I'd be interested to see yours — to learn, you understand.

You did this?

No. Not this one. I confess I bought it. So I would have an excuse to come and see you.

Peyre gave him a look that Rochas could not quite read. Was he so transparent?

To be honest, I thought you would not mind a visitor, living here alone.

Not quite alone.

Rochas hardly dared to draw a breath, the impending revelation seemed so close.

Come.

Peyre pushed his chair back and Rochas followed him out of the kitchen and across the courtyard. Rochas felt an unpleasant surge of adrenalin as his journalist's mind set down a tale of captive children and a deranged keeper — not to mention the reporter who died investigating them. But they walked to the octagonal annex with its glazed roof and walls. Rouff opened the door for him. It took Rochas a moment to register what he was seeing.

But this is extraordinary! His voice rode a sigh of relief that he hoped would be taken for wonder. He was surrounded by trees and shrubs and they were inhabited. The more he looked, the more he saw. And so lifelike. It rivalled any museum in Paris. *Extraordinary* was no exaggeration. The man was an artist. Tucked away up here in the middle of nowhere, no one to view his creation.

This must have taken years to build. You must have every possible inhabitant hidden here. Except man! He turned for a response, but his host was busy back over by the door, carefully picking up leaves that had blown in when they entered.

I have Man, said Peyre.

Rochas looked back at the diorama, scanning it methodically. To one side stood a tripod where, in place of a camera viewfinder, a pair of binoculars were fixed in the back wall of a large box. The front of the box faced the tableau.

Rochas walked over and bent down to look. The binoculars were focused on the painted backdrop, or at least they appeared to be, though he guessed there were mirrors involved.

There seems to be a... He was going to say 'smudge,' and then he had it—the figure of a girl. So real it seemed, he pulled away and looked directly at the backdrop. He bent and looked through the binoculars again, frowning. There it was, the figure of a girl. And now his eyes knew the trick. She stood out as in life from the background. She was naked and she was in the act of running off, her face turned to look back at the viewer. He pulled away and was about to speak—but Peyre was already outside recrossing the yard. Antoine Rochas's sense of unease returned. He hurried to catch up to his host. It seemed preferable to keep him in view. He did not want to appear one day as part of this extraordinary tableau, his only trace in this world an indistinct smear on a glass plate.

Without waiting for an invitation he followed Rouff as he went back into the house by a different door. The kitchen was vast, but Rochas could see Rouff only used a corner of it. The great fireplace was cold, the marble-topped vaisselier empty. The only pan in evidence was on a little iron stove near the sink.

Rouff stood by a small table. He was already pouring a glass of wine. He set it beside a broken loaf and a few olives.

Rochas took a risk and pulled out a chair, again without being asked. Nothing seemed to draw a response from this extraordinary man.

You will be needing something before you leave.

Rochas ignored the comment.

Well, he said. That is indeed extraordinary work, monsieur. Extraordinary.

Peyre Rouff blinked, perhaps nervously, and gave the slightest nod.

I dare say you don't feel the least bit lonely up here. With your creatures, I mean. I'd hazard a guess they're a kind of company?

Peyre, pouring wine from a pitcher, shrugged.

The girl on the plate I viewed, who is that? He could hear how his voice betrayed his suspicion of any explanation. The answer took him by surprise.

The wild girl.

As if it were the most natural thing in the world. No inflection, no explanation.

She lives here, in these parts?

Rouff opened a drawer in the table and took out a yellow account book. He began writing what looked like an invoice. Perhaps the answer to the question was too obvious to merit a reply. Rochas tried a different tack.

How many times have you sighted her?

Never had he come across so impassive a subject, so immobile a face. A slight and fleeting contraction of the eyebrows was the only sign that his subject was considering the question and then he shook his head just slightly to dismiss it.

Approximately, I mean.

I couldn't say.

She comes here regularly to visit?

Not visit. You cannot say visit.

But she comes here regularly?

Peyre shrugged. He had been asked a question in a foreign language.

That will be eight francs.

Antoine Rochas knew when he was being shown the door.

And when —?

Saturday. Au revoir, monsieur.

Four

MATHILDE CAN SEE the corner of the newspaper quivering as she reads the article again.

> The child is reported to no longer be running wild but to be wandering at liberty, albeit in a state of nature, in the grounds of Chateau d'Aveyrac, the residence of the de Villiers family.

Her hands are not to be trusted.

> She is sustained there by the steward, Peyre Rouff, a man who had the misadventure, fourteen years ago, to shoot his own son during a duck shoot. Monsieur Rouff, a recluse whose wife left him at the time of the alleged accident, has a reputation for eccentricity. The authorities in Gougeac are expected to conduct an investigation.

She puts the paper down carefully. She feels as if she has his name still in her mouth, like a host melting slowly on the tongue. She busies herself with the fresh white bread on her plate. She had almost forgotten she has a husband. The day he flinched from her touch, the pheasants glowing on the table, was the day a gulf opened between them and there was no crossing over. She had almost wanted to turn on her heel right then, turn her back on him and walk away. Not because she did not pity him, but because she did. Her pity that day, soft and generous, had overwhelmed her. It was compassion itself—and he refused it. They could have clung together in its tenderness, let themselves be laved, be saved together. But he let her succumb to it alone, while he stood, obdurate and dry, already a husk, a shell, drained of flesh and blood. When she turned away, she too had begun to harden. By the time she reached her room it was as if a rock had been set upon her heart. Under it a seed of shiny hatred split open.

Afterwards, when she left and moved away for good, she tore out his memory by the roots.

Her father's house had been nothing more to her than shelter from the weather, her father no more than a confused interloper in the domain of her grief, always looking for a way of escaping the dangerous ground, while her young stepmother, resentful, had been barely able to hide her desire for it all to be over. The women of the village had come to offer what they could, as women do. Mathilde begrudged them their intact broods. She had been told too many times that she would feel better once the new baby came. They were anxious, all of them, for her to be a mother once again. As if her boy could be replaced, like a mule or a pig. She did not want a substitute for her son, and most of all she did not want her husband's child. There was no one she could tell. Only one of the women, an ancient dame, freckled all over like a hen, guessed at the root of her misery. When the woman leaned and whispered in her ear, Mathilde listened. To allow what the woman suggested would be a way to destroy the nightmare of her past. To walk away free. But the secret was as burdensome as the child itself, and when the time came for her baby to be born, Mathilde could not allow it to be done. She had gripped the freckled wrist of the old woman who attended, and who already held the child in her hands, and hissed: Leave it. Just leave it. But perhaps the damage had already been done. It was as if the mere thought of such a thing had decided the infant's fate, for only hours later it was fighting for its breath and nothing could be done to save it.

The days that followed were wretched and tearless. Mathilde would see none of the neighbours, refusing them her misery the way her husband refused them his grief. She left after three weeks — grateful that no one tried to stop her — to go to her aunt Hélène's apartment in Montpellier. There she saw at once she was an imposition, for her aunt had a companion. The lady, who called herself Cousine Agathe, was ten years younger than her aunt. She had a certain evasiveness when she greeted Mathilde. It made her feel uncomfortable and she did not know why until she woke one night to noises in the dark and it came upon her that the woman was a companion who served her aunt in all ways.

For several days, the three women lived uneasily together. Clearly Mathilde could not stay. Her aunt's companion had connections in Paris. She knew a place where Mathilde could lodge cheaply but respectably. If she wished, of course.

The next day, Mathilde told her aunt she wanted to go to Paris to work. Her aunt immediately and happily agreed to find the means to support her for six months while she looked for suitable work.

In Paris Mathilde lived as a widow, which she felt to be truthful. And a widow's chances of employment in service were always greater than those of a single woman of obscure station. She took a position at once in the house of a certain Docteur Alain Derangeur, a doctor for the deaf. He was a quiet man, intelligent, reserved. She could tell he had embarrassed himself when he asked how her husband had died. She guessed that he probably knew she had run away.

He was older, much older than I. His heart failed him.

The doctor said, I'm sorry. And then he smiled and she knew she had obtained the post — housekeeper with room and board — on the strength of her pleasant looks. After a month he came to her in her room at the top of the house. After two months she was rarely in it, rising before dawn so that she could be up before the parlour maid's arrival. He was besotted. After Peyre's brooding abstinence, it was incendiary. She walked in flames.

On the maid's day off, they breakfasted together, eating the fresh white bread that she purchased early from the baker's cart, pouring each other coffee like man and wife. On the first of these mornings, Alain had looked up from his paper. She felt him staring as she cut the bread.

My heart fails every time I look at you, he said.

She was saved at last the ignominy and the isolation that would surely have come her way when, a few months later, the doctor put himself forward for a post at the Sorbonne and was, after interminable interviews and appearances before tribunals and committees, accepted.

On the day that he received the news of the appointment, she bought a little joint of lamb for their supper, his favourite, and he opened a bottle of champagne to drink while it was roasting.

Afterwards, as they sat on at the table, still savouring his success, he said, I have something else to tell you. I told them I am a married man. You will have to be my wife.

She did not know where to look, and turned her face away, her mind racing to salvage her situation. The possibility of marriage had certainly occurred to her, but every time she considered it, the thought of Giles intervened. Not Peyre but Giles. It was not possible. To live a life of bigamy would somehow do him dishonour, in some way make his memory invalid. It was many times more serious than what she did now, taking love when it was offered. She turned her face away.

I cannot.

I know that.

Their voices were whispers, thieves in the dark.

I know that, he repeated. I knew from the beginning. But it doesn't matter. He put out his arm to stop her from rising.

It doesn't matter. You will appear to be my wife. We go there, that's all. We present ourselves as Monsieur et Madame le Docteur Derangeur. The university is on the other side of the city. No one knows us there.

So there she sat before him, exposed, all pretense fallen away. And yet he had been perfectly serious, had never looked more grave.

She had said, for the sake of some kind of decorum, Let me take this in. Let us each think on it, sleep on it. Let us talk about it tomorrow. Though she knew already what she would say.

But it was one thing to confide a secret in the dark, quite another to expose every detail years later to the bright morning light. Now, here at the breakfast table, she can hardly keep from glancing at the newspaper. She has placed it so that the story lies face down on the table. She would not be surprised to see the letters burning through.

Alain reaches for the paper.

He cannot fail to be interested. More than a year ago a short article about a rumoured Enfant Sauvage had rivetted his attention.

She remembers how he had snapped the backs of his fingers against the page of his journal.

Look at this, will you: *WILD GIRL AT LARGE IN THE HAUTE GARRIGUE*. The two of them, at the breakfast table just as they were this morning, had pursued a whole conversation on the subject: how the girl ran entirely naked, how she might have lived her entire life in the cover of the maquis, and how she showed no desire to re-enter civilized society. Mathilde remembers his excitement.

What an opportunity!

She hoped he was not thinking of going there.

An opportunity? She had asked. For?

The world! The advancement of knowledge. I can think of a dozen men in Paris who would like to get their hands on such an innocent.

It said *sauvage.*

Same thing. These creatures are innocent of influence. They can tell us volumes about the true nature of man.

Things we need to know?

Of course. Things about knowledge itself, how it is acquired, the nature of attachment, the source of language. It's endless.

And Mathilde now, staring at the broken bread, the smear of butter on the knife, remembers her next words, for when she spoke them she had no thought of Peyre, considering him as safely buried as if he lay beside their son. She had said, But knowing changes nothing. We are still all victims of accident. And he had replied, That is a brutal way to put it. You could at least say 'hostage to fortune.' But life is brutal, she thinks. To that she can testify on all that is holy — and unholy.

Alain picks up the dangerous newspaper. She wants to rise and leave the table but is afraid to draw attention to herself. It seems important to behave normally.

It may rain later, she says.

Hmm?

It may rain later.

Mmm.

She waits.

So that child...

He continues reading. She waits and says nothing.

So...that child has turned up again.

Yes?

In the paper here. That enfant sauvage in my journal. They say she's believed to have attached herself to an eccentric, a recluse. In Aveyrac. A recluse, one with a sensational history. Another poor soul who finds society too demanding. He laughs and looks up.

Oh, yes?

Well, they would be a fine match, wouldn't they? Neither of them inclined to speak, I dare say.

She feels as if the very walls of the house might crack apart under the pressure of this conversation, might fall away to reveal the rocks and grasses of home in place of Paris pavements.

Life would be peaceful at least, she tries.

She smiles. She has made a joke. Now she can rise. She clears their plates and carries them out to the scullery herself. Her hands, shaking as she sets the dishes down, seem not to belong to her. She is back at their house by the marsh again and he is there before her in his devastation. What can he possibly be doing with a wild girl? What on earth? Her mind cannot begin to approach the question.

THE COMMISSIONER AT Gougeac did not have the opportunity to read Rochas's article until eighteen days after its publication, when the *Méridional* in Montpellier had time to reprint it. The whole business of the girl rattled the commissioner. He did not like the report at all. The *Méridional* had reproduced the original article exactly as it had appeared in the *Gazette*. It painted his department as a backwater of half-asleep simpletons who not only did not recognize the scientific significance of such a girl — a girl who would offer countless opportunities to unlock new knowledge about the development of civilized man — but who had allowed one of its own to maintain her as a piece of property, and in a fashion no civilized man could countenance. No, the whole region came off as a backwater, a backward, forgotten corner of France. The paper even spelled out certain embarrassing questions, asking why the local mayor had failed to see the opportunity for the advancement of human knowledge and why the authorities had failed to reclaim the girl for the common cause.

He could see it all, the arrival of condescending Parisiens, men with too much time on their hands, who would think it a diversion to come south, and engage in some effete form of hunt; men dressed in knickerbockers and carrying alpenstocks, delegates from some obscure society — he could see them — who would more than likely expect a free bed for the night; men who would take up his time asking the same questions, who would need directions, refuse a guide, get lost themselves, and generally cause him grief.

He reached for his writing paper, dipped his pen and wrote quickly.

> *Chers Messieurs, In response to your article of the 14th instant concerning the so-called "Wild Girl of the Garrigue," I feel it is my duty to inform you, as Commissioner of Gougeac that the Mayor of Freyzus has already been requested* — not entirely accurate but it soon would be — *to locate and deliver the girl into my custody here at Gougeac for care and study.*

He wrote another three paragraphs that amounted to little more than balm for his self-esteem, and then he signed and sealed the letter and took it himself to the post office along with a note to the mayor in Freyzus, which suggested in a comradely manner that he renew attempts to locate the wild girl who was once sighted in the area.

His letter to the *Méridional* was in its turn reprinted in the *Gazette de France*. Three and a half weeks later, he found himself the recipient of a request from the Minister of the Interior to supply as many details as he knew of the so-called Enfant Sauvage of the garrigue. The Minister requested, in particular, an up-to-the-minute investigation of the recent sighting at Aveyrac. A full report would thereafter be made available to The Society of Observers of Man, the proper body to undertake a full examination of the case. Apparently he had stoked the very fires he had tried to quench. He passed the whole thing over to the mayor of Freyzus.

In his reply, Ramon Pailhès wrote to the commissioner that none of the sightings, including the last, had ever been substantiated by a third party. In fact, he added — pleased with the rebuttal — in fact, one of them was the report of a less-than-trustworthy schoolboy. Altogether, he wrote, it seemed unlikely that the girl, having got as far as Aveyrac, would have remained in their Departement. Then, feeling that he had in some manner regained his autonomy, he told his wife he would be leaving early in the morning for Aveyrac on an important assignment from the Minister of the Interior.

It was time anyway that he paid Monsieur Rouff another visit. The question of restoration of the Freyzus mill was one the people never forgot. And he could understand why. He had promised them a rerouting of the water years ago when Rouff took over at Aveyrac. The man's only reason for withholding permission at the time seemed to be a desire to be left alone. It could not possibly matter any longer to him. The inhabitants of Freyzus, on the other hand, would be forever grateful — and the commissioner at Gougeac far more polite.

The orangerie was a sizeable building and the diorama almost filled it. The light that poured in gave the illusion of day; the trees and plants seemed to be growing there. Ramón Pailhès was impressed, but he suspected he was being given this tour as some kind of inept consolation, for he had met with no success. Or perhaps this was insult, for the glass house stood in the centre of what was once the walled reservoir whose outflow, through a system of sluice gates, had once fed the millrace.

Peyre Rouff had been as uncooperative as ever on the question of water. That was settled long ago by the seigneur, he said. He, Peyre Rouff, as steward had no authority to alter the arrangement. On the subject of the girl, however, he had been surprisingly forthcoming. Yes, the girl, he said. She came and went as she pleased. He did not seem to think there was anything uncommon in the fact. He said he had tried once to take her down to Gougeac, but she was too wild. He had not realized that she came from Freyzus, for she did not speak. She was a free agent, he said, and he was not responsible for her. He certainly could not guarantee she was still in the area, though he was sure she was out there somewhere.

Mayor Pailhès had never heard him utter so many words at one breath. Rouff had finished by asking him if he required anything for his journey back.

At this, Pailhès thought there might be hope and he had replied that he certainly wouldn't say no to a little something. He considered himself lucky when a plate of cold broth was set before him.

And your famous creation? Pailhès asked, setting down his spoon. Your reputation — as a taxidermist, I mean of course — is spreading, you know. A traveller spoke to me only the other day.

Rouff's expression — barely altered — had implied a shrug.

Your work has impressed people.

You want to see it.

Pailhès had resented the offhand manner and disliked being put in the position of accepting a favour, but it had not seemed reasonable to say no and, besides, he was curious. And so the two of them had left the unappetizing meal and walked over to view the diorama.

It was impossible to guess how many hours Peyre Rouff must have devoted to bringing the outside in, turning nature into artifice and artifice back to nature, fixing the colours of the living leaf, fixing even flight. The space nearest the viewer was carpeted with thyme and immortelle, behind it, rock rose and stonecrop, wild sage, rosemary and Spanish broom. Farther off stood the evergreen oak, box, and juniper. A canopy at the back — a tree limb offering shade from the leafy hands of a chestnut tree — suggested the darker wood beyond. And all seemed to pulse with life, even the silence. And yet death was present too, in the detritus of the earth, the dead leaves and dry fragments of flower heads, the husks of seeds. Snails appeared to climb the fennel stalks at one side. Their empty white shells scattered the ground. The longer he stood, the more he noticed. The birds at first were not visible at all, and then there they were, at one with the shrubs and trees on which they perched, or in the grasses where they foraged. And into those same sparse tufts the tail of a snake was disappearing, and a scorpion watched from beneath a tilted stone. The mayor wondered why he did not see the badger straight away, for there it was, frozen in the act of snuffling and rooting at the base of the juniper. He looked beyond, scanning the shade in front of the painted backdrop, and was rewarded. What seemed at first a patch of denser shade was the face and breast full on of a wild boar peering from the leaves. The camera set in front of it all was irresistible. He bent to look through the eyepieces. The lens was focused on the backdrop to the right of the boar. He straightened up to check. There was nothing there to see. Nevertheless. He bent again to look. Perhaps if he slid the plate into the box... The pale form of a young girl appeared against the leaves, blurred as if she was moving, running away from the glade, the orangerie, the house, running away from him. He had to check this illusion again against the silent dark of the painted wood.

The mayor drew a breath and blinked. He had once visited Paris and seen there the notorious *Bazaar des Delices*—a harmless entertainment that, for a small addition to the bill, primed its patrons for their visit to the brothel above. He remembered the charge of arousal that came about when he entered that darkened room, the even darker tent in the centre. Once he was inside, the canvas door was hooked in place and a second piece of canvas allowed to fall down, cutting out all light. When Madame was ready, she lifted a small flap on the front, low down, and a hole no bigger than a sou shone a beam of light onto a mirror, angled to project an image onto the wall. He saw blurry shapes moving there. And then his eyes made out what they were seeking. A young woman wearing a corset was placing her foot on a stool and bending to remove a stocking. He could not count the number of times he had seen such an action, yet never in the protection of the dark like this, spying. Just as the young woman was removing the other stocking, the flap fell back into place over the hole and he was again in utter blackness.

The mayor needed to look at the girl again. Perhaps it was merely a marking, no more than a smear on the glass. And now he was a little embarrassed. The camera was of course a mere prop to place the spectator in the proper role—as if he had rambled into the garrigue for the express purpose of photographing the landscape. Of course. He did not wish to appear foolish, far less reveal his most private fantasies. He said nothing, thinking it the safest stratagem for his dignity. And besides, if he did not speak about it... The vision seemed particularly his, to savour. Peyre, he noticed, made no comment at all.

Two days later, the commissioner from Gougeac came to see Ramón Pailhès in Freyzus. The girl was without doubt the mayor's responsibility—and it was his responsibility, as commissioner, to see that Pailhès did his duty as a public official and as a decent, responsible man. He had a report to make out for the Minister of the Interior.

The commissioner's visit irked the mayor. He could not agree that simply by tearing through his little town and hurling herself off the cliff the girl was his responsibility. Nevertheless.

Pailhès always knew how to get a job done. It did not take many drinks to persuade the men of Freyzus to turn out on the next full moon. They would take lamps with them and nets, ropes, and dogs. Setting out in daylight, they reasoned, would only diminish their chance of success, for the girl, in her roaming over the heights around Aveyrac would surely be alerted to their presence and most certainly outrun and outwit them long before they come close. Nighttime, they unanimously decided, was their best hope. They would wait until after midnight when the moon would be up and they would take the quickest way up to the ridge. They might be able to surprise her while she was still sleeping, the leashed dogs being certain to pick up a scent so rare and lead them straight to her before she had a chance to run. Some of the men would bring their guns because, well, it might not be hunting season, but this after all was a hunt.

ON THE NIGHT of the full moon the men are a while in the tavern. Henri is pleased with the evening. Every man has a full flask of cartagène in his pocket. Their wives at home in bed can hear the laughter as their husbands come out of the tavern. Leaving the village the men might almost be heading up a charivari, their spirits are so high. The dogs they have brought along run ahead, pleased to be out so unexpectedly. Gustave Thibéry's dog, the most experienced and the largest, leads them. Others, belonging to no one in particular, follow at a distance. Dogs left at their chains bay in protest as the others pass. The rising moon shines down on the band of men, making the pool of their shadow waver beneath their feet. Raoul walking among them feels himself at last a man among them, a soldier perhaps marching to some great victory, and he laughs to himself at the thought of other, lesser, boys, tucked in their beds ready for school.

The men leave the narrow walls of Freyzus and take the road down to the bridge, its stone shining white in the moonlight. Conversation dwindles as they make their way onto it. The dark river chatters on, its waters gleaming and flashing below, white foam spinning on the surface.

The girl sits in the mouth of her lair and watches the moonlight pour down the face of the cliff. She has found a small cave on the other side of the ridge behind the house. She likes to sleep there sometimes, high above the gorge. Tonight something wakes her just as the moon springs above the mountain to the east. She crawls forward and sits up to watch. To sit like this, to let the world enter, is her pleasure. The girl is never blind or deaf to the offerings of the world. There is always something—if not moonlight, then cloud, or rain, or wind or the foundering sun. These things can open her heart the way the man's voice did when he moaned for his dog, the ways his eyes once did when she saw them watching her drink. But a man's voice, a man's eyes, are not to be trusted. She lets the moonlight wash over her. Sitting there in the vastness of the night, she watches the mountain appearing as if just for her. And the light continues to pour. She holds out her open palms and then she cups them to her face as if quenching a great thirst.

It is one of the dogs she hears first. She thinks it is a wild boar rooting, until she hears a whistle. The whistle, unlike the call of any bird, tells her there are men on the cliff. And if men, then dogs. What she took for the snuffing of a boar in the distance is the harsh panting of a dog climbing toward the path that she must take to get off the cliff face. She does not want to meet it here. But there is no path on the other side of the cave mouth. Below is a tangle of trees and scrub that has taken root in a narrow rift running diagonally down to the dry stream bed above the mill. She takes a deep breath, as if she is entering water, and prepares to let herself fall into the risky embrace of the trees. At the same moment the dog breaks through onto the path to the cave, its barking hysterical as it catches sight of her. From the corner of her eye she sees it lengthen its stride to lunge, even as she springs. The weight of her body carries her down past the clawing trees onto a smooth chute of rock where there is nothing to stop her. It flings her, gasping with the speed of the descent, into a shallow trough near the entrance to the old stream bed. The dog on the ledge above yammers. From where she is she cannot see any path that will take her up again on the other side of the stream bed, but on her own side she can see a light just below her and she can hear the voices of men whispering low. She is only closer now to where they are climbing, and not one but two dogs are baying somewhere not far below her. Though she cannot see them she can visualize the bodies that match the ululations — medium-sized, heavy-chested, the two of them. Their breathing tells her they have saliva hanging from their jaws. She tries to double back, pulling herself up higher in the hope of finding an opening on the other side of the stream bed, picking up rocks as she goes. As she regains the trough she sees that the great dog that was almost on her at the top has made its way down and is breaking from its track through the scrub. And now it barks to see her, its voice marking time with its stride that devours the ground between them. A tree is growing from the edge of slope behind the trough. A spiny shrub at its base blocks her access to it but she has no choice. She lets the rocks go and pulls herself across it.

The men have trouble keeping up with the dogs crashing through the scrub ahead of them. They come now converging from three directions.

The hunters know by the racket of the dogs what is happening. The yaps of exhilaration have given way to a barking full of intent, and the men know the dogs have the prey in their sights. Gustave Thibéry calls to his dog, his voice lost in the tumult of snarl and snap. Stéphane comes on the scene first and sees how the girl has overreached the thorn bush and gained a hold on an arbutus tree behind. Thibéry's dog has her ankle in its mouth and has braced itself to pull her down, while the others snap and leap uselessly. He swings into them with his satchel and beats them about their faces until they back off, cowering. Thibéry joins him and has a stick and together they subdue the dogs. The girl clings to a branch while Raoul laughs aloud at her plight.

Oaf! says Thibéry under his breath and stretches up and across to grasp her good ankle. She struggles frantically and in her panic loses her hold. Thibéry tries to help her. He talks to her as he does to his dog when he rubs it down after an arduous hunt, using the soothing voice he would use if it were injured. The girl lets herself be extricated from the punishing spines. He holds her by the wrist while Stéphane takes off his jacket. Together they get her arms through the sleeves. Pech has a rope and ties it round the jacket to close it. The girl watches as he does it and she does not resist.

What now? Raoul is wide-eyed, looking from one to the other.

Not what you're thinking, you randy monkey, says Pech.

One of the men laughs.

What's your name, girl? says Thibéry

Look at her! Do you think she even has one, for God's sake?

She must have a name. She was born.

What are you thinking? Look at her! Pech says again. She's not understanding a word we're saying. She doesn't even know she's bleeding. She's more animal than human.

Stéphane is bending to look at her leg. A strip of skin hangs from her calf. The damage at the ankle is laid bare, raw as a knuckle of lamb.

We need to bind this. Who has the oldest shirt?

And now it seems all right to laugh with the image of torn shirts and angry wives and mothers comfortably domestic among them.

Early in the morning the boy Felip sees them bring her in. They have tied her inside a coat. Its sleeves are crossed in front and tied together at her back. She walks like one about to fall and she holds her head rigid as if afraid that in turning it some danger might strike from the blind side. But her eyes are agile, he sees that. When three dogs run forward barking she stops suddenly, rocking to keep her balance. One of the men curses. And there is Raoul walking just behind her. He gives her a shove. The boy feels as outraged as if he himself has been pushed. People, still bleary-eyed from sleep, have begun to gather at the tree in the square. The boy goes and stands with them. They are watching in silence, still unsure what to make of the sight, reluctant to release their judgments to the common air before they have delivered their verdicts in private. For really, what to make of it? Criminals and felons, murderers and thieves are escorted in this fashion, bound, and yet the impulse is for pity, as for an orphan, or a crippled child. Is this girl dangerous? It can hardly be, she is so slight and must have been so easily overpowered. Is she a thief? Of course she is a thief. One or two have the impulse to jeer or hiss, but they keep quiet all the same. For, what if they are wrong? What if this is not a sinner but a new variety of saint? And so the girl progresses through the silent stations of her personal cross, flashing her eyes to left and right with a rapidity all will speak of afterwards. The dogs circle and run behind to nip at her heels. Before he knows he has even reached to pick it up, the boy hurls a rock. The yellow dog yelps and jumps away, its tail plastered to its belly. The other two cower and increase their distance, and the small party goes on to the mairie. A few townspeople linger, hoping for more, and then they too drift away to their kitchens.

Felip spends the next two hours sitting on the steps of the church opposite the mairie, hugging his knees against the crisp of the spring morning. His lips are numb by the time the door opens. When they bring her out she looks more like the girl who inhabits his dreams. They have untied her sleeves. Though she still wears the coat, she walks, half runs now as he remembers her, hurling herself into the future, away from her present predicament. But she is not going anywhere of her own choosing, for the lead rope is still tied around her waist. He wants to tell her not to struggle, that it will only make matters worse.

So where did they take her? his mother asks when he gets back.

They all went into Doctor Ayash's house. Then they came out without her.

He does not add that he waited after they had gone and that only minutes later he heard a high-pitched wailing coming from somewhere at the back of the house. To speak about it might be to somehow speak against Doctor Ayash and earn a clip on the ear. The misty-haired Doctor Ayash is nothing if not venerable. His credentials, though no one knows exactly what they are, are unassailable. Felip had walked round to the back of the house to investigate but the garden was walled. He did not like to listen longer. Something inside him coiled and writhed at the sound, like a worm struck with a spade.

She's in good hands then, says his mother. Doctor Ayash is a learned man.

Without Doctor Ayash and his scientific interest, Ramon Pailhès does not know how he would handle the girl, for someone has to care for her while he goes through the process of trying to find her parents or her family. He writes to each of the four mayors situated in a fifty-mile radius of the town and describes for them the girl's appearance and condition, her general demeanour, and the location of her discovery. He asks them to post notice of her capture with a request for anyone with information as to her origins to come forth at once and make themselves known. But he knows that word of mouth is the fastest means of communication at his disposal, and to encourage its spread, he decides to have the girl herself displayed for two hours each morning on the steps of the church. He judges that a period of one month will be long enough for anyone connected to her to come forth and present themselves.

In his letter the mayor describes the girl as 'untamed but placid and pliant,' and an observer passing the steps of the church in the first few days would agree. She arrives with an eager air and readily lets herself be tied there to the iron ring, even using the tension on the rope to lean backwards and observe the swifts circling, circling. She seems to like to keep her face to the sky. Those who stop and try to speak to her are disappointed. She looks in their direction certainly, but she does not make eye contact and only scans their persons, looking, it is generally agreed, for food. If none is forthcoming, she has no further interest, but goes on with her sky gazing.

People bring her apples, a potato, a piece of sausage. Each time she wolfs down the offering without seeming to chew. When she defecates on the steps, the mairie issues a prohibition against feeding her. But for this incident, interest in viewing her might have waned. Instead, it rouses the curiosity of the coarsest souls, and lads and girls alike come to jeer, and have to be reprimanded and sent away—unless they are lucky and find her momentarily unattended.

By the second week, when the curious begin to arrive from neighbouring communes, the girl is exhibiting many more traits that accord with the mayor's description of her as 'untamed' and fewer that support his view of her as 'placid.' At times, bent over at the waist and repeatedly heaving her stomach back toward her spine, her mouth hanging open, she seems to be doing her utmost to make herself vomit. She begins to growl when anyone approaches. If the spectator persists, she alters her voice and sends it rising to such a pitch, such an in-human scream of protest that he will step back, reconsidering, while the cry rings from the stones of the surrounding walls. Doctor Ayash says he has read that wild cats in the jungles of Peru make just such an untrammelled high-pitched wail at times of mating. He notes it down beside his other observations. She is, he confides to the mayor, exhibiting behaviours more and more uncivilized.

When I lock her in her room, you would think there was a thunderstorm. She must be hurling herself against the door, he says.

She will hurt herself, the mayor says.

I have fixed a mattress to the back of the door.

But her face? The marks there?

When she is in distress she beats her head on the floor, sometimes the wall.

And now the idle gawkers come. The newspaper report encourages them.

Ramon Pailhès and Doctor Ayash begin to think four weeks too long.

IN THE TWO days it takes for her to reach Montpellier, Mathilde has not once asked herself why she is returning. She had acted on impulse one morning when Alain had resumed the topic of the Enfant Sauvage. He said one of his colleagues had heard unconfirmed reports of her capture from a member of The Society of Observers of Man. The Minister of the Interior, it seemed, had heard from the commissioner at Gougeac down in the south somewhere. Some young girl had been brought down from the hills.

Let's hope they send her here to Paris, he said. Or at least to the Institute in Montpellier. She should be somewhere she can be studied by all.

Why? But Mathilde did not really want to know why. The question merely covered for her thoughts, which had flown home, flown back to her other life, her other husband.

The opportunity, my dear. We talked about that. She is the original innocent. You know what that means for science.

A human child developing in the wild, free of influence, free of society.

Surely not free of society. Didn't you say — she hesitated, seeing how close she had approached — that she was being fed by the steward . . . or someone?

That would be negligible. It said he is a recluse. And she was still living out of doors, in the wild. In any case they should get her to some kind of civilized society. Montpellier first, perhaps.

And then it was almost as if her body were acting of its own accord, divorced from all rational consideration.

You know, by the way, my aunt is worsening, don't you? She heard herself say it. She continued with her breakfast, pleased she had found a change of subject to support her indifference to the story of the steward.

I had a letter yesterday with the midday post, she went on. She says she longs to see me. And then to her surprise here suddenly were real tears, shed for her young husband of years ago, falling amid the flakes of pastry on her plate.

Alain reached across to put his hand on hers.

Would you like to go? You know I'll help you if that's what you want. But you would have to travel without me. My work . . .

It was not what she had intended. She had meant only to escape the perilous subject of the girl that threatened to split apart the solid walls of the house in Rue Saint-Etienne and reveal a view clear into her past, where memory had so suddenly and mysteriously transformed to desire. But now here it was, this opportunity offered to her on a breakfast plate.

The train can get you there in two days and is quite safe. I don't like to see you so unhappy.

So that now anything was possible. She closed her eyes and said quietly, Thank you. Thank you, Alain.

But Alain Derangeur was already considering opportunities of his own. A lacuna of two weeks, perhaps more, without a faithful wife waiting each day patiently for his return might hold in store for him any number of delightful possibilities.

In Montpellier, Mathilde does indeed go to visit briefly with her aunt Hélène. And there she does indeed find her aunt much worsened. Cousine Agathe, opening the door herself, recognizes her at once, but her Tante Hélène, through all the long afternoon in the high-ceilinged salon, addresses her as Amélie and smiles in a meaningless way as if in private she would dearly love to know what business has brought this Amélie to her door. Cousine Agathe pours a tisane from a pitcher of tilleul. Like the tisane, she is pleasant but far from warm. She has not cared for her failing lover these last long years only to have a niece manifest out of the blue, carrying with her, perhaps, some new consideration regarding the bequest of a handy little parcel of land in the Hérault. All three women are glad when the visit limps to its inevitable conclusion.

From the grimy window, Agathe watches Mathilde walk quickly to the corner of the street. She turns and pours two glasses of absinthe. They have done well. All three of them.

In her hotel by the station, Mathilde pens a note to Alain Derangeur. Her aunt was overjoyed, she writes. The visit is bound to have a tonic effect on her health. She cannot thank him enough. She will write to him again in a few days' time.

In the early morning, with her bank notes safely out of sight in the little cloth purse she wore round her neck, and with a grubby-looking boy carrying her travelling wares, Mathilde leaves her small hotel and walks back to the station forecourt, where the diligence for Lodève waits for its passengers. It will take the road west and make the climb up to Ceresc, then down to Soulières, before turning northwest again on the road to Lodève.

A woman outside the station is selling violets. Mathilde buys a bunch and keeps them on her lap in the coach.

It is not long before the diligence leaves all sign of civilized life behind. It climbs steadily. Leaving the slate roofs, the iron-work, and the plane trees of the city's perimeter, it rocks and sways up to a windy plateau where wiry blue-green scrub is bossed with pale grey rock and all is open to the sky. Mathilde, like the other passengers inside, begins to feel the cut of the wind and draws her coat closer at the neck. Outside, hawks fall obliquely to their prey, like pieces chipped off the wind and rendered visible. To get out and walk here would be to walk toward one's soul. To see it clear and bare. She looks across the plain and can see no house, no tree, no clue to help her know the reason for her journey. There is only the reflection of her barren heart, endless. Has she come for her son — or for her husband? On the train from Paris she had avoided the question, intent as she was on maintaining the pose of the traveller on important pressing business, occupying herself with the mechanics of the journey. She had been playing a role: the role of reading her book, of looking at the landscape, avoiding those who seemed too forward, eating her lunch, inspecting her gloved fingers. She had busied her thoughts with rehearsing what she would say to her aunt in Montpellier, building her story of her life in Paris, all the while wearing the guise of one who knows her purpose in life, one who knows where she is going and why.

From a sweetheart, then, are they? says the man beside her in the diligence.

I beg your pardon.

From your sweetheart. The man nods toward the flowers. Pretty lady like you.

She did not answer.

You'll have to write him a letter when you get where you're going.

I am going to see my mother, she lies.

He glances down again.

She'll like the flowers, he says.

Mathilde closes her eyes. She feels fragile suddenly, like one recovering from a long illness. She is grateful to the woman opposite who interrupts the man's next attempt to engage her.

Madame is sleeping, monsieur, she says.

Mathilde opens her eyes once to smile at the woman. On the long climb up to the Font-Froide mountains, she listens to the man describing everything outside the window to the other travellers, all of whom can see perfectly well for themselves. It is a luxury not to be present.

In Soulières, a carrier with a gig is waiting for the diligence. Mathilde is his only patron but he does not seem to mind. He says he has been busy lately. People are going up to Freyzus all the time now.

Is that why you've come? he asks. You know, to see the girl?

Mathilde shakes her head.

I've seen her, he says. Poor creature. A savage, he says. No hope. They should have let her be. No hope.

I'm going to see my mother. Over in Gougeac, Mathilde says, anxious to leave the subject of the wild girl, whose life seems to have suddenly become entangled with hers.

Oh Gougeac. I can take you over there.

Thank you.

Not at all. Then you won't have to go over with le Boulidou. He winks as if she should understand exactly what he means. He's the local toper — carter, I mean, he says.

Mathilde wraps herself in the scratchy brown blanket and sits in the seat behind him.

So Gougeac. There's talk they'll end up taking that girl there. For good — if you can call it that. Getting itself a reputation is Gougeac. The place is jinxed if you ask me.

Oh but she does not want him straying into history, anything but the past and herself there centre stage, become a figure in an old tale, the grieving mother. She tries to keep him pinned to the present.

And what, then? she says. What about this girl?

But even as he began recounting the wild girl's escapade in Freyzus, Mathilde realizes there is no avoiding her husband's place in the rumour-filled story of various sightings and searches. It does not take long. The carrier is already offering his opinion that there is much more to the story than meets the eye.

Living up there with that man who killed his son? What was *he* up to all that time? Why didn't he bring her in before? You answer me that.

He looks over his shoulder at her.

If you're cold, he says, there's another blanket in the back.

Mathilde is still shivering when they arrive.

She pays the driver and walks with her bag to the house of Madame Maurel, who had been so kind.

Alice Maurel, thinking it is her neighbour at the door, sings out, Come in. She puts her hand over her mouth when she sees Mathilde standing in the wedge of light. There is no way now to know how to behave, what to say. She offers her tea, soup, a bed, a chair. Oh dear, oh dear! she says. And then again, Oh dear, oh dear!

For the first time on her journey, Mathilde softens and feels her blood run as it should in her veins, feels her breath rise and fall as it should.

Have I become a ghost? she says and laughs. She is going to say 'I too' referring to her husband, her son, but she holds it back. It seems kinder.

Oh, a ghost, heaven forbid. We are all haunted enough by the past without ghosts. But come and sit.

Despite Alice Maurel's brave words about ghosts, Mathilde cannot help noticing that her hand shakes as she pulls up the chair.

And tell me where you have come from. We wanted to get in touch with you but your father's wife could not find an address to write to.

And then Mathilde knows there is something more here.

You did not know about your father? Oh, I am sorry to be the one to tell you. You really don't know. He passed away two years ago.

Mathilde shakes her head. I heard nothing.

It was a fever in the lungs. The wife is remarried now. You haven't been there?

Mathilde shakes her head again.

She said when a year had gone by that he had written to you and that you had never answered.

Mathilde smiles.

Oh, Madame Rouff, I'm sorry. We did not know what to think.

I've been in Paris. Paris is far. Perhaps she does not have the address. I think I need to walk now. I've been sitting too long. Will you come?

They do not take the road to the marshes but follow instead the high road that climbs the slopes behind the town.

On their walk, Alice Maurel apologizes again. Mathilde says it really is of little consequence. She really had not come to see her father. I was going to our house, she says. And then I was afraid and so I came to you.

Afraid of?

I don't know. What I might find. I don't know anything any longer.

Your husband is not here. You know that?

The newspaper said he was at Aveyrac. They said he kept a wild girl there.

They brought her down two weeks ago, Alice said.

I heard that. I thought he would have come down. I don't know why. I imagined he came here often...

They took her to Freyzus. He hasn't been down, not for a long time. Your house here is all closed up. Who knows what state it's in? You shall stay with us tonight.

Mathilde thanks her and accepts. After a little while she returns to the subject of her husband.

Perhaps he is waiting for another manifestation from the wild. She is trying for levity, but Alice Maurel is not smiling.

Oh, one is enough. You'll hear. People are saying she brings bad luck wherever she appears. But that would be witchcraft, don't you think? I don't believe it. It's coincidence, that's all. She was seen up in Ysolt and a fire broke out in the carter's barn. Then after she jumped in the river up at Freyzus, three children were taken sick. And then your husband. His dog died right away, or so they said.

What else did they say?

They said he was feeding her in place of the dog. But he cannot care about her, not sincerely, if he hasn't come down. But perhaps no one has bothered to tell him and he waits for her every day. She does not add that others have their own theories about his continued absence: that perhaps, so their salacious minds tell them, he used the girl and stays away for his good reasons.

Frédéric is at the house when they come back. He hesitates.

Madame Rouff.

He looks pale, Mathilde thinks.

Monsieur Maurel — Frédéric.

You've come back.

He puts his hands on her shoulders and the day no one has mentioned comes hurtling at her through time: her husband's arms heavy at his sides while Frédéric holds her away from the bed.

Her voice is unsteady when she answers him, and Madame Maurel can see it is no use pretending that the most important thing of all does not exist.

Yes. I came back. The violets are for Giles. I'll go there tomorrow.

I'll help you arrange it, Frédéric says.

Madame Maurel speaks softly. I can come with you if you like.

No. I prefer to go alone. I'll walk.

Mathilde is aware suddenly of the two of them looking at her.

You can't possibly. You'll need someone to take you up there. A conveyance.

No, no. I used to make that walk all the time, when I went home from the market. Mathilde gives a wry smile to think of those times. But the two of them are staring so. There is something else. There is something they know, something she doesn't. She puts her hand on the edge of her chair to steady herself.

Alice Maurel gets up and goes to the window. It is obvious that Mathilde has never been told. She is suddenly furious with Mathilde's father. She was sorry to have had to break the news to her of his passing, but this, this dismal duty should not be hers. To tell a mother they came with shovels? Tell her, They came with shovels and they dug up your son.

He is not in the cemetery, not in the one at Freyzus, she says at last. I thought you would have known. He's at Aveyrac now. He was moved. They moved him. They had a priest. It was all done in accordance. Peyre stays at Aveyrac to be close to him.

In the morning Mathilde walks out early. She takes the track that leads up into the garrigue, winding between stone walls until it reaches an open expanse where ruined walls mark some ancient habitation. The walls are not high enough to keep out the tireless wind. Wild irises and woody herbs have sprung up around them, between them, and she sees how once plants have a footing they take on the power to tilt stones.

She walks farther up the hill into the wind.

She is hollowed out. She had buried her loss so deep, so deep, afraid it would overwhelm her. And now there is nothing left. The wind could blow right through her. She is a shell. She had let the fires of Paris consume her pain. Now that they have cooled, she can see how they have consumed her loss and therefore her love too, for they are the same. There is a cavernous emptiness at her heart. Is that loss? She has memories certainly. A horror there, certainly. A nightmare that still sometimes surfaces and returns her to the single moment of obliteration, her whole being an expression of no, and no, and endlessly no. It is a terror she would not wish on any man or woman. But a loss? She lost her son years before his death. Peyre had reached out long before and spirited him away to the woods, the marsh, the hill, showed him how he could walk abroad in the world and need nothing more than the wild world itself, its groaning creatures, its lovely light. She could see it in his eyes, when he came home from a hunt. His heart was in the wild world. He did not need her. No, Giles before it happened was already out of reach, launched into his own life where she figured not at all. So, loss? The wind strips her of all relevance; the loss belongs wholly to Giles, his life wrenched from him before it had been lived. The imperious wind, the blue sky, the birds.

Madame Maurel is waiting for her when Mathilde returns. She says she has something to put to her.

It is delicate, she says. Can you stay with your husband?

Mathilde tries to ignore the small panic. Alice Maurel cannot possibly know how she lives in Paris as a married woman. Though she might guess if she hesitates.

Of course.

Well, then my brother can take you up to Avèyrac tomorrow. He's going all the way over the pass to Bresailles. But he could bring you back down the next evening. He needs no payment, Alice says. It is the least...

Mathilde hears the catch in her voice — just a small break, barely noticeable. And now the clarity the wind brought has misted over and the pity of others comes crowding in, and she understands for the first time how a great loss belongs to all, and how she abandoned her friends, depriving them.

She will need to be ready to leave before dawn, Alice says, if Léon is to make Bresailles by nightfall. She offers to go with Mathilde. If it is a question of honour, she says.

It is not a question of honour, says Mathilde. I am his wife still. There is no need.

Madame Maurel wonders to herself if Mathilde might want to move back. It is not the time to ask.

They take their meal with Frédéric when he comes in, each one of them feeling that they sit at the table only days after the accident, for the missing years have been erased, and the memories loom real and uncontained. Mathilde concentrates on her dinner. No one has an appetite.

And this wild girl, Madame Maurel says, suddenly inspired. You would not believe the stories.

Frédéric pushes his plate away and says they are best left for the lies they are, and Alice becomes flustered and sees how she cannot repeat some of them to Peyre Rouff's own wife.

I did not mean...

If you will excuse me, says Frédéric, there is something I have to do before the morning. Good night, Madame Rouff. I hope you have a comfortable journey tomorrow. Please tell your husband he is welcome here at any time. He knows that, but it is years since we've seen him.

I'll tell him, says Mathilde. And she sees how Frédéric too has lived a kind of loss for fourteen years. And now here is his wife looking resentful at the way she has been slighted. Mathilde feels a little sorry for her.

Have you seen the girl? she asks.

Madame Maurel shakes her head. No, I have heard, that's all. They say they are bringing her here next.

From Freyzus?

Yes. She lives at the house of the doctor and from what I've heard she causes nothing but grief. They're sending her here in an effort to find the parents, they say. But if you ask me it's to have her off their hands for a while.

What does she do?

Oh, she eats and she empties herself and when she's not doing either of those, as far as I can make out, she's either looking or rocking. What is she supposed to do? She can't even speak.

Mathilde sleeps that night with the violets in a jar of water on the table beside her. She is awake for a while with her dark memories, her son's death like a hard cold stone at her side under the covers. But the last thought she has before sleep is of a lonely wild child rocking, rocking.

In the morning she dresses by candlelight while Madame Maurel wraps the flowers in damp paper for the journey. Mathilde stands outside in the greying light listening for the sound of the cart.

A mist lies above the surface of the river like a long roll of lamb's wool. There was always a mist lying over the marshes when Peyre took the hunters out. She would see from the door how it turned shell pink before it began to lift, the pale grasses wet beneath it.

Léon, older than his sister, brawny and rumpled, arrives a little late and keeps his eyes from meeting hers as he apologizes.

It is not until they have driven out of the town that he risks a question.

You haven't been back, he says.

It's very difficult.

He nods. What can he say?

After a while he says that if she wants to sleep he can arrange the rugs for her in the back of the trap. She will be quite safe. She says thank you, no. She is quite happy to watch the countryside. It has been so long.

You'll see the harrier hawks, he says, when we get up a bit higher. Wonderful hunters, those birds. They stay all through winter.

Can I help you? Peyre Rouff's tone says it had better be a sensible request. He is not smiling. Unkempt, dirty, he looks, Léon thinks, like a worker after a long day in the quarry, or the vines.

I've not come all this way to ask a favour, monsieur. And 'Bonjour' would be more in order, after all this time.

He climbs down from the trap.

I've brought you a visitor.

Peyre folds his arms.

She's following. She got down to walk. She wanted me to come ahead to warn you. Though Léon did not imagine when he made his offer that he would have to be the one to break the news to Peyre.

For a moment Peyre thinks he means the girl, and something like joy flickers at his heart. But the girl would not be giving orders. He looks past the trap to the road. From the steps, the avenue of elms obscures most of it.

She?

Madame...Léon's mouth opens and he draws a breath. He tries again. Four breaths, five.

Monsieur Rouff, he says, it is your wife. Later he will have to invent Peyre's reaction, for his own sister as soon as they are alone and then for others, because Rouff turns away at once and Léon cannot see his face. When he turns back, he is as impassive as before.

Take your gig into the yard, he says. Gesturing, recovering. There's water there.

He goes to meet her. Dishevelled. His hair wild, his face unshaven. He wears a brown jacket, frayed at the cuffs, a rag of a kerchief round his neck. His trousers are splashed with pale clay at the ankles and he wears no shoes.

They stand facing each other in the yellow drive, the bare branches rubbing somewhere above them, high. She glances at him once, but he will not meet her eyes. She sees his hands at his sides, the fingers curled into fists, the faintest of tremors running over them.

Mathilde, he says. So low she can barely hear. And still he is not looking at her. Come.

They walk together to the house. She tries not to let him hear her breath, though she can hear his, heavy, as if he has been hurrying. At the steps he reaches and takes her hand, places it on his arm. It is courtesy, she knows it, and she takes her hand away when they reach the top. She cannot even manage 'thank you.'

He shows her into the reception room off the hall and pulls a sheet from one of the chairs.

Sit down. Please. I'll come back.

She sits on the very edge of the chair and waits. She cannot shake the sense of being watched. She gets up and goes to stand, uneasily, at the shuttered window. How did she think that this would be possible? She can hear him, she thinks, somewhere in the back of the house. And then nothing. She remembers Léon. Peyre will see to him first, of course. See him on his way with something for the road. But he is so long. She goes back to the chair to wait, surmises he is making himself respectable. She would have liked to check her own appearance.

When she hears him coming, she smoothes her skirt and folds her hands in her lap.

But Peyre is as dishevelled and unkempt as before. Bits of chaff stuck to his sleeve now. He looks more than ever like a man who has been living outside. He looks, somehow...hunted. Perhaps he has been living outside with the wild girl, the two of them lying down face to face to sleep, their dusty hair tangling.

What have you done? she says, thinking of the girl.

He flinches.

Your first words to me? You need to ask me again?

She realizes how it had sounded. Can he believe she has come all this way, after all this time, to repeat those words?

I have not come to lay blame.

He seems not to hear her.

I was alone, he says. I was alone amid people. I had to leave.

She does not say anything to help him.

Giles is in the churchyard. He nods toward the window.

She walks over and stands a long time looking out.

Beyond the courtyard, the hill rises gently. Past the cypress trees she can see the domed roof of the chapel with its iron cross.

Why here? We shall not be buried with him.

I wanted him near me. I could not abandon him, he says.

Now you accuse.

He says nothing.

She turns round suddenly.

I could not stay. I could not. She tries in vain to make him meet her gaze. I wanted you dead. I longed for it.

But there is grieving…

I did not want to grieve. She is crying now without restraint. I wanted to kill you. I wanted to leave him for you. For you to suffer endlessly. Alone.

He waits.

Where did you go?

Quieter now, she goes back to her chair, takes a breath. She unpins her hat and holds it on her lap. Strands of her hair fall free. She hooks them back. Wipes her face with the flat of her palm.

I went to Montpellier. And then I went to Paris.

How did you live?

I lived. How did you live?

I lived. I lived by not believing.

The newspaper said you are an eccentric, a recluse.

The newspaper? His laugh is hollow.

The *Gazette de France*. It named you. It described you.

He laughs again and shakes his head.

But this poor savage. She returns to her first question. What are people to think?

He looks past her, through her.

The girl, she prompts. The wild girl.

People are to think nothing. She came here. That was all. And she was sick. She stayed nearby. Perhaps she was grateful that I helped her. He shrugs. I put food down.

As for a dog?

Yes, as for a dog. She eats her food like a dog, from the ground.

So what happened?

I've not seen her here for weeks. She may come again, I don't know.

Mathilde sees that he was telling the truth.

Has no one told you?

He looks at her suddenly.

No, Mathilde says. She's not dead. She's alive and in the custody of the mairie.

In Gougeac?

In Freyzus. She sleeps at the house of the doctor there by arrangement with the mairie. Alice Maurel told me all about it. They have put her on display outside the church of

St. Eustache. She is on a leash. People gather. Some of the people, Alice heard, come every day just to gawk. No one steps forward. No one claims her.

Is she all right?

She hears the concern in his voice, the sense of attachment, and she resents it.

All right? No I would say she's not all right at all. She is completely mad. She is chained there, Alice said, like some lunatic.

She's not mad.

Perhaps you've lost your ability to assess madness. Or sanity. Perhaps you are not qualified.

When he does not respond, she continues.

She tears at her clothes. She spits if anyone approaches. Peyre, she defecates.

She hears him swallow.

Peyre, what were you doing with her?

I told you. She came here, that was all. I fed her. He shrugs. I believe she was finding sanctuary. Finding rest. Before, she used to run all the time. Everywhere.

Mathilde is waiting for more, but he has nothing to offer.

She is to be moved to Montpellier.

And why?

For purposes of study, I believe.

He frowns.

She is not a specimen. She is a person.

A wild girl.

A person. No one has the right.

Her parents.

Who are her parents?

They are not discovered. I told you. No one has come forward. But stop this, for the love of God. Never mind the damned girl. You show more interest in her than in the memory of our son.

Perhaps because she brings him closer to me.

Oh, but you talk rot. As always you talk rot. She gets up and fixes her hat again. Please bring my coat.

Without a word he fetches it. She puts it on and winds the thick muffler at the neck.

I want to go to his grave. Her words a whisper now, barely audible. I do not need you to come with me. I shall find it.

But Peyre puts on his coat and they walk out together into the wind that is blowing down from the hill.

You can see kites circling here, he says, on a calm day.

She pushes open the iron gate without waiting for him to lead the way and she walks at once toward the stone. He wonders how she knows, not realizing the path he has worn over the wiry grass. At the grave she kneels down and draws a small packet from her coat pocket. She unwraps it and lays the withered violets at the head. And then she is down on her knees, huddled over and rocking, her hands reaching repeatedly to sweep in arcs across the white stone, drawing all that is not there toward her heart, as if she would embrace the grave itself, take it to her as if it, the cold stone, were her child's flesh. As if her breast could flow with new life.

He turns away. The hopelessness of the gesture is abhorrent. He has found a way to manage. He has found a way to live. This is a return to the first day. He leaves her and walks back down. If he stays a moment longer he too might find himself on his knees, clawing at the stone.

He is in the kitchen when she comes down from the hill.

I've warmed some soup, he says.

A little bread will do, if you have any.

Will you not eat soup?

She says she will be pleased to try.

They sit together.

As she concentrates on her soup, Peyre tries to read her face. The same beauty there, but hardened. Her lips more sharply defined, her eyes more hooded, more deeply set. But the same beauty. He cannot stop watching, so long has he kept himself from the company of women. The mesdames who pestered him with their inquisitive sympathy that first year did not qualify. They had been to him as flies he wanted to swat away.

Her long fingers, he sees, have turned white, as if the wind has sucked the warmth from them.

Why did you come?

I came because I remembered. You seemed so close. He seemed so close.

I have spent the last fourteen years trying to stay close. You have only just thought?

The Giles you brought here is not my son. That is a remnant, a rag.

You cannot accuse. You cannot.

And you can?

Their words now like heavy blows about the head long after the cause of conflict has disappeared.

You who killed him. You who tore him out of his grave.

There. With unhinged limbs and a bloodied face stark in the air between them. It is out.

Sleep in the bed. I shan't bother you. It's upstairs. You'll see.

He leaves her at the table and goes outside. And there in the fading light, he stands in terror of what more she might conjure between the two of them — the three of them. For here is his son again, or not his son as he knows him now in all his careful memorizing, alive and running, but his son in ruin and all the world turning to night as if the trees are bleeding darkness from their leaves.

The day had begun like any other. The men and the boy with them quiet as they walked out, the dogs tense with excitement, but the dogs quiet too, contained and already working, paying mind. The pup, more than a year then, was showing all the signs of growing into an excellent duck dog. It was his third outing with shooters. Peyre had already taken him out with Giles, just the two of them, and Peyre's own dog. It had obeyed his orders, lain quiet when commanded. Toward the end of the second hunt, Giles had been allowed to give it the command to fetch and it had sprung into the water like pure joy. It might itself have been propelled by gunpowder. It had plunged through the shallows, wings of water flaring up on either side, making repeatedly, unerringly, for the fallen birds until it had brought back all four. Even so that morning, that third day, Peyre was going to leave it at the cottage when he took de Villiers out, for de Villiers had brought along a young dog of his own and Peyre did not know how mindful it would be. But Giles begged, and Frédéric, who was coming too, said, Let it come. It will learn. And so they had walked together through the dawn, feeling the cool air on their faces like water from a stream.

Giles set out the decoy ducks. He had made one of them himself and was proud of it. And Peyre was proud of his son for not announcing the fact. The boy was all business and attention. They settled together on the two wooden pontoons Peyre had built there in the cover of the reeds. De Villiers was impressed with the improvements Peyre had made by adding a sturdy rail in places. The hunters could now lie prone, resting their firing pieces on the rail so that they could take the birds as low as possible, or they could kneel, bracing the bent knee against the rail for stability. When everyone was ready, Peyre and Frédéric began to call. The marsh was very quiet. The rosiness in the east was giving way gradually to blue. Giles whispered to his dog whenever it showed signs of restlessness. You try, said Peyre. You're a good caller.

Frédéric and Giles called together, their voices calling and answering on the early air. It was a kind of music. And the ducks came. They saw them coming in high and they waited until the birds were all but committed to land, and then de Villiers's dog was up and before it could be stopped had leapt into the water. Peyre shouted, 'Hold fire,' and in silence they watched the ducks wheel and rise, the dog still thrashing in the water.

He can remember Giles's face as he watched de Villiers beat his dog. Then he saw the boy cover his mouth and bend to whisper something in the pup's ear. The pup licked him.

After that de Villiers was more careful. They waited for about twenty minutes and then began to call again. Giles saw them first, new birds this time coming in from the opposite direction and already low, perhaps already headed for the marsh. The boy and the dog were so quick, so quick. The dog pulling out backwards from under Giles's arm where he lay and Giles at the same instant beginning to rise to block him. The dog launched itself from Giles's shoulder as he struggled to push himself up to stand. It was already too late when he turned to shout. Frédéric and Peyre were firing.

Peyre can remember how the world darkened in an instant as if his own head, his own eyes, had suddenly filled with blood. His ears were filled with its booming, and the sounds of all the world — cries, gunshots, ducks, dogs, men, wind and water — became the sound of his son's name in his throat.

And Giles unmoving. His red blood pooling, mercifully masking.

He remembers his desperate panic, his self inside himself clawing to escape his slow body, clawing to get out, to be outside himself and to haul what was happening, what would always be happening, what would have always happened, back into the moment before. But his body refused to free his self and his mouth was willfully crying out the words he can never forget: *I have shot my son!* But in memory now he hears another voice, not his, detach from the booming, and another word, not his, shake loose and forge onto his own. It is a word he did not speak, would have no reason to speak. It is his own name: *I have shot Peyre's son!*

Peyre feels a constriction at his chest. It is hard to breathe. He begins to recite a list in his head, searching for a way not to see more, searching for refuge. It is no use. He needs to look. He needs to see it all: Frédéric's white face, his shaking hands, de Villiers taking aim inexplicably at the dogs, Giles's dog running, running.

He stands outside until he is exhausted with looking. There is nothing more to see. Every star in the universe is shining overhead.

Later, staring out of the kitchen window, as he washes Mathilde's plate, he holds his thoughts steady. He had never abandoned the list, only put it aside. His refuge. And she has driven him to it all over again. He may make a new list. There are other things than bee orchids and birds' wings to consider.

THERE IS NO restoring what is lost, Mathilde. I do try, you know. It is what I do.

She draws in her breath sharply and looks away. She has been up to the churchyard again this morning. When she came down, Peyre had prepared warm milk, set out fresh goat cheese for her and some dried figs.

Will you let me show you?

Your stuffed animals?

Yesterday she had had to go back into the hall to confirm what she thought she had seen when she entered—a fox curled in a chair, two magpies at the top of the stairs. The wolf.

You know I hated all that.

It fed us, helped to.

I hated it.

He wants to say this is not the same.

Stay there?

When he comes back he is carrying something in his cupped hands, like an egg. He sets it on the table in front of her. I can pack this for your journey back. Or I can send it.

It is a nest of grass, thick walled and finely woven, its sides bowing out and slightly in again at the top to form the shape of a bowl. Inside all is movement, for it is lined with the blunt, round feathers of an owl. Their down lifts and waves under her breath, a mist moving airily over whatever lies concealed there.

She uses the backs of her fingers to move it aside.

You're giving me a dead mouse?

A dormouse. It is preserved. Though he might have said, It is my heart. It is for you.

It is very small. Curled there it is not as big as a plum. She withdraws her hand. The down settles again over the mouse.

As I said—

But she cannot say it again. She has seen his eyes.

You can parcel it up for me.

And she does not know if she is mad at herself or mad at her maddening husband — who surely knew how so small a gift would create such vast uncertainty.

You know there is no forgiving, don't you?

It is not from you I need forgiveness. I'm not looking for forgiveness. Not from God and not from you.

And how has he done that, taken the dart she aimed and deflected it? Its path leads somewhere else altogether.

I'm not talking about the accident. You live with what you have done. But moving him, Peyre...moving him. You desecrated his peace. There is no forgiving that.

Then she sees herself suddenly as he does, blind and helpless, stranded in her own pain with no help ever, for he comes to her without a word and draws her to him. And where she had thought to feel the thin satisfaction of pity for him she feels only an unexpected warmth, and does not know the source of it.

Peyre thinks of many things to say, standing there, his eyes closed, his arms around his wife, his heart breaking open with pity for her and for himself too, his heart breaking with love of who they had been and could never be again. The words are too many. They are too dangerous. But life might expand for them, make room. Nothing stays the same. That is the only certainty.

After a while he says, Would you like to walk? We can watch for Léon on his way back.

At the grave again, he leaves Mathilde alone with her memories and her prayers. Afterwards there is little to say until Léon arrives like some envoy from the living bringing the clatter of wheels on stone, the creak of leather and iron. It is a relief to be able to listen to his news of his journey that interests them not at all. When the horse is fed and watered and Léon has taken his own refreshment, Peyre goes with Mathilde to the cart. He kisses her on both cheeks with great formality before he helps her up. As Léon snaps the reins, she says, Dieu te garde, Peyre. He cannot tell if it is love or pity that moves her.

He walks after that for most of the afternoon, no longer needing to submit to the urge to return to the grave, wishing he could lie there until the sod folds him under, wishing he had died in place of Giles. She had brought it all back with her. And he had looked without flinching at what he needed to see. He walks for hours over the hills, conscious of the unforgiving blue above him. He walks until he can see the sky for what it is, a gift of great beauty. He walks until he can receive its blessing. For Giles. For himself and for Mathilde.

The light is failing fast by the time he returns to the house. He goes into the kitchen and out of habit reaches for a bowl, a spoon. He ladles cold soup from the day before and carries it to the table, training his mind on the features of the linnet. But even as he sits down to eat, the contours of the bird vanish and he sees his own mind, clear and pure as the pale green sky beyond the window. Slowly, insistently, an image of his son's face takes shape on its limitless field, and he allows it. His son's twelve-year-old face, whole and perfect.

He is calmer when he goes with a lantern to the orangerie.

He lights a few candles and sits for a long time in his created, flickering world seeing its beauty and seeing for the first time its lack. For perfect beauty is a state of change. Always about to vanish. That is its power. Giles young again, years before the accident. Giles so young that he held his hand while they walked. Giles too young to frame the question every child must ask. They were walking back down to the cottage from the hill where Peyre had been hunting rabbits. They had two for the pot. The question had arrived swiftly, like a falcon dropping from the deeps of the sky. Me too? Giles had said. Shall I die also? And Peyre remembers looking down and seeing Giles's upturned face and seeing there the answer his son already knew, alive in the boy's eyes, like darkness roiling, about to consume the last gleam of gold.

Peyre rubs his palms up over his face, as if he has just woken up. He gets up. Every creature seeming to watch. He goes to the stereoscope he has set up and looks through the eyepieces. There she is, the girl, caught eternally in the act of escaping.

And the words come from nowhere:

As I am.

So suddenly the words arrive, and so clearly, they might have come from someone in the room. He sees himself, forever escaping, not just from the past, but from the moment, the moment of his habitation, the moment of his life. He had promised his son he would live for him, would know the world for him completely. And yet he is not living, not here in his workshop. He was living when he had watched the girl eat. He was living when he had set the gift in front of his wife.

The parcel lies unwrapped at the bottom of Mathilde's box. She has had to stand on a chair to place it on top of the armoire out of sight.

Sitting down to dinner with Alain, she expects it to melt through the piece of furniture, through the rug, the floor-boards. She almost expects to see it melt through the ceiling above them.

How did you find your aunt?

She is not well. She is not well at all.

Are the doctors no help?

A little. They give her something for the pain in her heart, but she breathes so little. She is getting weaker all the time.

I'm sorry to hear that.

It is difficult.

Have you ordered the meat for tomorrow?

I have not. I'll see to it this morning.

Good. I have to be at the college until four. Make sure you pay the dairyman. Berthe says he has been asking.

He kisses her lightly on the cheek, drains the last of his chocolate and leaves.

She goes upstairs. When she is sure he is not coming back, she climbs on the chair again and takes down the box. She takes out the package from her husband. She cannot keep it. There would be no explaining so strange a thing or why she wants it.

She unties the string and opens the paper to look at it again. Something alone, terribly alone. And yet protected. Enveloped by softness, hidden in it. The vitality of the down softens the pain of the loneliness. She wraps it up again carefully and carries it downstairs to write a note, tucking it under the string when she has finished.

A curiosity for your collection. Anonymous.

Then she takes it with her to the Jardin des Plantes, where she slides it through the bars of the gate to rest on the gravel inside, before she goes back, calling at the butcher's on the way.

Alain says that night that it sounds as if her aunt needed some good red meat.

She does not answer, but says, after a few moments, I may well have to go back.

Five

ALMOST EVERY DAY after the girl's capture, the boy Felip was late for school. He knew she was put outside at nine o'clock and so he dallied with purpose, taking little detours until he arrived at the square at five past nine. And there she would be, her leash attached to a ring in the wall of the church.

They had cut her hair off at the neck. It belonged to neither boy nor girl now, sticking out stiff and crazy just above her shoulders. They had dressed her in a white nightshift, a leather belt around the waist to which her leash was tied. The shift was splashed and stained, its long sleeves hanging down to her knuckles. Her brown shins stuck out below. They had a sheen to them.

He saw that she liked to sway, standing with her weight against the leash, pulling it taut and sawing at the air with her stiff body. Lately, he would see her squatting down, hugging her knees and rocking back and forth, clumped, staring, always staring though she seemed to see nothing, certainly not him. Slumped there, she might have been a marionette waiting for the puppet master's hands. She did not look like anyone who could outrun a village and leap into a gorge. Still, he was fascinated, hoping always to see the flash of fire return.

The schoolmaster grew tired of Felip's lateness. He kept him after school for every minute that he missed. It did not make any difference. Once or twice Felip had seen the girl when she was neither rocking nor swaying. Wildly alert, she was then another girl entirely. And when once she met his eye, she was the girl from another place, the girl he was looking for. He could not stay away.

And then one morning she was not there at all. It was raining and he thought that was the reason, but the next day was clear and fine and the steps were again empty. He wondered what they were doing with her, hoped outrageously that he would find her at school and ran there faster than he ever had before.

I see she is gone then. His mother fished out shreds of rabbit from the pot, ladled onions to place beside them on his plate. No one's claimed her. And just as well. For her, I mean. You can imagine the parents.

He could not. He could not imagine parents of any kind. For him, she had come fully formed from the mountain.

Someone should have taken her in, his mother continued, and his father — winking aside at Felip — said to her, Why didn't you?

Someone who could afford to keep a girl, his mother said. Someone who could train her, civilize her.

Did you see her?

I see her — said Felip and quickly stopped. I saw her one Thursday on my way home.

His father ignored him anyway. She was like a beast, dirty thing. You wouldn't want her crawling all around your house, smearing her filth over everything. And you especially would not want her near your chickens. He laughed aloud and all of them could see again the girl as she lived now in local legend, tearing the head off a chicken with her teeth.

Madame Maraval shook her head. Very sad, she said. But they're taking her to Montpellier.

Well, that would be the best place, if you ask me. Somewhere she can be kept apart and not endanger others.

The boy saw his father mouth the words 'lunatic asylum.' He'd heard the words before. He would ask next day at school.

In the morning Felip dawdled yet again. The steps of the church seemed somehow special now, as if she had left her shadow there, or her taint. But it was a hollow feeling he had. As if the idea of angels was suddenly lifted out of the world, leaving only himself and others — everyone else — like him. Poor humans.

When he arrived at the school, Raoul was there under the olive tree. He had a crowd of boys around him. The boy pressed in to see. Raoul had a slate and chalk. He had drawn the figure of a girl with tiny pointed breasts. She was leaping from a cliff. One of the boys said, Here, took the slate and the chalk, and drew a stream of piss between her legs.

IN HIS WORKSHOP Peyre felt the ghost of Mathilde's cold gaze over his shoulder, and each day he achieved less. When he walked through the house looking for validation, some reminder of why this work of his was important, he did not find it. The house was filled with dead animals. They had lost their mysterious power to speak to him and the world they beheld behind the glass eyes had vanished. He was haunted by questions concerning the girl — where she was, how she was being cared for; if she were being treated well, or punished for her brutishness. And did she keen still? Was she mourning her liberty? Or did they let her run somewhere, free to breathe the air? For him, the girl had meant possibility. Possibility where none before existed. The simple fact of her existence had once been a comfort, connecting him to something vital in the world. And now there was no possibility, none.

His solitude now was vast as the massif across the valley, empty and without end. He walked up to the churchyard and there under the wind it seemed to him the boy too was sleeping, with his face turned away. Even pain had fled, and his heart was a blind creature, turning its face this way and that to catch the sense of another.

He thought of journeying down, going over to Freyzus to tell them what he knew of her, how she suffered if she was contained, but how she was quick to learn — and then he saw quite clearly the averted glances of the townspeople, their overt stares at his back as he walked away. He heard their whispers and told himself he could not do it—when what he really feared was to look the girl in the eye and then to have to leave her.

But then came the day Arthur Trochet thought it fine enough make his postman's journey up to Aveyrac, bringing with him a piece of mail that had been languishing, against all the regulations, in his house. Peyre made a sudden decision.

The letter was from Mathilde. Folded inside was a page of the *Gazette de France*. She wrote that she did not know if he would be pleased to hear from her, but she expected he might care to learn the piece of news she had for him. She had enclosed it, she wrote. And that was all. He sat down to read the article.

WILD GIRL OF FREYZUS

The Wild Girl of Freyzus, exhibited without result for a period of four weeks in the towns of both Freyzus and Gougeac, has now been delivered into the care of the esteemed doctor of the deaf, Doctor Bizeul in Montpellier. While it is regrettable that her true parents did not come forward, it is exhilarating to consider the benefits that might accrue to mankind from the study of one so uniquely placed to teach us the hidden origins of our nature. Study of such...

Trochet waited patiently for a reply.

Peyre said there was none. He offered a glass of wine and in his turn waited. When Trochet had finished, he got up to go. Peyre walked with him to his horse and held its head while he mounted.

One thing you could do for me, though, said Peyre. Could you put out word that I need to go away for several days? I'll be bringing my animals down when I come. My aunt is no longer living. I'll need someone for them.

Is it bad news?

Peyre frowned. When he answered, he looked the postman in the eye. I don't know, he said. I really don't know.

The postman picked up his cap, thinking it was perhaps the first time he had seen Peyre Rouff so defenceless — and the first time he had looked him in the eye.

You can leave your animals with us, he said. My mother never has enough eggs. He brushed the dust off his cap and put it on.

That night Peyre stayed at the churchyard late. He did not take a bottle with him. He listened to the wind and watched until the moon had silvered the grasses. There was no one here. No one.

In the morning, while he was dressing, he put what money he had into the inside pocket of his jacket. He packed a clean shirt, a flask of water, a cup, and a few potatoes in a haversack, and tied a piece of sacking over his back. With his chickens closed in a basket and hoisted over his shoulders, he set out down the hill, the goat running ahead of him. He thought about taking the shortcut over the top and down to the bridge but decided against it, the basket too cumbersome for the steep descent. He did not look back.

Madame Trochet, when she saw him approaching her house, let the two dogs out. The chickens in their cage made a racket behind his head as he turned and turned to protect them. Madame Trochet came running, finally, shouting at the dogs.

But you look like a tramp, she said, smacking his arm with the back of her hand so that it seemed to be smoking in the sunlight where the dust flew. Look at you. Am I supposed to know who you are in this state?

She called to the dogs again for now they were barking at the goat, which had fled up the embankment at the side of the road.

We'll go in, she said. She'll come down eventually.

She shut up the dogs and took Peyre inside. The chickens inside their basket shifted nervously, complained, and finally settled. Madame Trochet wanted to know what he did to encourage them to lay.

He shrugged. They lay when they want to. He said he did not expect anything from her. If they produced chicks from her rooster she could keep them, he said, and raise them for her own, if she had the inclination.

And where exactly are you going for so long? Across the sea?

I'm going to Montpellier, he said.

To look for your wild girl? You know what people are saying?

He shook his head.

That you conjugated.

~~Her face turned crimson and for her sake he looked away.~~

And some say she is a daughter of yours, born the year you went up to the chateau. That there was a serving girl up there at that time.

And now he felt he owed her nothing and turned to look her directly, brutally, in the eye.

And others? Others might say she is the reincarnation of my son? No? Yes?

So that it was her turn to look away, shamed. He felt a little sorry.

But the chickens, he said. You know what makes them lay? Salt on their tails, just a little, but every day. He stood up. Salt, now, he said. You won't forget? He smiled.

She brushed his sleeve lightly and said, I have a coat of my husband's still, Monsieur Rouff. It would fit you.

He put his hands to the lapels of his jacket and tugged it straight and as he did so saw the stains and the frayed cuffs as if for the first time.

Would you like to try it?

Do you have trousers too?

He looked more sane as well as more respectable, she thought, when he had changed. The coat, green velvet, was old and out of date but still in good condition. Her husband had worn it to mass. She had always made him take it off when they got back to the house, the material so expensive, the desire not to spoil it so strong.

She watched Peyre walk away and begin climbing up into the garrigue. The coat bulged noticeably even from a distance. He was walking all the way up to Ceresc, he had told her, and at Ceresc he would board the coach for Montpellier. Good luck, she thought. You will look like a vagrant by the time you get there. But, so! She had a good story to tell. How he had rolled her late husband's trousers in a ball and put them in his haversack to wear later. How she could see they would be thoroughly rumpled when he drew them out again. And how, then, just when she thought he was all ready and looking quite handsome too, he had felt in the pockets of his old jacket and had drawn out—wait for this—several small potatoes, which he carefully transferred, one by one, to the pockets of her husband's coat. They did not improve the look of it at all.

THE CONCIERGE AT the Institut des Sourds-Muets in Montpellier looked this visitor over.

When the man said he would like to see Doctor Bizeul, he told him firmly that all patients were required to report round the corner at the door on Rue Saint Croix.

Peyre said he was not a patient.

The concierge said all the relatives of patients reported there too. And some of them, he wanted to add, would do well to commit themselves too—by the looks of them.

At Rue Saint Croix an elderly valet answered the door.

The concierge sent me. It was not the best introduction Peyre could have made. He removed his hat, but the valet stood firm.

To see the girl.

The door was already closing.

In the care of Doctor Bizeul. She was found on my property.

The valet stopped. He had expected another cooked-up story about a long-lost daughter. The men who had come to the door so far had been particularly unconvincing.

Oh, yes? he said and one white eyebrow snagged high on skepticism. You will have to see his assistant. You are?

Monsieur Peyre Rouff. From Chateau d'Aveyrac.

Come in. The valet closed the door to the street. Follow me.

He led the way along the corridor and showed Peyre into a small panelled room, furnished only with a chair.

Please sit down. The doctor will be a while.

Peyre listened to the sound of the man's footsteps receding down the hall. In the quiet that followed, he could have fallen asleep, but the sharp smell of lye kept him alert. He was hungry. A fly spun on its back in the sunlight on the window ledge. After a long while it was still, the silence then a release—until it began again. Twice he heard footsteps, people conversing, but the steps receded and he could not hear what the voices were saying.

He had no idea how long he had been sitting when at last he heard footsteps approaching the door.

An energetic young man looked in.

Are you waiting to see someone?

Doctor Bizeul.

Doctor Bizeul is entertaining a group of visitors from Paris. I believe they've just left for Le Cerisier.

I'm actually here to see the girl from Chateau d'Aveyrac.

I can take you. I'd be happy to.

They left the room, the tiled corridor, the tall windows, and followed several passages. They passed an open door and he glimpsed a group of young women in identical blue gowns, blue ribbons in their hair, a man pointing to letters on a blackboard. They passed another and he saw a table bearing a pyramid of oranges, another blackboard filled with rows of carefully drawn hands, gesturing. They climbed a short flight of stairs to an open walkway and descended again into what appeared to be another building altogether, the walls here bare, the small windows high, the floors flagged in stone.

When he heard the noise he knew it was her. She was keening, the sound high and chilling and filled with the grief of all the world.

The assistant laughed. Quite the opera singer, isn't she?

They stopped at a door. The assistant called out as he opened it.

It's only me, Monsieur Étourbes. Don't worry, he said under his breath, there are bars.

And the door did indeed open onto the bars of a cell. The air was foul with the girl's waste. She stood on the other side of the small room with her back to the door. She was dressed in a brown shift and her head was shaved. She had her face raised to the high window as she wailed. Peyre could see red welts and what looked like blood on her scalp.

I think she's been scratching again, said the young man. *Virginie!*

She did not turn round.

It's what we've called her, he said, Virginie. But she doesn't answer. *Virginie!*

What's wrong with her head?

Her head? Oh, we had to cut her hair. She was pulling it out. Yes, I mean it, in handfuls. She would just take a handful, a whole clump, and tear slowly until it came away.

He shook his head. Handfuls! She scratches now. And I believe the doctor said she's started on her eyebrows. If we can get her to come over, we can see. *Virginie!*

The girl stopped crying and turned her head slightly.

I think she's—

But there was no one beside the young man to hear his opinion. He closed the door and hurried back the way they had come. The visitor was not in the waiting room. He went to the front door. There were potatoes—good potatoes—lying on the ground.

PEYRE WAS A presence in the town. He more than filled the vacuum left by the girl. The sight of him in the street was a challenge to be negotiated. For you had to acknowledge him. You could not just look the other way. That would be too obvious. It would all have been so much easier if only he looked a little more normal. He had on the coat old Trochet used to wear to mass and when he raised his hat you could see his hair was all in tangles. Even the way he walked drew attention. He strode, covering ground as if he were a travelling player on stilts, the long coat flaring out behind. But still it was not that. No, it was the look that had come upon him. The unsettling blankness of his gaze had been replaced with something driven and wild. No one would want to stand in his way.

Ramon Pailhès, when Peyre went to see him, was conscious that he was sitting across from someone who had discarded all the usual courtesies and civilities. Here was a man who had surrendered all rational thought to the dictates of some private delusion.

She's your ward. You can do something.

She's out of my hands.

Then get her back.

Pailhès looked at Peyre Rouff. The way he was talking you would think the girl was his own flesh and blood. He considered the blunt demand. He thought about Rouff's need and he thought his about his own interests and he decided to continue the conversation a little longer.

And what would I do with her here?

You would set her free.

The mayor shook his head with a sharp movement like a terrier, as if having the idea between his teeth, he would like to break its back at once. Are you mad?

You have to bring her back. She is your responsibility.

Ramon Pailhès was getting tired of the refrain. I beg to differ, he said. The Institute is the proper place. Somewhere she can be studied, somewhere she can be taught.

She is turning into a savage.

She *is* a savage, if you remember. The town's duty extends only to her physical needs. She is being housed and fed.

Her physical condition is deteriorating. She is in a state of neglect. If you could see her...

I repeat: she is being housed and fed.

In the name of common decency bring her back.

There is no home for her here.

She wants no home. Just bring her back. Proceed from there.

There is no reason, Monsieur Rouff, for me to do so. No incentive. I'm sure you understand.

But it's in your power.

Of course. But without some incentive... Cooperation works both ways.

For a moment Peyre thought he was being asked to contribute to the coffers. But the pause was gravid, a rolling train coming to a stop, the weight of all the carriages behind almost palpable, and all that they contained in the way of past discussions, arriving in the present. Peyre knew what he was expected to do.

If, for instance, said Pailhès, we were to see eye to eye where water is concerned...

The seigneur—

Monsieur de Villiers will not be back. We both know that. You have the chance to make restitution on his behalf. Right a wrong. And get what you want at the same time.

It would mean changes...

Of course. For my part, I might be able to help. The girl would no doubt thank you — if she could speak. I know the town of Freyzus would. And the town could supply all the necessary labour too. That goes without saying. An incentive makes everything so much easier. For both of us.

It will take time. She should be removed now.

The mayor tried to keep a steady gaze, tried at all costs not to betray the perfectly sharp and clear impression he had that he was taking advantage of this man slightly astray in his mind.

I'll send the men to help you. And I'll write to Doctor Bizeul.

You'll write today?

Of course.

Pailhès looked down at his desk, as if his letter were already composing itself on the dark surface of the wood. There really was no need for Peyre Rouff to know that Doctor Bizeul had already notified him of the girl's immediate return from the Institute. They had no further use of her. She was, the letter had said, quite untrainable.

And I'll engage an engineer to work with you.

Peyre Rouff nodded, looking him straight in the eye, Pailhès noticed. Surely a good sign.

They shook hands at the door.

You are a good man, Peyre Rouff. You have always been a good man.

THE MAYOR ASSIGNED six labourers and requested the services of an engineer from Gougeac. Two days later the men were at work restoring the walls of the old reservoir with stones and with clay they dug from the hill. The engineer in service to Mayor Pailhès might have found his work easier if only he had had access to notes and drawings from the time when the first comte d'Aveyrac harnessed the waters, but all records had disappeared when the family fled the Terror. Still, the engineer was hopeful that the reservoir's water supply could be restored.

He made an investigation of the entire east-west ridge behind the house. His findings suggested the place where the stream had once emerged from the hill to feed the reservoir. It should be possible, he said, to re-establish the original flow of the water. They would have to close off the sluices at the upper level and trust the water to rediscover its original course underground. It might take a while. Meanwhile they would prepare a new wooden béal at the outlet in the west to carry the water directly overground to the reservoir. Where gates had seized, they would have to be freed with a sledge and would likely be broken. New gates and gears in any case would need to be forged for the new reservoir. The engineer left orders for the construction of the new béal and returned to Gougeac, with a promise to come back after two weeks.

And so Peyre found his sanctuary, his shelter from the world, open suddenly, like a patient laid open under the hands of the physician, to the world's intrusion. A forge was fired, stone broken, mortar mixed. There was a small amount of board in one of the outbuildings, not nearly sufficient. Peyre surprised himself. He heard his own voice suggesting that the cypress trees up at the church had outgrown themselves. They could be thinned to half their number.

He opened two rooms in the house for the men to make their beds. The men behaved at first with wary reverence, as before the offerings of a madman. They skirted the she-wolf in the hall and passed politely by the line of rabbits on the landing, resisting the urge to entertain each other with growls and barks.

While they drifted to sleep composing tales to tell at home of the grandeur and the strangeness of their lodgings, Peyre lay awake, and knew himself cut loose, like a boat drifting from the harbour mouth. He gave himself to the swell.

As the preparation of the reservoir went ahead, Peyre turned to his own work. He started on the orangerie first, where he swept the floor, which would soon be underwater. He had intended to pack up the viewing apparatus and the plate of the girl to take with him but now he thought better of it. Her frozen image belonged in his Eden, forever running. He dusted off the mounts, content to leave them in their silence. They had told him all they had to say. He left them in their appointed places and locked the door on his created world. In his workshop, he collected his tools and equipment from the bench, selecting only his favourites for packing. He cleaned the shelves and drawers and put the rest away. He was a steward and he would leave all in good order.

By the time the engineer returned, a week later than anticipated, the béal had been constructed—but no water leapt to its channel. Instead, a dark stain had begun to spread in a thin line across the western slope to the right of the old outlet. It was not what they had hoped for. The engineer said without doubt the blockage could be remedied. Peyre said he would himself go into the hole to investigate. He did not get far before he felt solid stone straight ahead. Or perhaps it was iron. It was cold like iron, and it was wet. He backed out and brushed himself off.

It's a gate, he said. Solid.

They brought a pick to the place and hacked away the thin top layer of wiry sod and the soil under it until they found the stone housing, jammed now at an angle where over time it had slipped down onto the sluice gate itself. The engineer said it would prove easier than he had hoped. A moderate blast was all they would need to clear it. A man was sent to Gougeac for the powder.

The water that issued forth was muddy at first and full of debris. They let it clear before they closed off the upper gate again. Two days later the new béal was repositioned and the engineer himself went to reopen the upper gate. The stream flowed unimpeded. The men at their different lookouts shouted to one another, no one hearing what another was saying, but smiling and knowing anyway.

The engineer stayed on that night to drink to the health of the project. Peyre opened champagne and listened while the men told stories. None of them had ventured beyond Soulières, but stories have a life of their own and travel from place to place like journeymen. They told of mining and road-building, disasters on the new canal, and black powder that ignited of its own accord. Their stories loomed and magnified like shadows on the wall, until by midnight tales of witches were thickening the air and the whiff of the devil had entered the room.

In the morning Peyre and the engineer walked out. A thin stream of water sparkled in the conduit. The ground in the reservoir was beginning to darken. The engineer had done all he could. He shook hands and rode back down.

There was work still to be done. Peyre took the labourers with him to the churchyard and there, despite their grumbling, they began to cut down the remaining trees that blocked the view down to the house and out over the valley. From here a traveller, before he turned to read the headstones, would be able to stand and look out across the reservoir, and marvel at the orangerie rising from the centre of its shining patch of sky. They left the trees where they fell, as if the dead had decreed it.

Peyre had a knife with him to cut away the grass that grew round his son's grave. Instead, he left it as it was, preferring the thought of grasses bowing before the wind, alive with whispers, the sheen in summer on the dry stems, insects buzzing.

The men were anxious to get back to their families, but the reservoir was slow to fill. Peyre sensed that something was amiss, the water rushing as it did to fill the higher pool, and only a thin stream issuing from the hill lower down. He asked the men to stay, and set them to work finishing the waterway that would carry the water from the reservoir and send it on its way to the mill. When they were not working, they roamed the slopes for the last of the wild figs and the first of the almonds and for the tiny red berries that yielded a mealy goodness. They filled a sack that they planned to take back to their families.

Peyre spent his time putting the house in order. He cleaned every room. Some had not been opened in years. He shook out the dustsheets and swept the floors, not replacing the sheets but folding them carefully away, preferring to leave the rooms as if ready for an important visitor, the beaten rugs laid down on the tiles. It was for his son of course, he knew that. He left the doors standing open, the animals keeping watch over the empty rooms. He disturbed only the fox, carried it away to the workshop and there crated it, packing it carefully in shavings and tying the box with a stout cord. It would serve as notice of his skill when he looked for work in the city. Montpellier, he thought, or Paris.

He polished windows and mirrors in the high-ceilinged rooms, imagined the water outside reflected in them, flashing as if a swallow in flight dipped its wing. Attracted perhaps by some trick of the light, a hawk flew in through one of the tall windows of the salon. Caught in the shimmering cage of the chandelier, it clashed its wings against the shining droplets and sent tears of glass crashing and skidding on the tiles. He looked for blood when it was gone and found none.

At night the men drank great quantities of wine and told one another tales of the hunt, not thinking it strange at all to be doing this in the house of Peyre Rouff. And then one night they drank nothing at all and when Peyre got up at dawn they were gone.

He packed a knapsack with his tools and a few belongings. He wanted nothing. He did not need this place or anything that it housed. In a few days he would be able to leave.

From the hill he watched the water while he waited. The floor of the reservoir shone back at the sky, only the tips of the grasses standing here and there above the surface. Still the stream that fed it remained strangely unequal to the supply rushing into the upper pool. Peyre climbed up to where the stream tumbled and hissed. He checked the gates. The upper sluice — that once channelled water away to the south to waste itself in the marsh farther along the valley — was closed fast, the stone of the spillway pale and dry, only traces of weed pasted to the sides. The trout pond was empty, the gate dropped into position. He went back down and inspected the new conduit that carried the redirected water down to the reservoir and he found no fault. He began to think it all an illusion, a discrepancy attributable to the respective inclines of the two water courses. But the engineer had left and he had no way of knowing.

For the second time in a month he walked into Freyzus. He took the long route, carrying the crate on his back.

Madame Trochet was surprised to see him.

She listened and said she thought his plans were good, and she agreed after some persuasion to keep the box for him in, not in her barn — Fox among the chickens, eh? — but in a little stone hut at some distance from the house. Peyre saw her unease and understood the cost of her offer. Her offer was in its own way a gift — in the way the coat had been a gift, and Mathilde's letter, and Blind Henri's silent presence in the tavern. He could see them now for what they were and he was grateful.

But your plan is good, she said again, covering her discomfort. She said he could not live there all alone forever — even with his son. It was, she said, living his life with one foot in the grave.

My son has long since left the grave.

That, she thought, was an ungodly thing to voice, but she kept her opinion to herself.

What will you do? When you come down for the last time?

I shall find my way.

Where will you live?

Where I can find work. Perhaps Montpellier. Paris, even. Somewhere I can teach my craft to younger men.

They need it?

No one needs it.

So, then, why?

Why the flowers? Why the birds, madame? The blue sky? Why your son, Arthur?

My son was a gift.

Exactly.

Madame Trochet did not see the connection at all. She suddenly regretted befriending Peyre, she regretted the fox on her property, and she told herself to be more careful how she embarked on a conversation with him. She hoped sincerely he would choose Paris as a destination. Paris was another country.

Ramon Pailhès sighed and wiped his hand across his face as if removing a cobweb. He said he had written. He said he was expecting her daily. Like the water.

Peyre said it could be many weeks of waiting for the water. The reservoir was proving slow to fill.

Then we must all be patient.

The girl meanwhile is held like a prisoner. You know that.

The mayor tucked his chin in to his chest and drew a deep breath.

Monsieur Rouff. Peyre. I am expecting her. I have told you. But when will you understand she is not our responsibility. Not mine, not yours.

She is a fellow human.

Barely.

And you do have a responsibility. To me. A promise to keep.

Here is my suggestion, Pailhès said. You return to Aveyrac. You watch over the water. When there is sufficient, you release a small stream into the millrace as a sign. We shall then make the journey up to you to see that all is in order and to supervise the opening of the millrace. In the meantime I shall search for a suitable family to take in the girl when she is returned to Freyzus. If one is not found, she shall be sent up to the orphanage at Saint-Affrique, where she will be cared for properly.

Peyre did not answer. This was something new. It was not what he had imagined for the girl. He had imagined the sky lark rising from the high garrigue, the shadow of the kite's wing passing over the grey thyme, the girl running.

The mayor kept his eyes down.

You'll be returning tomorrow, I take it? You need a bed for tonight. You will find one at our house and be welcome to it. He twirled a pen between his fingers as he drew breath for something more. You are like an orphan yourself, he said, gruff with the effort of risking the truth. It is the same thing.

And Peyre, seeing the mayor's effort, and that that too was a gift, could only nod.

The day was not yet over and Peyre had no way to fill the empty hours. The mayor's words resonated. He walked by the church where the girl had been kept and he thought of her there displayed like a curiosity. Thought of her alone among people, as perhaps he was. He was indeed an orphan. The evidence was all around, in the voices of the children at play, in the companionable pipe smoke of the old men under the marronnier.

Peyre sat across the square and watched them. They were simply smoking, gazing into the space before them. There was no need for them to speak. They knew one another's lives as they knew their own bootlaces. He got up and walked on. A young girl at a window was talking to a caged bird that hung there in the last rays of the sun as he passed, while at the door a woman set down milk for a weaving cat. Everywhere he turned this cast of players performed for him. Children running together shouted names at one another and then fell to laughing. Someone in a kitchen knocked a spoon repeatedly on the rim of a pot, stirred again, and called sharply to a child to come and help. Outside Blind Henri's, men who had laboured all day had finished two bottles of cartagène. Two of them rose up from the bench, tussling awkwardly, one falling back, his hand to his face, others shouting. Peyre watched. The man who had been knocked in the face was examining the blood on his hands, but stopped when he realized the others had turned on his friend.

Hey, leave him alone, the man shouted. What are you thinking? He's in his cups, that's all.

Everywhere he turned.

Peyre did not see the mayor's wife when he went to the house. Pailhès greeted him, gruff as before but with words of welcome. His wife had prepared a terrine packed with meat, a plate of bright tomatoes. And then she had gone to her sister's house. To be out of his presence and more at ease, Peyre guessed. Not an orphan but a ghost.

~~He had not eaten such food in years and said so.~~

Madame le Maire says you are to take a slice in your pocket tomorrow.

You are married to a good woman, Monsieur le Maire.

Both men smiled, aware, both, of the courteous reply the mayor could not make: *As are you, Peyre Rouff.*

Mayor Pailhès poured more wine. Peyre Rouff could match him glass for glass.

When they finished the third bottle, Pailhès remarked that they could have come to terms and begun this friendship long ago.

But there's no going back, eh? We go forward from where we are.

The two them raised their glasses and drank to the brilliance of the observation.

So, I'll get a message to the engineer, said Pailhès. Let him know there's a problem and he may have to go up there again. And meanwhile I'll send you a couple of lads. You can put them to work for a day or two.

Now. A nightcap to finish, don't you think?

It was early when Peyre set out again for Aveyrac, the pockets of the green coat filled this time with the chunk of terrine wrapped in a cloth and six boiled eggs. Madame Trochet, when she passed, had not yet opened her shutters.

The day arrived pink and gold, a half moon still visible, hanging in otherworldly blue on the other side of the sky. He climbed up through the old watercourse above the mill, taking the shortest route. A sharp edge to the air made him think of chestnut woods, the crunch of leaves underfoot, smoke. If he looked down and back, he could see the telltale twist of mist along the bottom of the gorge. When he came out at the top, he rested before he went on over the ridge.

The orangerie stood in its shallow lake of sky. The devastation Peyre had wrought in the churchyard looked from here like the work of a petulant child. But he had not been angry, only anxious to leave the churchyard open to the valley, the sky. He would take off some of the limbs while he was waiting, saw them up for fuel. Perhaps someone would come up from Gougeac when he was gone and haul it away. Someone should.

He walked on down to check on the water. He saw it had risen, for he had been marking the level in the stone wall each day, but it had a way to go before there would be enough to release.

The mayor sent the promised men up to Aveyrac. He chose Stéphane, who was good and solid in all he did, and Raoul. No one really knew what to do with Raoul this year: big enough now to be called a man, trouble enough still to be mistaken for a schoolboy. Stéphane might be an influence for good.

Raoul did not want to go. Life in Freyzus was just getting interesting again. He had seen the girl arrive the day before, when Doctor Ayash and the carter from Gougeac bundled her into the doctor's house. He had gone to the school gates that afternoon to impress the lesser mortals there.

He told them he had a plan.

It will be easy, he said. She's only guarded by the old woman. I don't have to be here at all, he said. I'm finished with school. I just come sometimes because Monsieur le Professeur needs me. But I'm free. Not like you. I'm free to go wherever I please in the world and make my way.

The happy knack he had never lost. Standing before an awed group of the not-quite-grown, making himself the sole attraction. Turning young lads' eyes into saucers, their mouths into ever-open beaks receiving his holy word.

It's easy. When I put my plan in place no one will even realize she's gone until it's too late. I'll be halfway up to Ceresc with her before they even know she's missing, or perhaps down past Soulières—I'm not telling you where we're going. I'm not stupid, am I? And I'll have the world at my feet when I've got her. People will pay, you know, good money to see a wild girl. The Wild Girl of the Garrigue, I'll call her. And I'll take all her clothes away and make her go on all fours...

But Raoul never did get the chance to even attempt such an escapade. His father agreed with the mayor. He said he had to go to Aveyrac. It was time he made himself useful.

You may have to be up there for a while, the mayor told Stéphane before they left, but as soon as there's enough water I expect to see it turning that wheel. He'll act in good faith, I know he will. You're just there, you understand, to assist in any way you can.

Raoul and Stéphane took their time at first, going the long way round, enjoying a meal, stretching out on the warmed ground afterwards, and enjoying the thought that they were being paid for their time. But as they went on, they felt a coolness in the air, and they noticed the bank of cloud massing over the hills to the north. The prospect of staying under the same roof as Mad Peyre Rouff began to impress itself on Raoul and he was not the same bold youth who had stood at Peyre's door last year. When they arrived they saw the piles of displaced earth, a small mountain of rocks to move who knew where. Raoul hoped Stéphane would do the talking, but he hoped too that Stéphane would keep quiet about the mayor's instructions. He could see they would lead straight to the mountain of rocks.

Peyre Rouff came out to meet them and they shook hands.

The mayor says, said Stéphane straight away, that we are to help you in any way we can.

Good, said Peyre. A man can always use good help. Nor did it seem to him so foreign, this new language of amenability. He smiled.

Come. I'll show you where.

They walked to the tunnel the engineer had located in the ridge. Peyre said he wanted to reinforce the wooden béal that would carry the water from the reservoir to the tunnel. He showed them the new-sawn planks, the tools standing by, and he left them.

At least we're not hauling rocks, said Stéphane.

You just see, he said to Raoul that night in their room on the third floor, we'll be home in a couple of days. As soon as that water's high enough.

Not soon enough, said Raoul from the bed. He did not like the work and he did not like the place at all, the taxidermy, the huge furniture, the chairs with the high backs, so you weren't really sure there was no one sitting there. And the pairs of staring eyes everywhere you turned. Including Rouff's.

Do you think this place is haunted? he asked while Stéphane was undressing.

By?

The girl. Some people say that girl we caught is not human. She is the ghost of herself.

Don't listen to such stupidity.

By the dead boy, then. Ah, I've been shot! I've been shot!

Raoul rolled grotesquely with his hands over his face.

Stop it, Raoul. Say a prayer. Stéphane blew out the candle and Raoul was quiet.

I've heard that Peyre Rouff is loaded, he said before he fell asleep. When Stéphane didn't reply he said it again. Stéphane roused.

Loaded with birdshot in his own brain, Raoul whispered, giggling. He's mad. A raven on the maudit bedrail, didn't you see? Right down there at the foot of the bed. But he had his own eyes squeezed shut as he turned over.

From his perch in the fig tree in the Chemin des Ramparts behind Doctor Ayash's house, Felip can see into the garden. Like the other boys, Felip had taken in every word of Raoul's that afternoon outside the school. But the others had gone into their class and had forgotten all about it as soon as the daily torments of the classroom closed in. Unlike Felip. He watches the garden.

The doctor's wife brings her out. They have dressed her in a bright white shift. Her hair, no longer than the bristles on a scrubbing brush, sticks out from her head in all directions. The boy thinks of stubble in the fields after it has been burned, some of it still standing. She is no longer on a leash. Where, after all, would she go? The garden is contained by walls of its own that butt up against the wall of the old path behind. Madame le Docteur watches her for a minute or two and then goes inside. The girl continues to stand in the very centre of the garden. She raises her face to the sky and remains perfectly still. Breathing. As if her eyes are breathing sky. Felip makes himself small on his branch, watching her carefully. Afraid she will see him and attract attention, he slips down in one smooth movement and regains the path.

All day he thinks of her. The rhythm of his body has changed. His pulse has quickened. In the afternoon he runs to the ruined tower next to the church. It is farther off, but it still gives some view of the garden. She is not there. It does nothing to settle him. His belly remains charged with energy. It upsets his appetite and keeps him from sleep.

He leaves the house early next morning and half walks, half runs along the passage behind the houses until he reaches the wall of the Ayash garden. The fig tree seems ready to scoop him up. He jumps to grab hold of a low branch. Fragments of stone from the wall come loose under his feet as he pulls his way up and hauls himself onto the next branch. Perched there again waiting for her appearance is its own excitement. His breath takes on a ragged rhythm and he fights to control it.

And there she is, ambling listlessly, with the way of a shackled bear, to the centre of the garden. She lets her hands fall to her sides and gazes skyward again, turns once, twice, and stands still. She stands a long time there. He is about to leave when he sees her start toward the wall where a bird has landed farther along. He does not move. When she draws near the bird, she raises her arms and it flies off. She takes another step and lets her body fall forward against the wall, flattening herself, measuring herself against its height. Her fingertips reach almost to the top. The last he sees, before he ducks out of sight, she is still there. Still reaching for the bird.

She is like no girl or boy in the town. He has never seen a girl so clothed. It makes her seem an angel, or a saint in a church. But no angel has such a strange, mad appearance as she with her wild hedgehog hair. He longs to put the palm of his hand on her head.

He thinks of the stories of the girl flinging herself against closed doors. And then he thinks of her leaping clear in the shining air above the water.

I shall not be here in the morning, the schoolmaster says on Wednesday. The priest is coming to take roll call and then he will oversee the calculations I am about to give you. Those being completed, you will study our three verses of the *Aeneid* until noon.

At his desk, the boy begins to dream. He sees the girl reaching up from her side of the garden wall. He sees himself, one foot hooked for safety on the limb of the fig outside, reaching down. And he sees — no, he feels — their fingers touch.

The dream consumes him. Nothing occurs between the sound of the schoolmaster's voice and the touch of their fingers. Nothing. The world stands on its axis while the sun and the moon and the stars pass overhead. His heart runs on. That is all he knows. His heart running and running beyond the classroom walls. Running toward possibility. Through leaf and stone, through water, light, through darkness and through void. His heart carries him past the voices of his family, past his doubts and fears and into that bright clear Thursday.

Doubling back from the road to the school, the boy takes the Chemin des Ramparts. No one sees him. He puts down his bundle and leans against the trunk of the fig tree to catch his breath, and then he climbs.

Madame le Docteur is with her. He draws back and lowers himself behind the wall again. In a little while he hears the girl's voice rising unnaturally, laying out a high-pitched plaint upon the air. Again and again she returns to the note, her voice a stone on a string whirled about her head. Around and around and no rest ever.

She reels him in. He climbs back to his vantage point. The doctor's wife has gone. The girl sees him at once and she pitches her voice even higher. But she does not move or turn toward the house — out of which at any moment Felip expects to see Madame Ayash come running.

But Madame le Docteur is well accustomed to the girl's strange noises signifying nothing she can comprehend. Even when Felip joins his voice in perfect pitch with the girl's, she hears nothing to be concerned about. Or perhaps she does not hear. But the girl hears. She stops her noise at once. He rummages quickly in his pocket for one of the apples he has brought. And just as he dreamed on his bench at school, he hooks his foot on the branch for an anchor and leans down over the stone wall. He takes care to hold the bright apple by the stalk so she can clearly see it.

She runs low to the ground and stands at the base of the wall looking up at him. He shows the apple, then hides it again and stretches down farther from the tree. The girl reaches up. She stands high on her toes. She reaches with both arms, like a small child, all ten fingers spread. He stretches farther and the fingertips of his hand graze hers. It is as if lightning travels between them. He feels the charge. He leans farther still, and farther — and she lets his hand spider its way down to hers and close around her wrist. And she must have been anticipating, for she has one foot lodged in a crevice of the wall. He hauls on her wrist and she heaves herself high enough for him to grab her other arm. Then, just as if she has done this before, she opens her hands and grasps both his wrists, splicing herself to him in trust. He is afraid of being dislodged, but her feet push and climb the stone and there she is walking, simply walking up the wall. The two of them cling at the top, balancing, teetering. He lets go of one of her wrists and at once she releases both of his and springs for a branch. His hold on her other wrist stops her short and the two of them fall, bumping and scraping to the earth.

She looks him up and down, searching, and then begins to claw at his clothes, her hands like animals running, crawling all over him. He keeps his wits about him and pushes her away with his free hand and takes out the apple.

In the bundle he has a cap and a pair of ragged trousers. While she is occupied with the apple he takes off his own jacket and puts it on her, right over the nightshirt. He picks up the trousers and she sticks out her arms again. He has to hold the trousers up against his body, show her where they belong, mime stepping in. It is very awkward and he sees the length of her skinny legs, the fine fuzz at the top, and he grows weak and tries not to look because how then will he be able to run? He ties the trousers in place and sticks the cap on her head. She snatches it off. He holds her shoulders so that he can look directly in her face. He has no words to speak to her. All he knows and feels swims in his eyes. It is for her. Everything he risks is for her. He loves her more than he loves himself and he will not harm her ever, only protect her. And she sees it. She sees at last the look she saw in the man's eyes when he held his dog. As her own tears begin, he gently puts the cap back on her head.

He tries to explain, gesturing as best he can, that they are going to run. She seems to want to stay where they are. He shakes his head.

Come *on*!

He points away to the other end of the narrow thorough-fare and tugs at her wrist. She resists at first, leaning back, and then she takes him by surprise and leaps forward. It is awkward running together in fits and starts but they get themselves to the end of the passage. And here she seems to forget him. He sees the change in her eyes. She turns her head and looks all around.

There is no one in the street, for which he is grateful. Dogs bark as they run past, but no one comes outside to see. The old men in the tavern are deep in discussion and would not have seen a pair of charging bulls go by. Just past the tavern, the girl begins a low, distraught whimper as she runs. They slip across the road and he scrambles with her down onto the wall of the gorge, praying she will not jump, and from there they make their precarious way along to the bridge.

They cross and still no one has raised an alarm. On the other side, he pushes her on toward the track that leads directly up and she knows it, he can tell. He puts his hand on her arm and stops her. He takes his jacket back and unties the trousers, mimes what she must do. She steps out of them and he gathers them up and reaches for the cap but she claps both hands to her head and stands perfectly still. And now it is for him this time to read all that is in her eyes. You cannot take it. It is the sign that I was loved, that I am loved. It is for me to love in return.

And the great mystery that lies sheathed in layer upon layer of darkness begins to open, unfolding to the light. It blooms over both of them like the moon.

NO ONE KNEW how the disaster came about. The mayor's first reaction had been to blame one of the two young men he sent up there. It was not hard to imagine Raoul opening the wrong valve at the wrong time and releasing a flood of such destruction. The townspeople had their own ideas. They blamed the girl and her reappearance in the town — and when Peyre Rouff appeared they blamed him. But up at Aveyrac, Peyre had been uneasy even before the trouble arrived.

He had walked away from the reservoir and climbed up high again to an outcrop on the eastern hill to investigate. The water was still pounding down the rock face above him before disappearing underground — as intended — yet the water that was issuing lower down the hill was still no more than a thread running into the chute to the reservoir. He checked the upper pool again to see if the waters had found a new way to return to it. Everything was dry, as before. There was no escape of water at this level, yet lower down it remained a trickle. It had not increased in volume since the completion of the work. The rest of the water was somewhere, making its torrential passage in darkness, under the hill. He listened, thinking he should hear its thunder.

It was then that he heard a sound that was not rock or water or wind and he knew it was iron. And he knew that iron to be the gears of the sluice at the reservoir grinding open, and he guessed that one of the workers, impatient to be home, must have taken it upon himself to release the water into the cut for the gorge. Peyre took the path in great uneven strides, loose rocks and pebbles skidding from under his boots. Before he was halfway down the ridge, he heard a new sound, a monstrous, high-pitched whistle, a shriek. He stopped again where the track swung out briefly above the gorge side of the ridge. From his vantage point he saw it all. How the water sprang like a tiger from the rock, surging from the mouth of the cave where it had pursued the shriek of air. How it crashed down into the mill-lead where the water from the reservoir was now already running and surged on toward the cliff edge. And he saw the two young men, who had wandered down to the conduit to watch the water's progress from the reservoir, saw how they were taken by surprise as the wall of water reared up like a horse.

The girl too had heard the warning whistle and she stopped. She was in a narrow neck of the track climbing up beside what had begun as a trickle and was now a steady stream. Men on the hillside called their dogs to them with such a whistle...but it was spiralling and the next instant had risen to a shriek no man or bird had ever made. She felt the tremor. And not just underfoot. The very air was shaking. And then the roaring and the thundering began. She looked up to the head of the track and saw the white oaks shaking, tilting, and then unbelievably leaping toward her. A great cloud rose in front of them and then she could not see them anymore. Whatever it was, was almost on her. She clawed her way up the side of the track to get away from the deafening roar and she was suddenly wet, her hands slippery, her feet losing ground. She grabbed on to the trunk of a small tree and hauled herself up, clasping it with her arms and legs and clinging to it in her terror as the wall of water arrived. The tree lurched and tore free and she found herself upside down and somersaulting through the air with her gangly partner. The topmost branches took the force of the rock where the tree jammed and shook her free. Her only thought was to protect herself from the terrible deafening din and the battering rocks, so she drew in her knees and covered her head and let herself be carried in one long held breath, rolling and tumbling. She did not see the approaching drop, for she was still wrapped tight, but she felt the fall, the sudden absence of grinding rock against her skin, and she drew another breath before the rocks came up to meet her and the water, rolling her once, swept her on. And here a great wedge of basalt split the torrent in two and she was rolled, gasping to one side while the main flow of the water churned through on the other. The stream pushed up in waves along its curving bank before it swirled on to rejoin the flow. She found a handhold, clung there while her legs swung out from beneath her, and at last pulled herself dripping and naked from the flood.

The water bore down the old stream bed, boiling and seething as it went, spitting debris that ricocheted from the rocks. The sound of it had entered her head and filled it with thunder and it shut off the noise of the world she knew. But then as her breath began to return and her heart stopped its racing, she began to regain her hearing and she could make out another sound mixed with the water's din, as of some giant wagon creaking and grinding on a free run down a hill. She saw how far back down the cliff she had been carried. And now she saw too how the shift had been torn from her by the waters and she had no covering. She looked down. Her limbs glistened. She hardly recognized them for they were blotched and bruised with the colours of the storm. Trickles of blood ran everywhere, her body deluged with its own scarlet rills that had surfaced. She had a sudden urge to defecate. When it was done she climbed away from the bank and stood up.

Below her, she could see a shelf over which the water was leaping down to the mill. Her intent came back to her. She had been making her way up to the man again. The track she had been ascending had disappeared and there was no passage for her either up or down the cliff. To the side, a seam in the rock offered a path through the scrub onto the high slopes above the gorge. She could see that it narrowed in the distance to no more than a scar across the rock face. But it led away from the punishing water, and she took it. And the path received her. It narrowed almost at once to a ledge, and then her foot assumed a deep intelligence, feeling its way forward to the next place that offered a sound grip. And her obedient body followed. What looked unachievable became possible. She walked facing the rock, progressing crabwise. She did not think about the gorge below—why would she? She was intent on listening to the feet that took her away from the falling flood. And the cliff too practised obedience to her desire, for in measure that the ledge narrowed to a mere scratch, so the steepness of the cliff declined and softened. The hill itself took breath and leaned back a little for her, offering her the chance to lean against it, so that at last she was indeed a lizard hugging the rock, crossing it, and gradually climbing it, gradually, gradually, plastered against its generous breast. Her toes found snags and cracks and from these she levered herself, higher, and still higher until she came at last to a level place where she could stand.

She saw then how the cliff was no more than a nightmare and she stood in another part of the world altogether. She had not been in this part of the country but she knew its fragrance. It was all rock and scrubby herbs and heather and hardly a tree to be seen. Now that she could walk without fear of falling, her limbs felt suddenly weak and she found that she was shaking as if currents of lightning were travelling from the crown of her head to her heels. It became hard for her to walk and keep a straight course. She found a rock and sat at its base out of the wind. The warmth of the sun began to penetrate. She did not like the sight of the blue bruises on her legs, and she closed her eyes. In a little while she curled on her side and slept.

IT WAS THE boy's misfortune that the first place the doctor and the mayor had chosen to look for the girl was down at the bridge where he had just left her. The men had been standing in the roadway as Felip approached and there had been nowhere for him to hide as he came back over. He had tried brazenness but 'Good morning, messieurs' did him no good.

I think you need to tell us where you've been.

Doctor Ayash had his arms folded across his chest. Clearly he had made his assumptions and nothing would dislodge them.

Across the bridge.

Pailhès lifted his hand to strike and then disguised the impulse by stroking his moustache.

Now, now, said the doctor. Let's not be cheeky.

I'm just telling you, monsieur.

And what business had you across the bridge? Going to do a little milling?

The boy shrugged.

Well? said the mayor.

I was walking, monsieur.

Taking the air?

The boy shrugged and this time the mayor did cuff him.

I think you've got more to tell us.

You were seen climbing the fig tree at the back of my house.

Now the boy felt the dread of exposure.

And you know the girl is missing. You know that, don't you? Don't you?

The boy felt the blood rush to his face and neck, giving him away. It drummed in his ears. Even the world in front of his eyes seemed blotched with it.

So where is she? Did you take her across the bridge?

The boy almost whispered his reply.

She ran away, monsieur.

When?

Just now. She ran. She ran up high. She's very fast. He gestured vaguely to the old stream bed that came down above the mill.

She had best be fast. There'll be water sliding down there in a day or two.

Ramon Pailhès scanned the cliff. For the first time he realized his great good luck. He had never wanted the girl's return. The orphanage at Saint-Affrique had replied to his inquiries with elaborately worded but emphatic regret. Housed in the town again she would become a kind of totem, an advertisement of retrogression, of sorriness, marking it forever as a backwater. Word of her would get about again. People would come from afar to see for themselves. And then they would return to their towns, smug in their own superior civility. And one day — he knew this too — there would come a traveller who would tell a long and complicated story of a daughter lost many years ago on a journey across the mountains. Or perhaps the traveller would pose as a doctor, have poorly written proof that he came from The Society for the Improvement of the Mentally Unsound or The Institute for the Enfeebled and the Lame. What did it matter? Then, tired of the whole affair, he would choose to believe the traveller's story simply out of exhaustion, grateful to see the girl led meekly away. He would willingly accede, knowing all the while what lay ahead in the towns the traveller would visit on market days, the crowds, the gawkers, the propositions later in the tavern. Would know all this yet not permit himself to imagine what might happen on the road between towns. Would complete the pretense, the charade with 'Thank you, monsieur. I hope you will be able to help her. It is a service both to her and to science that you do.'

So, yes, this nuisance of a boy had saved him a great deal of trouble — saved him from himself as well. And saved him face, for people would have talked if he had released her to Peyre Rouff, he was sure of that. He could hear them: his poor decision, his shelving of responsibility, the poor dumb dependent. It had really been a most difficult position. He began to love the very existence of this impetuous unthinking boy who had solved everything at a stroke. Nevertheless, some semblance of a search must go forward.

You, he said to the boy. You'll take us to where you left her.

The boy followed miserably as the two men strode onto the bridge.

She may still be in the vicin— The mayor stopped talking, distracted by the sound of a train approaching the gorge. The sound of a train was unmistakable. But the nearest railway was at Montpellier. The noise was almost on them before he could place it and allow himself to look up above the mill. It was not the water they saw first, but the mass of moving debris like the head of a dragon, a mist flying above. They watched the mass descend, churning under and scooping up whatever standing thing was in its path, tossing it rolling onto the waters of its back, shearing trees and bushes from the banks as it passed. At the cliff it plunged. The mill wheel below sent two boards shooting skyward like thrown javelins as it broke apart. The mill itself stood like a rock at sea, waves breaking at its back, white water spewing from its single window.

The waters of the gorge churned as they rose. Doctor Ayash looked down and dizzied at the sight. The suddenness of it. The impossibility of what they had just seen. The mill engulfed in an explosion of water and rock. The mill as the streaming ruin of itself standing amid the wreckage of its own walls and all that had come down upon it from above. They continued to watch, willing the mill reconstruct itself stone by stone, whispering God's name. The boy was the first to realize their danger. He had already turned and was on his way back across the bridge as the air began to vibrate.

It seemed they had always known what they would see when they too turned: the bridge already in danger, the water breaking high against its stone. Not even space for the head of man between the water and the stone. The roadbed was already wet. The mayor, feeling nauseous, thought his bowels might give way like a feeble dam. The boy did not hesitate but ran right across. Doctor Ayash and the mayor followed, holding to each other like a pair of old women on winter ice.

They went a little way up the road before they turned to watch. The stones of the low parapet were no longer visible in the flood.

On the way up to the town, the boy looked back often, his eyes narrow, hurt. His vision of the girl climbing swiftly and melting like a wraith back into the garrigue had been swept away by the violence of the flash flood. What had come about was not his intent, yet it seemed in some strange way to be his fault. He looked back again. The waterfall looked like any other. He told himself the girl would have had time to get away. He had to believe it.

The turmoil now lay ahead of him, in the town, he knew it. He felt instinctively that he would be implicated, though the two men seemed to have forgotten all about him for the time being. For something in the air must have changed. Some reverberations must have announced the disaster, to bring these men and women down the hill toward them. The boy saw his fate descending. He wanted to run away. Instead he ran toward it.

The bridge! he screamed to the men and women approaching. And the mill! All gone!

No one took a boy seriously. He screamed the news again, louder this time, and then he was crying hysterically, uncontrollably, as if he had indeed like some ancient giant wrought the destruction himself.

Then all was confusion and some were running back to spread the news, others running down to see for themselves. And some were holding each other tight because it made the world stop reeling.

And now, in the very centre of the vortex of shouts and cries and arms and legs, his mother was suddenly before him like a mad woman escaped. She yanked him by the collar of his coat and jerked him right and left and slammed him to her breast. And to the boy it was the safest place by far.

PEYRE HAD SEEN the water issue from the rock and boil as it met the waters in the millrace. When he looked again toward the young men he could see only one. He yelled to the remaining figure to get away, get away, and he tore down the hill in great lurching strides and flung himself at the wheel that closed the gate of the reservoir. Then he turned and ran again, following the watercourse, keeping to the line of the channel that cut through the ridge to emerge above the gorge.

He found Stéphane on the ground, white-faced and shaking. Water from the cave was still crashing into what was left of the mill-lead.

What happened?

Stéphane stared blankly ahead. He was breathing hard through his nose as if it could not possibly draw in the quantity of air he needed. He made no answer.

Where's Raoul?

Stéphane had his head in his hands.

Did he go over?

Peyre took off his coat and placed it round his shoulders.

Tell me what happened. Did he go over?

Stéphane covered his eyes.

I don't know.

Come on, Stéphane. We have to move.

It took them a while to find a way onto the cliff face. The flood had made the descent more impracticable than ever. Peyre tried to stay close to the falls but was repeatedly driven back by the tangle of scrub or loosened rocks. They found a place where they could stop and safely see right down to the mill. The mill wheel had gone. The mill itself was unrecognizable. They had hoped for the sight of Raoul still alive, waving for help. They saw only the endless plunge of the cataract and they continued down.

A path is twice as long with a silent companion. Peyre

would have preferred Stéphane to talk, even if he did nothing but accuse himself. Stéphane made his way down carefully, bowed and slow as if he carried the youth on his back. Peyre felt the weight.

Below the mill, where debris had been flung up at the flood's entry to the gorge, rags had caught in the broken branches wedged in the rock. Peyre climbed down. There was a cap too. Peyre held it out.

Stéphane shook his head.

He didn't wear a cap.

Peyre folded it into his pocket and they went on. They could see now that the bridge too was gone. It shook a man to see such a thing. A boat was pulled up on the opposite shore. Queasy with apprehension they continued searching downstream.

Stéphane's silence was oppressive.

After a while, feeling hopeless and defeated, they walked back up the river and settled opposite the boat to wait there on the bank. Peyre went over the sequence of events. Again and again he saw the water leaping from the cave, the force of it. He had seen such a thing in an engraving. He remembered the night he had shown the book to Giles and tried to explain it.

He looked at Stéphane, but he could not see his face.

Listen, Peyre said. It wasn't your fault. Did you see it, the water?

I opened the gate.

No. Did you see the source when it broke through? Just above the mill-lead? That wasn't the water from the reservoir.

Stéphane looked up.

It wasn't your doing. You have to understand that. No one could have predicted. No one.

They continued to wait, not quite knowing what for, their faces turned downstream, away from the sight of the ruined mill. Before the sun went down le Boulidou and some others came down to the water and Peyre hailed him to take them across.

You will ruin my new ferry trade, he said to Peyre as he stepped into the boat. The whole town is after your blood. Where's Raoul?

Silence once would have been a choice, a luxury. Walls of silence to keep the world at bay. But his duty now was to Stéphane.

There was nothing anyone could do. It came from nowhere.

It was not the time to discuss who had opened the gate at the same moment.

From nowhere, eh? And Raoul?

Stéphane drew in his breath sharply and tried to speak, his mouth opening and closing on the invisible shapes of words. He began to weep, silently at first and then in sobs that shook his chest.

That girl, le Boulidou said. She's at the root of this.

She was nowhere near.

You get out, said le Boulidou to Peyre as he beached the boat. We'll take him up when he's fit.

Peyre watched Stéphane's convulsions.

Get on out of here! said one of the others.

Peyre turned, hoping they would not disturb the young man's private act of salvation. The sound of weeping followed him. The sobs had taken on voice. Stéphane, without shame, was crying remorse to the waters of the gorge and to the vertiginous depths of the sky. From a distance it might have been laughter.

Some of the people closed their doors and shutters when they saw Peyre entering the town. One—a woman who had reviled the girl, though he did not know it—spat at him and called him the agent of the devil.

Clarius Pech came forward and stood firmly in his path.

What are you doing here? People are upset, he said.

I've come to see the mayor. Stéphane Foix is down at the crossing, he said. Unhurt. Raoul is missing.

Pech called to a boy to run and tell the mayor.

You have a lot to answer for, he said. They were searching for the girl when it happened.

Peyre looked at him.

The wild girl, man. They're saying the Maraval boy let her out. I didn't search. I hope she drowned. But Raoul...I hope for your sake he didn't.

At the square a small crowd had gathered, waiting for answers. Peyre heard his name again as he went into the mairie.

Ramon Pailhès was in his office with a thin, worried man who was repeating the same indignant phrases in a high-pitched voice: Well, how will I? Tell me that. How will I? Pailhès saw Peyre and stood up.

Monsieur, he said to the thin man, I will have answers for you tomorrow. I promise you. Though the expression in his eyes belied it. It was the look of a man who has lost the key to his house.

The man continued repeating his question on the way out.

Peyre Rouff and Ramon Pailhès stood facing each other. They listened to the man's voice receding.

Well. Water, said the mayor. We have that. Sit down, Peyre. There's a lot to discuss. He poured a large glass of aqua vitae for both of them and sat down.

So. A life lost. For water. Water, but no bridge and no mill. A good joke, don't you think, Peyre Rouff? Oh and no girl, either. I forgot to mention that.

Peyre listened in silence to the mayor's account. It was without doubt a disaster for the town. And yet he could not shake a small voice in the midst of all the chaos and destruction that told him one thing at least was as it should be.

There was not time to hear more. Everyone, it seemed, needed the mayor. Raoul's father had arrived and would not be kept away. He shouted first at the mayor. You! You sent him up there. With that lunatic!

It was an accident, Gregor.

Gregor turned to look at Peyre. Yes, an accident. And not the first you've been the cause of. Murderous bastard. Damned drunk.

He cursed Peyre Rouff deeply, heaping damnation on his soul until he was led away.

Peyre was shaken. So much pain in the world. Everyone looking to inflict it to assuage their own. As if sharing it could make it less.

He left the mairie not knowing where he would spend the night. If there were a bridge he would have gone over to Gougeac to Frédéric's house. The mayor had said he was not able to offer him a bed. His wife was sick, he had said without conviction, embarrassed that she should have her way.

But go to Henri's, the mayor had said. Henri's wife will not say no.

He said they would meet again in the morning. The whole town, he said, was meeting in the morning.

Peyre turned and walked down the street. Before he reached Henri's, he heard footsteps behind him and turned to see Madame Trochet.

I'm just going home, she said. I saw you go to the mairie, and then I saw you walking back. Do you have a bed for the night?

At the inn.

She smiled. Not the place for any self-respecting citizen to sleep. Only strangers. I'll give you a bed. I wouldn't want to be in the town right now, she said on the way down. Not if I was you.

Her son, Arthur, was at the house. Peyre smiled at the son briefly and nodded in his direction as Madame Trochet showed him to a little room under the rafters with clean sheets upon the bed. She did not ask him any questions. Instead she offered a silence kind and full. In the narrow bed he closed his eyes in gratitude.

There was not a citizen who was not up and about by dawn. At seven o'clock there was a small crowd waiting outside the mayor's house. The mayor sent his wife outside with a jug of warm milk and a bottle of eau de vie. It seemed only wise. By eight o'clock le Boulidou, who had taken a messenger across the river to the road to Gougeac, was walking up the street with Raoul. He was smiling triumphantly as if he had just fished the youth personally from the depths of the gorge and not found him sheepish and cold waiting on the bank to come over. Raoul concentrated on looking fraught and mildly injured. He rubbed his knee from time to time and clutched his shoulder as if in pain, but when the doctor tried to take a look he fended him off, frowning. When asked why he could not be found and where he had been, he could give no satisfactory explanation, for the truth—that he had run, that he had not waited to see if Stéphane was all right, that he had not cared to help Peyre, that he had spent the night shivering on the spur of the hill, awake and watching for the ghost of the she-wolf to come thundering, ten times larger than life—the truth was ignominious. He was relieved when the mayor stepped forward and suggested that everyone move to the church. He took the chance to slip quietly out of the crowd.

Ramon Pailhès was beset on every side by those who wanted answers. Who was responsible? How were they to get out of the valley with the bridge gone? Would the stone in the quarry be suitable for rebuilding? Who would undertake to organize it? Who transport it? And was it even worth repairing the mill? And again and again the most pressing question of all: what would happen next time water was released?

Peyre stood up. It was as if a thieving wind had swept through the church, stealing away every human sound and leaving only faces turned toward him, silent, even their breath held. Peyre assured them that the gate from the reservoir had been closed. But that was not the point, he said. The great volume of water that had come down so suddenly had not issued from the reservoir. It came from within the hill. Yes, the gate had been opened, but that was not the cause—

Someone, looking for blame, interrupted and asked him who had opened it.

I opened the gate, he said. And the lie must have contained some power of its own, drawn perhaps from its good intent, for it was as if a door of a kind opened inside him and he let it.

I will be glad to help, he said. I do not have to go anywhere, not anywhere at all. I'll be pleased to stay and help you. And to his surprise, he found space in his heart and still more for the world and its troubles, which yet were not his.

The church fell silent, his words at odds with his reputation. And then the objections began. Those who voiced them gave courage to others. Lingering doubts, secret suspicions, and sudden thoughts were fireworks to be set off immediately and simultaneously. The mayor tried, in the uproar, to explain what Peyre had just said, that the floodwater did not originate at the reservoir. The volume of the water and the force of its arrival was too great. But that was only confirmation of what the loudest objectors were declaring. It was all the evidence they needed: Peyre Rouff was in league with the devil.

The priest put out his hands to calm the uproar.

My dear children, let us be mindful of Our Lord's house!

The mayor waited, his arms across his chest, one hand propping his forehead, shielding his eyes as if to relieve a terrible ache in the head.

The noise subsided and Gustave Thibéry took advantage of the lull. He raised his voice. Did no one remember the girl? Had they forgotten all about her? It was the girl Peyre Rouff wanted and the girl had been set free. Were the two events not connected?

And suddenly there was consensus in the church, everyone solidly in agreement with his neighbour, because they were badly in need of a scapegoat, and this one — unlike Peyre Rouff, who was disconcertingly in their midst — was naked, vulnerable, and most conveniently absent.

My wife, said the mayor's brother-in-law, huge and slack and sounding as he always did, a little drunk, My wife always said this man was the agent of the devil. And what's he done now? He's made a pact. When did this water come down on our mill and tear away our bridge? When the girl was returned to Peyre Rouff, that's when. Tell me that's not a pact with the devil.

Ramon Pailhès, deeply embarrassed by this display of backward thinking, asked his brother-in-law to sit down. Someone asked what the next thing would be to come down that cliff. And then the mayor could not make himself heard at all. He leaned to Peyre and suggested they meet again in private. He had not thought to see the day when Peyre Rouff might be the most useful man in the room.

Peyre got up. Several people moved back to let him pass, leaving space enough for a sulphurous companion beside him.

.

It was not the devil but the girl who walked beside him when Peyre went down to the gorge — or the town's memory of the girl. He began to piece together the disconnected remarks of the meeting. And when he thought about the girl's escape and the different accounts of it and tried to picture what had happened in the town, he began to see that she might once more be at large. Certainly she was at large in their imaginations. She might even be at liberty on the land, but despite the possibility, he knew for certain he was not going to see her. Perhaps because he no longer had the need.

The waters were placid now. Across the gorge, a steady silver stream was falling.

Peyre sat for a long time in contemplation. Everything he had heard about the history of the building of Aveyrac, all of his conversations with the engineer, began to make sense. The water they had tried to channel had found a new route underground. Instead of surfacing to be channelled obediently to the reservoir, it had entered an underground cavern. If the water could be made to arrive instead at the reservoir without entering the cavern, the people of Freyzus could have their working mill. Water at their command. All they would need would be a gatekeeper. Someone who didn't mind living in such a remote corner of the land. Someone who was content to be there.

The mayor reconvened the meeting for three o'clock. He sent men in le Boulidou's boat to make a preliminary assessment of the damage. He sent a man over to Gougeac for the engineer and he called for all skilled artisans and willing citizens to a meeting the following morning down at the bridge site. And he felt strangely elated. He finally had some important work to do.

They have already named the new bridge, he said, when Peyre came in to see him. Even though it's not yet built.

And?

Le Pont du Diable Sauvage. She is not going to be forgotten easily.

Oh, Le Diable Sauvage, said Peyre. That almost ensures she *will* be forgotten, said Peyre. Le diable sauvage was not the girl. She was a poor thing. You know that.

But she had power. You, Peyre Rouff, you have to admit she had power. And you weren't the only one. She had a hold on that boy. He shrugged. A tremendous hold. But then. He's young. He was infatuated. She made him believe his own lies. Pailhès shrugged. Perhaps that's what we all do. Ah, but there! I think he's telling the truth now. He says he climbed the wall behind the doctor's garden and he helped her make her escape. He may have planned to run with her, then changed his mind, said the mayor. Who knows?

Peyre thought he knew. He had no trouble imagining himself a lad again, seduced by a wild child like a sprite from the mountain beckoning — a real wild child, not to be tamed by any father or priest, or schoolmaster, a child free to run forever.

Probably only the boy, he said.

Peyre smiled as he spoke. He looked, the mayor thought, for the first time in many years like a normal man. And he suspected that Peyre too, for whatever reasons of his own, might be equally glad that the girl had been let go.

From what the boy said, she was making her way up to you. But she was too fast and he couldn't keep up — lucky for him. That was when the water came down.

So sudden, the weight of water. Always so sudden. The ineluctable weight. Peyre could feel it. How did he not foresee it? The girl in the brief act of running, the sudden water overtaking her, swallowing her. It was always her fate.

I'll tell you this much. The mayor passed his hands over his blotter, smoothing imperfections away. We are not going to search again. Our assumption — and this is official — is that she was lost in the flood. He made the gesture again, clearing away all trace of the girl. I'll prepare a full report as soon as I have the time. For now, the matter of the bridge is the most pressing. We'll accept the offer of your help, along with the engineer of course. We need to start rebuilding as soon as possible, but we can't even begin without finding out what happened and making sure it won't happen again.

It will happen again. The water you see flowing now will stop. I don't know for how long, but I do know it will start again. And I know you can control it.

With new gates?

With additional gates. A new arrangement. The gates didn't fail. You must understand that. Here. Let me show you. He reached for the piece of paper in front of the mayor and Ramon handed it to him.

Look! Peyre dipped the pen and began to draw on the back of the paper. It's nothing to do with the reservoir. There was always water under the hill, a lake. See! And we were feeding it. Peyre was drawing rapidly, scribbling. Through the old watercourse. Raising the level, you see? That's why the reservoir — up here at the house — was slow to fill.

He continued to draw. His attention was complete, focused. Pailhès thought again how useful such a man might be.

Imagine an underground lake inside a hill — here. Imagine the channel that drains the lake running uphill — like this — a certain way under the ground before it descends again — like this — to make its exit — at a cave mouth, here — to the outside world. The channel becomes a siphon. If the water level is allowed to fall, there will be an air lock inside the passage. Only when the water inside it is pushed high enough will the lake begin to drain, and then it will continue until it falls below the entrance to the channel. But a siphon, you know, can be controlled. After a few experiments, we would know roughly how long it takes for the lake to fill with a reasonable supply.

We'll see what the engineer says.

Perhaps like me he will see an underground reservoir, there for your use in times of drought. Controlled with a gate at the outlet. He scribbled in a gate. And then seeing how Ramon

Pailhès was looking unconvinced and seeing how furious was his drawing, he laughed.

I'm sorry. There will be other ways too, perhaps with less risk attached. He put down the pen, a little exhausted. You will just need a good man up at Aveyrac.

The mayor leaned back and drew a breath. He ran his hand over his moustache.

We don't even have a mill.

The mill can be rebuilt. You'll find a way. And the bridge. I can oversee the system of béals and locks.

It is something to consider. But perhaps not now.

I'm prepared to wait until you're ready.

You think you'll get workmen up there again?

Are they afraid of the water or are they afraid of ghosts?

They're afraid of the devil.

And you're not?

The mayor took his time answering.

I think there was a time, I'll be honest with you, when the devil was at your heels. I don't see him now. Only his shadow. Shall we go back?

He did not like it, Felip's father said. He did not like it at all. That girl had been part of a bargain with the eccentric at the chateau. He'd been thinking about it ever since the morning. She had been like a token in some diabolic pact. Did she think, he said to his bemused wife, that a man like that, a man who had killed his own son, was going to let things go? Just like that? Provide the water for nothing? Of course not. There had to be a price. Why did she think the water had come down in such a flood? Well? Well, why did she?

But his wife had not given it any thought at all. It was as natural as any flash flood was natural. As normal as a lightning strike or the ague running through the town like fire. And the man Peyre? Peyre Rouff was normal too. Just unlucky, though more unlucky than any one of God's creation should ever have to be.

I have no idea, she said.

But you are a dense woman! You always were. Because of *him*. It was his doing.

He pointed at his son sitting red-eyed and pale in the corner.

He's interfered in a most dangerous situation. And he's drawn the attention of a most dangerous man.

Did Peyre Rouff mention Felip?

No. But he spoke for hours with the mayor. And what do you suppose the mayor spoke about?

Water?

And now he felt like hitting his wife too.

He spoke of course about the young thief—pointing his finger now, shaking it—the young thief who stole away the girl. And where do you think Peyre Rouff will look when he wants to exact compensation for his loss in the bargain? He'll look to us, that's where.

She was glad he had answered his own question, for she did not follow his logic at all.

Then...? she said, hoping to hurry him to his conclusion. She had to go out to find potatoes to scrub for their dinner.

Then we need to make some kind of restitution, of course.

Like an offering?

~~If you want to call it that. A wrong has been done. By~~ *him*—
your son. And *he's* going to have to put it right.

He's a boy. What is he supposed to do? Go and find the
girl? All by himself? Or are you going along with him?

Thomas didn't answer. It was an appalling thought. The
familiar landscape where he loved to net the small birds
transformed at the mere idea of the girl. The dark chestnut
wood. The summit where the wind howled. The girl alive as
terrifying as the girl dead.

Why don't you take him a chicken?

A chicken?

Two then. You said he's supposed to be going back there
to live. His own hens are to stay with Madame Trochet. She
told me.

His wife was clever. For all that she was stupid, she was
clever.

You, he said to the boy. Get up. We're going out.

The boy Felip did not appreciate this venture at all. The
hens seemed to know his intent before he even got near. He
began to sneeze uncontrollably in the chaff he was kicking
up. His father's silence helped not one bit. When Felip's
hand finally closed around a cold scratchy leg, he had almost
given up. His father held out the sack and Felip pushed the
hen inside. The second bird was more trouble. She kept her
wings in constant motion and when he finally collapsed her
enough to push her in the sack, the first bird pushed her

way out. Now he was more ruthless and hurled himself on the bird, working his hands under his own weight to get a hold of her.

His father stood and watched. When both birds were finally together in the sack, he tied the neck of the sack tight.

Hold it here, all right? Don't let it come loose.

Won't they suffocate?

That's a big word.

But won't they?

Not if you're quick, they won't.

The boy wondered how Peyre would be quick on the long journey back to the chateau.

They waited outside Madame Trochet's house. When the door opened, the boy's father poked him sharply in the back.

Bonsoir, madame. I have brought something for Monsieur Rouff, said Felip.

Well then, you'll have to be quick, Madame Trochet said. He's already left. He said he's going up there tonight. Le Boulidou's already down there to take him over.

The river was turning the colour of lavender as it did when the gold had faded. Peyre was sitting on a rock, waiting for le Boulidou to finish talking with his friends.

The boy held the sack out to him at arm's length, though clearly it was heavy. His father gave him a nudge.

Felip had been silently rehearsing the Act of Contrition all the way.

I'm heartily sorry, he said.

The sack weighed heavily on his outstretched arm. Something moved inside.

Peyre looked up. He was smiling.

For—?

For letting her go.

Peyre searched the boy's face.

The girl? She was not mine, he said, and he felt as if he were suddenly revealing a great and important truth to himself, and it extended beyond the girl. Beyond now, beyond then.

He's sorry for the trouble, said Thomas. He's brought you these chickens. He pushed the boy closer.

That is very kind. What's your name?

Felip.

Thank you, Felip.

Peyre looked at the boy's father.

Thank you very much. His eyes met Thomas's, telling him tacitly in front of everyone that he appreciated the kindness of this unlooked-for gift, telling him he understood it was not really atonement, just an excuse for an act of kindness. Telling him all men are good creatures at heart and want only to be kind.

The boy's father read every word in Peyre eyes correctly —and was confirmed in his opinion that the madman of Aveyrac had no grasp at all of reality and was just as mad as ever.

But two of le Boulidou's friends had also caught the look, and thought to themselves that yes, it was indeed a good thing to do and wished they had thought of such a thing themselves.

Maman said give them this. Felip held out an apple. Give them small pieces and they won't be thirsty.

Shall we give them some air too? said Peyre, and he took out his knife. He carefully made two small cuts in the burlap before setting it down at his feet.

By the time le Boulidou had the boat in the water, both of the birds had their heads stuck through the burlap and were drinking the extraordinary sight of the river just before sunset.

Peyre took the road around the long spur of the hill. He watched the colours of the land deepen with the low light. The ochre earth glowed rich orange, the pale rocks were suffused with pink, and everywhere the grass was vibrant with mauve flowers that by day passed unnoticed. And then the sun was lost to the purple hills in the west and all around the richness cooled to grey-green, blue-grey. Peyre walked as far as he could in the twilight and then walked on some more in the first blue-washed dark of the night, until he came to a small wood, the road ahead uncertain now in the dusk. When he began to stumble, off balance with the sack, he sat with his back to a rock and waited for the moon to rise on the hillside. He thought about Madame Maraval. He saw her calling the boy back on an afterthought to give him the apple. The hens were quiet and had pulled back into the sack. Sleeping, perhaps. Chickens down the hill, chickens up again. He had not expected it.

There was no end to the surprise of people.

And the boy. He found he could contemplate the boy without pain. He guessed Felip was twelve, perhaps younger.

There had been a time when he would not have been able to look at him. Twelve. Yes, Felip was the right age to feel his soul scorched by the girl's wild passage. He thought of his son and the young falcon they had trained. And Giles came back to him, whole and unharmed, and he gave himself to the memory for the truth and the beauty that it offered and because it was deserving of its own place in the world. So that there on the hillside the moment bloomed in the darkness before the moon and in memory he watched again the bird in flight, his hand still outstretched frozen in air before them, while, above, the bird sliced sky to carve a canted arc and stoop, swifter than the eye, snatch the thrown mouse and soar again. The beauty of the thing, its precision and its power. Peyre gave himself wholly to the memory. His son's quick intake of breath. He had drawn in his hand and squeezed Giles's shoulder and looked down, smiling. Giles's face that a second before had been upturned, a perfect offering to the broad sky, was changed. His jaw was set unnaturally. Peyre had leaned forward to read his expression. Giles's eyes filled suddenly to overflowing. Peyre had drawn him to his side. Had said, It's all right. The mouse was already dead. But Giles was shaking his head and wiping his tears with the back of his hand. It's not the mouse, Giles had said. It's the bird. I want to be the bird.

Peyre was not sure how long he had been asleep. His eyes were fixed on the wood on the other side of the track, where the risen moon was silvering the leaves. The girl had slipped between the tree trunks and out of sight, he was sure of it. Those skinny limbs, made bone white by the moon. Or was it his own memory of her he had glimpsed, that familiar lurching gait as she ran? He told himself it was a dream. And perhaps it was. Perhaps a dream from another time re-membered only now. And did he dream Giles too so real? Or remember him? He closed his eyes and again he was standing beside his son, again the two of them were turning their faces up to the sky, and again the falcon stooped and in less than a heartbeat bisected past and future.

Peyre picked up the sack and went on.

His son a small boy again. His son alive again beside him there before the moon came up. His son was here on the hill and his son was in him. A life was forever. A life cut short was still forever. There was no end to love. If he could find his son in the wild girl, he could find him also in the eye of a hawk or the wing of a moth, in the bite of the wind, or the rilling of water over rock. For eternity is on earth as it is in heaven.

And Felip? Felip, he knew, would hold the girl forever in his heart, a wild heart hidden within his own. The possibility of flight.

ACKNOWLEDGEMENTS

Foremost thanks to John, as always. My thanks again to Leo for another generous and most timely read. Thanks too to Silas for the wild and inspirational art. And grateful thanks to Hélène Joucla for readily finding the time to be my first French reader.

I'd like to thank everyone at Goose Lane Editions for their care of the book. In addition, I owe special thanks to Hilary McMahon, my agent, for the initial momentum and to Bethany Gibson, the book's editor, for expert and infuriating attention to every last detail. So grateful.